———————— ★ ————————

The scarecrow wore a yellow flannel shirt, dark-stained in many spots above the denim overalls. Ten feet from the figure, Jon stopped. Clothesline rope wrapped several times around the waist secured the figure to the upright wood. Similar rope had been used to lash the arms. Jon saw that the darkest stains across the chest and upper portion of the overalls were blood that had seeped out from the rough gashes in the cloth and dried. Below the farmer's hat, the scarecrow wore the mask Jon remembered from the Harvest Hoedown of the night before—the bulbous nose and great buck-teeth above the mouth that was still arcing upward in an oafish grin.

The face of death.

———————— ★ ————————

"Bird lore and legend are woven effortlessly into the story, enriching it considerably."
—*Publishers Weekly*

Forthcoming titles from Worldwide Library by
RAY SIPHERD

THE AUDUBON QUARTET

RAY SIPHERD

DANCE OF THE SCARE CROWS

WORLDWIDE ®

TORONTO • NEW YORK • LONDON
AMSTERDAM • PARIS • SYDNEY • HAMBURG
STOCKHOLM • ATHENS • TOKYO • MILAN
MADRID • WARSAW • BUDAPEST • AUCKLAND

For
Anne Marie

DANCE OF THE SCARECROWS

A Worldwide Mystery/October 1998

First published by St. Martin's Press, Incorporated.

ISBN 0-373-26287-6

Printed in U.S.A.

Acknowledgments

With special thanks to Milan G. Bull,
Director of the Connecticut Audubon Society,
Fairfield, Connecticut; Lieutenant David G. Lydem;
Michael V. Carlisle of the William Morris Agency;
Neal Bascomb and Tom Dunne of St. Martin's Press;
and Gordon and Fran Shogren.

As the birds that are caught in the snare, so are the sons of men snared in an evil time, when it falls suddenly upon them.

—*Ecclesiastes* 9:12

ONE

SILENT, from within a thicket of low pines, they watched him through their binoculars and scopes. He was dressed in a white fisherman's knit sweater over brown wool slacks; a tall man, lean, with straight dark hair and deep-set eyes. Hands thrust in his pockets, he was studying a flock of black ducks feeding on the surface of the shallow bay.

The morning sea fog had begun to lighten. But enough of it remained to cover the calm water and to give the air a late-October chill.

The leader gave the signal and the ten of them moved quietly in his direction. Some carried heavy objects at their sides. Falling into single file where the breakwater began, they crossed it, finally descending downward through the beach grass to the narrow shoreline where the sand was wet and hard.

They were thirty yards away from him when he turned suddenly and saw them.

Ten yards from him the leader stopped. The others spread around him in a ring.

The leader spoke. "Good morning, Mr. Wilder."

The man looked down at the small, gray-haired woman with the walking stick. "Good morning, Mrs. Stives."

He turned to face the other members of the group. "For those of you I haven't met," he told them, "I'm Jon Wilder."

Hands were offered all around. He shook them, exchanging brief remarks and greeting the newcomers. The group numbered seven women and three men. The men were in their sixties. The women ranged in age from early thirties to Mrs. Stives herself, who admitted to no more than mid-seventies. Most were dressed in slacks and sweaters, except for Mrs. Stives, who wore a leather bomber jacket, jodhpurs, and high boots. A knapsack was on her back. All had cameras and binoculars or scopes that hung from straps around their necks. In one hand, each carried an artist's sketchpad; in the other, a blanket or boat cushion. Two of the men had folded wooden beach chairs.

Mrs. Stives plunged her walking stick into the sand. "We're grateful that you took the time to join us this morning, Mr. Wilder."

"I'm always glad to be with birders," he assured her. "Particularly my friends and neighbors in Scarborough."

"Before we begin," Mrs. Stives asked, "would you allow me to take a picture of you for our November newsletter?"

"Certainly."

Mrs. Stives removed her knapsack, withdrew a camera and pointed it in his direction. What the camera caught in close-up was a man younger than his rugged features suggested, weathered by the sun and wind. The chin was square and deeply cleft. There was also a small scar on his right cheekbone, the result of an accidental confrontation with a nesting falcon several years before.

Lowering the camera, Mrs. Stives turned and addressed the group. "On behalf of the Scarborough Friends of Birds, it is my honor to welcome Mr. Jonathan McNicol Wilder. Again this year, he has agreed to conduct a field class on the subject of bird portraiture. As you all know, he is an outstanding ornithologist and painter of birds and, fortunately for us, a resident of Scarborough. Please welcome Mr. Wilder."

There was a scattering of applause and Jon stepped forward. "Thank you, Mrs. Stives. And thank you all. It's my pleasure also to be here. I enjoy these sketching classes in the spring and fall especially, since this part of Connecticut is on the principal migration route for eastern birds. As you can see, this little bay and the marshy area at the far end of it have attracted a number of waterbirds this morning."

He waved a hand in the direction of the water. "Besides the American black ducks, there are a few grebes, as well as the usual seagulls and cormorants. So let's begin. Each person choose a particular bird he or she would like to draw. Sketch quickly, using two-B pencils. If you have a camera, take some photographs. After you've caught the essential outline of the bird, you can do finished drawings, checking the photographs for reference."

As Jon waited, a flock of mallard ducks appeared out of the morning sun. They flew in low over the breakwater, dipping rapidly, and landing one after another on the bay, directly opposite where Jon and the group stood.

There was a collective cry of pleasure from the Friends of Birds.

"Since these mallards have obviously come to have their portraits done," Jon said, "I suggest we make them our subjects. Later, we can look at the sketches and compare styles and techniques. Is that agreeable to everyone?"

The group murmured their assent and began unfolding beach chairs, or positioning their blankets and cushions on the sand. Sitting down, they put their sketchpads on their laps. Those who carried cameras snapped away, while the mallards swam and clucked among themselves.

For almost an hour the class worked in silence, photographing and sketching the ducks. Jon stood a short distance from the group, occasionally walking among them, offering suggestions, and answering any whispered questions they might have.

The mallards, for their part, seemed unaware of the attention that was being lavished on them. Mostly, they moved in small circles near the shore where their portrayers sat. Sometimes they plunged their heads beneath the surface, feeding on the bottom, with their tails pointed in the air. Once or twice brief skirmishes erupted between pairs of male ducks, until both tired of the battle or the loser judiciously withdrew. Then each resumed its search for food.

Across the bay a breeze was gently scalloping the water. The tide, which had been rising when the group arrived, was now pulling the mallards in the direction of the marsh.

Jon watched the distance between the amateur artists and their subjects lengthening. Finally, he decided the birds were too far away for photographs or useful drawing.

"Ladies and gentlemen," Jon said, "both time and tide seem to have deprived us of our models. So I suggest that we collect our things and head back to our cars."

The sketchers rose, replacing the lens caps on their cameras, gathering up pencils and covering their sketchpads. Mrs. Stives again assumed the lead, with Jon beside her. Together the group walked back along the beach.

As they reached the beach grass, there was a sound behind them. Two members of the group turned back to look, then whispered to the others.

Rising rapidly on beating wings, the leader of the mallard flock took flight. A second mallard followed. Then another, and still more.

As the flock rose one by one, the Friends of Birds hastily removed the lens caps from their cameras, or watched through their binoculars. Expressions of delight were heard: "How beautiful!" "Sheer poetry in motion!" "'Hope' is the thing with feathers..."

Suddenly the day exploded.

Two blasts from a shotgun shook the air.

A woman shrieked. A man dropped onto the sand, covering his head. The shots reverberated, echoing back at them from the breakwater and surrounding trees.

Then there was silence.

Jon and the Friends of Birds stood silent also, staring toward the water where the ducks had been. The flock had fled in wild panic. But on the surface of the water two young females thrashed helplessly, their death cries audible, blood pouring from the bills.

Unable to bear the sight, most of the group turned away. Jon Wilder remained, watching the two dying birds. Delicate brown feathers, blown away by shotgun pellets, floated aimlessly. Then, very slowly, one duck ceased her thrashing. Gradually, her head and neck stretched forward on the water. The other duck soon did the same. Side by side, and carried by the wind and tide, the two ducks drifted slowly toward the marsh.

Jon saw it then: the glint of sunlight on the barrel of a gun. From the cover of bulrushes and tall reeds a figure emerged wearing high waders and a hunting vest of mottled green and brown. A large cap was pulled down over mirrored sunglasses covering the hunter's eyes. A shotgun was held loosely in one hand.

Jon and a few others watched as the hunter waded knee-deep in the water, and splashed out to where the two dead mallards lay in a widening crimson ring. Switching the gun to the right hand, the hunter was about to reach down and retrieve the ducks. Instead, he looked abruptly in the direction of the group, as if aware of them for the first time.

At once, the figure turned and splashed back to the cover of the marsh, abandoning his kill.

The next moment, one of the women beside Jon stepped forward, hands cupped to her mouth. "Murderer!" she bellowed.

Others immediately joined her, shouting toward the marsh.

"Killer!"

"Butcher!"

"Wanton murderer!"

The man nearest Jon suddenly grabbed up his folded beach chair. "Let's get him!" he shouted, raising the chair over his head, and running toward the marsh.

A second man did likewise, brandishing a cushion as he ran.

"Stay here! Both of you!" commanded Jon.

The men halted.

"We can still grab him," said the first man.

"Maybe," Jon said. "But the hunter has a gun."

The two men stared at Jon, then turned and trudged back to where the others stood.

"As soon as we get back to town," Jon said, "I'll go to the game warden. If the hunter lives in Scarborough—and if he has a hunting license—he might be registered at the town hall. I suggest you go back to your cars."

Like children for whom a happy party had ended with some awful, inexplicable event, the Friends of Birds resumed their sad retreat. One young woman was now weeping openly. The man who had been brandishing the beach chair moments earlier had a handkerchief held to his face. Even the indefatigable Mrs. Stives dabbed at her eyes.

Jon watched them as they shuffled through the beach grass, over the breakwater, and into the pine thicket toward the path that led to the road.

When they were gone, Jon turned again and began walking back along the beach in the direction of the marsh.

THE SCARBOROUGH town hall was an architectural hybrid—the sedate combined with the ornate. Built of granite walls, with a frieze of prancing nymphs above the entrance and Ionic columns stretched across the front, it looked half like a staid New England bank, half a Grecian temple that exalted in Dionysian excesses.

Jon parked his dark-green Range Rover in the lot behind

the building and entered on the lower level, where the lesser administrative offices were housed. Along the hall he found the office of the town game warden, who also doubled as the animal-control officer. The door was partly open and Jon heard the tap-pause-tap-pause of uncertain fingers typing on a manual machine.

Jon knocked briefly, then went in. Seated at a wooden desk was a young man in a green uniform, jabbing with two fingers at an ancient Smith-Corona. He looked up as Jon entered.

"Got a minute, Tom?"

"I know, I know," the young man said at once. "Mrs. Stives was just in here hollering about the killing of the ducks."

"So what did you tell her?"

"I'd look into it."

"When?"

"When I get a chance," the young man said. "If I discover who the shooter was, we'll fine him on two counts: shooting ducks off-season and killing them while they were feeding on the water. If he's had earlier infractions, we can take away his license. Maybe."

"Even if he's the first selectman of the town?"

"Ramsey?" The muscle under the young man's left eye began to twitch. "How do you know that? Did you see him?"

"I saw somebody dressed in a hunting vest and cap," Jon said. "He also wore sunglasses. The reflecting kind."

"Hell, Jon—lots of hunters dress like that. I'll make a note of your complaint. All right? Now I've got a lot of work to do."

He resumed typing. Jon sat down on the corner of the desk and placed a hand against the carriage of the typewriter.

"Look, you and I know Ramsey has this macho thing

where hunting is concerned. He's up for reelection and he thinks it helps his image with the NRA zealots around Scarborough."

"Even so, I can't go marching up to Ramsey's office and accuse him based on what you saw."

"No, I guess you can't." Jon stood. "But I can."

He left the office quickly, walked to the stairs at the far end of the hall and sprinted up them to the main floor. He crossed the marble lobby to a set of offices that looked out on the town green.

A young blond woman in a cashmere sweater sat in the reception area, a telephone pressed to her ear. She glanced up briefly, seeing Jon, and put a hand over the telephone.

"I'll be with you in a minute, sir," she told him.

"Don't bother." Jon kept going.

"Sir, I'm sorry, but you can't—"

Jon pushed open the polished fruitwood door directly opposite. Behind a broad desk, feet resting on it, a boyish-looking man in a blue blazer and open white shirt sat talking on the telephone. At the front edge of the desk a small plaque said Roderick J. Ramsey, First Selectman.

Ramsey looked up as Jon stood there. "Gotta go," he said into the phone. "Somebody's here. Bye, love."

He hung up the phone, swung his feet around and stood, a finger aimed at Jon. "Hi. Wait. Don't tell me the name. It's Jim. Jim Wilder—the bird guy, right? We met at Madeleine Thoreau's last year."

"Jon Wilder."

"*Jon* Wilder. Right." The first selectman flashed a toothy grin that made Jon think of a television game-show host.

"What's on your mind, Jon?" Ramsey sat again in the cushioned leather desk chair, coupling his hands behind his head.

"I'd like to know if you were down at Mullet's Bay today."

"Today?"

"This morning. About ten."

A flicker of uncertainty crossed Ramsey's face. "What would I be doing there?"

"Duck hunting."

"Jon, Election Day is five days off. I've got constituents to talk to, campaign stops to make." Ramsey leaned forward in his chair.

"So you weren't anywhere near Mullet's Bay."

Ramsey shook his head and smiled. "Definitely not."

"Then why did I see your car parked on the dirt road leading to the marsh?"

The first selectman's smile faded. "What makes you think it was my car you saw?"

"It was a red Triumph with the letters 'ROD' on the license plate. I was doing a field class in drawing on the far side of the bay. As we were leaving, a hunter stepped out of the reeds and shot two female ducks while they were feeding. After the group left, I walked back along the beach and up to the dirt road. That's when I saw your car."

"Jon—Jon…" Again, the toothy smile. Ramsey spread his hands toward Jon, palms up.

"Correct me if I'm wrong," Ramsey went on. "But hundreds, probably thousands, of birds cross over the shoreline every year. And some of them get killed. Hunters shoot them. Or dogs catch them. I've even seen birds kill other birds."

"I'm talking about murder, damn it!" Jon realized his voice had been louder than he meant.

He noticed Ramsey's eyes shift past him to the open door. Jon turned and saw the girl in the cashmere sweater looking at them with a curious expression on her face.

"It's okay, Cindy," Ramsey told her. "Shut the door."

She retreated, closing the door as she went. Ramsey stood again, facing Jon across the desk.

"Listen, I'm a sportsman. I admit it. And now and then I go duck hunting. I admit that, too."

"Sportsmen don't kill young females while they're feeding on the water."

"Jon, they're only birds, for Chrissake! You're making a federal case out of a couple of dead ducks."

"Try telling that to Abigail Stives."

"Mrs. Stives is an eccentric. She's a fanatic about birds. And I must say, your profession notwithstanding, you're sounding pretty overwrought yourself."

Ramsey's smile now took on a malicious edge. "Besides, you saw my car. But you're not sure you saw me, are you?"

"No, but—"

"There you are." Once more, the open hands. "I could have driven by the bay, parked my Triumph where you saw it, and gotten out to stretch my legs."

The first selectman checked his watch. "Sorry, Jon, but I'm due over at the senior center in ten minutes. Gotta run."

He reached about the desk, collecting papers and stuffing them into a briefcase at one side.

Jon watched him, saying nothing. Ramsey finally looked up. "Was that all you had to say to me? Or was there something else?"

"I just want you to know I'm going to file an official complaint with the game warden."

Ramsey zipped the briefcase shut. "With Tommy Gunderson? I don't imagine he'll do much." He gave a laugh. "Remember, I appointed him. If I'm reelected to this job on Tuesday, I can reappoint the guy. Or not."

Jon stared at the man. "You really are the bastard people say you are."

He turned and started out of Ramsey's office.

"Does that mean I shouldn't expect your vote?" Ramsey called after him, amused.

But Jon was well across the lobby, heading for the stairs.

TWO

THE MOON, enormous and blood-red, rose slowly, cradled in the leafless branches of the trees. Appropriate for Halloween, Jon thought. The full October moon was also called the hunter's moon: a grim reminder of the killing of the ducks the day before.

Jon turned off the engine and stepped out of the Range Rover. More cars were parking behind him on the narrow country road. As their occupants emerged, Jon could see them in the moonlight. They were dressed in old-fashioned rustic costumes—the men as farmers for the most part, the women as farm wives. His own costume was a well-worn woolen shirt of red-and-black plaid, a pair of jeans with holes in the knees, and a frayed farmer's hat he'd found at a tag sale. Footsteps sounded, and a man and woman passed him, dressed as a farm couple. The man was carrying a pitchfork; the woman's hair was tied in a severe bun. Grant Wood all the way. Jon fell in behind them and began walking along the road. Glancing at the cars already parked, he noticed several displayed bumper stickers with the initials "RRR." They stood for Reelect Rod Ramsey; a reminder also of the man's continued popularity with many voters of the town.

The large wooden building toward which he and the other masqueraders marched was the Scarborough Grange—a barnlike structure set well back from the road within a grove of trees. Most of the year it was the meeting hall for the authentic farmers of the area; the place where they discussed farm subsidies on corn, cranberries and other crops, and heard lectures from state agriculture agents on subjects ranging from the virtues of new automatic milkers to the perils of the cabbage borer and related pests. But on Halloween, the hall became the site of what was called the Harvest Hoedown, an annual event intended to raise money for a variety of local charities. Inside the hall, the celebrants could do-si-do to the music of a six-piece country band, sip homemade cider, nibble at corn fritters, and in general rub flannel elbows with their social peers.

As Jon continued up the gravel footpath leading to the hall, the sounds of laughter and festivity grew louder. The country band was finishing a Stephen Foster medley, and was rewarded with shrill whistles and applause.

Jon stepped into the hall and looked around. Several hundred people filled it, although, from the sound of their relentless jollity, it appeared to be far more. The hall's plain barnwood interior had been decorated in the harvest theme. Sheaves of wheat and bundled cornstalks had been tied to the wooden columns that led up to the trestle beams above. Stapled to the beams were artificial leaves in autumn colors. Around the grange hall, set against the walls, were tables that sold food and beverages, as well as concessions offering Halloween-related games. Jon noticed a line of people waiting for their chance to bob for apples in a washtub, and he wondered if the game's popularity was a result of last year's hoedown, when someone had filled the bobbing tub with gin.

Jon also saw a line of men standing before a curtained booth. Above it was a sign advertising KISS THE WITCH— $5. The witches in this case were a dozen or so local women who disguised themselves as hags and witches and dispersed a kiss to any man prepared to pay five dollars to be thusly bussed. Since the first Kiss the Witch booth made its appearance several years ago, it had instantly become the evening's most popular attraction. Rumors still circulated that it had also been the catalyst for three adulterous affairs and one divorce.

Jon felt someone tap him on the shoulder from behind, and heard a voice pipe, "I know it's you! You're Binky Wellington!"

Jon turned to discover he was looking at a short, very chubby woman costumed as a milkmaid. Seeing Jon, she blinked.

"Oh, you're not Binky Wellington at all."

"No, I'm Jon Wilder."

"The man who draws those darling little birds?"

"That's right."

"I adore birds. Last month I bought a gorgeous hat with feathers from an Eskimo curlew."

"Did you?" Jon said. "I'm sure the curlew would be glad to know you like his feathers, if he hadn't been illegally killed to furnish them."

"Dear me. How sad." The woman blinked again.

"Excuse me." Jon turned back and began to mingle with the crowd. The country band of fiddlers and banjo players were lounging at an open door at the rear of the hall. He began to envy them. The crush of people and cacophony of voices inside the hall had increased since his arrival. He was debating with himself whether he should leave now or stay, when he felt someone kiss him lightly on the cheek.

"Hello, Jon," a woman's voice said.

He looked and was confronted by the green face of a smiling witch. Beneath the pointed hat and stringy wig, he also saw the sharp blue eyes of Madeleine Thoreau.

"That kiss won't cost you, by the way," the witch added. "I'm off duty."

"Hello, Madeleine. How are you?"

"Personally or professionally?"

"Whichever," Jon said.

"Professionally, the market for Scarborough real estate

is picking up. Yuppies have discovered this quiet little corner of Connecticut.''

"And personally?''

"Personally, the market's flat. I haven't had a bid in months, to say nothing of a closing. Maybe I should offer myself as a multiple listing. How are you, Jon? I haven't seen you in a while.''

"I've been traveling a bit. Australia last spring. A few weeks in Alaska in the summer. Next year, I'll be working on a nature guide of western birds.''

"But you're home to stay for now?'' she asked. "I mean, you're not about to sell your house on Plover Point.''

"No.''

"I'm glad. Give me a call sometime. Maybe we can have a drink.''

"Sure.''

"Promise?''

"Promise.''

"Good. Happy Halloween.'' She kissed him on the cheek again, then disappeared into the crowd.

Jon watched her go with an odd feeling of pleasure and regret. After his wife's death, Madeleine Thoreau had offered sympathy and comfort; albeit, he came to realize, for reasons that were not entirely selfless. A widow in her fifties, she was still a handsome woman and a friend, as well as being the town's most successful realtor. During the time they were together, he'd even thought of asking her to marry him, but rejected the idea. Still, he enjoyed seeing her from time to time. And there were few people in Scarborough he felt that way about.

He saw the country band was making their way back to the low platform that was the makeshift bandstand. Near Jon was a table behind which a woman in a plaid sundress sat knitting. On a hot tray on the table were some round flat brownish disks about the size of hockey pucks. A hand-

lettered sign leaning against the table identified the objects
as corn fritters.

Since there was not a waiting line, Jon bought one. The
moment he bit into it, he knew the reason why the woman
had no customers. The corn kernels were as hard as BB
shot, and the whole thing seemed to have been fried up in
a gummy sauce that tasted like shellac.

Jon took the fritter from his mouth and stared at it. As
he was wondering how to get rid of it, a door of the grange
hall directly behind him swung open. A woman with a tray
of candied apples entered, and before the door closed Jon
caught it with his other hand. He pushed it outward and
stepped out of the hall.

The fresh air filled him like a tonic and he took several
long, deep breaths. As his eyes readjusted to the moonlight,
he discovered he was standing in an open grassy area
strewn with dead leaves and bordered by bushes and tall
trees. Abandoned farm equipment was parked against the
trees.

Jon lifted the corn fritter and scaled it in the direction of
the trees.

"Hey! Watch your aim!" The voice came from the
equipment.

Jon peered toward it. On the high seat of a farmer's
hayrack was the figure of a woman.

"I'm sorry. I didn't know anyone was there."

He stepped closer to the hayrack. At the same time, the
woman jumped down from the seat. "No harm done, you
missed me."

He saw she was a slim young woman costumed in a
gingham dress. Her long blond hair was tied in two long
braids she had pulled forward, and which hung down to the
bodice of her dress.

"Before you ask," she said, "I came as the farmer's
daughter. A mistake. The first man I told that to tonight

turned out to be a traveling salesman. What was it you threw in my direction, by the way?"

"A half-eaten corn fritter."

"Then I don't blame you. Mine was awful."

She offered her hand. "My name is Lorelei Merriwell." She added quickly, "Mrs. Merriwell."

He shook her hand. "I'm Jon Wilder."

"Is that John or J-o-n, without the 'h'?"

"Without."

"Jonathan then."

"Yes."

"Excuse me for asking, but I'm new in Scarborough. Are you a somebody in town?"

"A somebody?"

"A local honcho? Influential in town politics? Anything like that?"

"I'm afraid not," Jon said.

"The reason I asked is—" She stopped abruptly, looking past him. "My God—who are they?"

Jon turned. From the direction of the road, six costumed figures walked in their direction, their feet crushing the dry leaves that lay along the path. As they approached, Jon saw they wore farmers' bib overalls. Masks hid their faces and farmers' hats were pulled down on their heads.

Passing Jon and Mrs. Merriwell, they marched to a rear door of the grange hall. The one who seemed to be the leader lifted a gloved hand and rapped three times on the door. The door opened and a head appeared.

The head nodded. The door was pushed aside, the six stepped through it one after the other, and the door closed again.

"You want to see the somebodies in Scarborough?" Jon said to Mrs. Merriwell. "Follow me."

He motioned to her and they moved together to a open side window of the grange hall that gave a view of the

interior. Pressing close to the window, they saw that a section on the dance floor near the country band was being
cleared. The partygoers had quieted considerably, and there
was a sense of expectation in the hall.

At last, the leader of the band mounted the platform and
whistled through his teeth for quiet.

"Ladies and gentlemen! Farmers and Farmettes! Hush
up now, please!" he called. "This is the moment everyone's been waiting for. The highlight of the Harvest Hoedown. Back for a repeat performance, let's give a big hand
to the best, goll-darnedest dancin' group this town has ever
seen—the Scarborough Scarecrows!"

The crowd erupted in applause. The banjo players stood
and twanged an introduction on their instruments.

From behind a row of cornstalks to the side of the platform, an overall-clad figure leaped out, arms spread above
his head, his gloved hands waving. Cheers and laughter
greeted him. Jon recognized him as the leader of the six
who had walked past them moments earlier. In the bright
lights of the hall, Jon saw he was costumed as a scarecrow.
Beneath his overalls, he also wore a yellow flannel shirt
with bits of straw protruding from the sleeves. Straw also
poked out from beneath the cuffs of the overalls. On his
feet were clodhopper shoes three sizes too large, and his
hands were covered by white work gloves, which he continued waving to the crowd. A battered farmer's hat with
a pushed-in crown was perched on his head.

But it was the mask Jon noticed most. It was intended
to be comical; to Jon it looked bizarre and even sinister.
Garishly detailed, it displayed the gross, exaggerated features of a simpleton. The painted outline of the eyes had
pupils that crossed inward over a grotesque and bulbous
nose. Freckles blotched the cheeks and forehead, and two
enormous buckteeth overlapped an idiotic grin that turned
upward from the lower section of the mask.

Jon felt a tap on his shoulder. "What's going on?" Mrs. Merriwell asked in a whisper.

"It's a comedy routine. It started at the hoedown several years ago. Six of the town's leading citizens dress up as scarecrows and do a sort of chorus-line routine. The one you see, his name is Rod Ramsey. He's Scarborough's first selectman; what passes for our mayor."

"I've met him. Bad news." She made a face, which surprised Jon.

The scarecrow stopped his waving. From a breast pocket, he produced a red bandanna and made an elaborate gesture of mopping perspiration from the forehead of his mask. The crowd roared with delight.

The scarecrow turned back toward a line of cornstalks near the platform. A musician played a rising note on a kazoo, and a second scarecrow jumped out from behind the stalks, his arms and legs akimbo. He was followed by another and another, until six scarecrows, all similarly dressed, stood side by side. They bowed elaborately to the crowd, to loud applause.

Jon inclined his head to Mrs. Merriwell. "The fat scarecrow next to Ramsey is Bernie Benjamin. He runs a restaurant near the interstate. Next to him is Justin Kittridge, the bank president. Then comes Lester Fitch, the pharmacist; then Aaron Peabody, who owns the lumberyard. Finally, the tall scarecrow with his finger in the nose of his mask is Chester Rill, the Congregationalist minister."

"You wouldn't catch an Episcopalian doing that," Mrs. Merriwell commented tartly.

The band leader gave a downbeat and the band launched into "Turkey in the Straw." At the same time, the scarecrows joined arms and began a series of high kicks, moving left, then right, followed by a cancan flourish of their legs.

"Not exactly the Rockettes," said Mrs. Merriwell. "Oh, look! The first scarecrow is losing his straw."

Jon saw it too. From below the cuffs of Rod Ramsey's overalls, straw was falling out and spilling on the floor. Unaware of it, he danced across it, slipped and landed squarely in a pratfall with his legs outspread. The crowd whistled and applauded. Enjoying the moment, Ramsey remained seated, waving his arms to them and pretending it was part of the routine. Following his lead, the other scarecrows executed comic falls, until all were down beside him on the floor. Finally, as the music ended, the scarecrows leaped up, dusted off their backsides with their hats, bowed to the applauding crowd, and trotted off behind the shocks of corn.

The applause continued and there were shouts of "Encore!" from the hall. Again, the scarecrows bounded out onto the floor. This time, prominently pinned to his chest, Ramsey was wearing an enormous white button with the initials "RRR" in blue. Most people laughed; some shouted, "Way to go, Rod!"—"Reelect Rod Ramsey!"

Ramsey gestured to the band, which struck up a chorus of "She'll Be Comin' Round the Mountain." As a group, the other scarecrows reappeared and joined Ramsey in a high-stepping promenade around the floor.

The encore went on for five minutes, encouraged by the crowd's rhythmic applause. When it ended, the scarecrows doffed their hats, bowed to the audience and then shook hands among themselves, before exiting again behind the corn.

The applause dwindled. The band began to play "Good Night, Ladies," and doors were opened all around the hall. People started moving toward them, talking and still laughing as they went. Jon and Mrs. Merriwell retreated to the farm equipment, as partygoers spilled out of the hall and headed toward the road.

While people drifted past them, Mrs. Merriwell leaned

close to Jon. "Do you know if there's a telephone inside the hall?" she asked.

"Yes. I think so."

"Good. I need to call a taxi to get home. The date I came with had been drinking when he picked me up. As soon as we got here, he went off to bob for apples, and I haven't seen him since."

"Well, Scarborough does have a taxi service," Jon informed her. "But it's an old car, and an old man who drives it. Besides, he turns off his telephone at nine o'clock."

They were interrupted by a figure retching near a rear door of the hall. When the figure straightened up and turned, Jon saw it was a short man with a brush mustache; he recognized him as a local builder by the name of Gustav Schiller. He was costumed as a goatherd, and wore a loose shirt that hung down over knee-length leather breeches. One hand clutched a herdsman's staff, which he leaned on for support.

Seeing Jon and Mrs. Merriwell, he started toward them. "Here y'are." He stopped a foot away from them, then spoke to Mrs. Merriwell, ignoring Jon.

"Looking for you everywhere. Le's go."

"I came outside for some air," she told him neutrally. "Gus, I'd like you to meet—"

"Know who he is. Bird man." Schiller's alcoholic breath washed over them.

"Hello, Gus," Jon said.

Schiller reached out and grabbed one of Mrs. Merriwell's pigtails. "Party's over. Time to go."

She took back the pigtail. "Really, Gus. I don't think you should drive."

"Can drive. Can do a lot of things tonight." He laughed.

"Gus, go inside and get some coffee," Jon said. "Then ask somebody to drive you home. They have people who'll do that."

"Fly away, bird man." Schiller looked at Jon for the first time. He turned to Mrs. Merriwell again. "Come on."

She backed away. "No, Gus."

Suddenly, the herdsman's crook shot forward, catching her around the wrist. "Come on!" he said again.

Jon grabbed the staff with both hands and held it, letting her withdraw her arm. "You heard her, Gus. The lady doesn't want to drive with you."

Jon gave the staff a shove. Still clutching it, Gus Schiller stumbled backward, tripped, and collapsed into a hedge of junipers.

"My car's nearby," Jon said to Mrs. Merriwell. "I'll drive you home."

She nodded, and together they moved quickly toward the road.

THE LINE OF CARS making their way to the state highway moved forward at a sluggish pace. As Jon drove, Mrs. Merriwell stared through the windshield of the Range Rover, saying nothing.

Several times, Jon glanced in her direction. Even in the dim light from the dashboard, he could see that she was lovely. Her large eyes had a golden cast; her lips were full. Silent, with her features in repose, she had the classic beauty of a Titian heroine. Yet also, in the eyes and mouth, there was a sensuality about her that suggested something more. Jon decided he had better pay attention to his driving.

At the state highway, a policeman with a flashlight waved them out onto the road. Jon turned, increased his speed, and began to watch for the road signs that would lead them back to town.

Mrs. Merriwell spoke at last. "I'm sorry," she said. "I haven't been very conversational."

"And I'm sorry about what happened," Jon said.

"When he's sober, Gus Schiller is a fairly harmless character. But he can be nasty when he's drunk."

"May I ask you a question?"

Jon nodded. "Sure."

"What did he mean when he called you bird man?"

"I study them."

"You mean, you're a scientist?"

"Not really. I write about them and I lecture now and then. What I mostly do is draw them. I've published a few illustrated nature guides."

"I always thought that grown men who draw pictures of small animals were—well, effete. You don't fit that description."

"I'm glad you think so."

"And is there a bird woman?"

Jon paused. He shook his head. "No. I'm a widower."

"I'm sorry."

"So how is it you came to be in Scarborough?" he asked, changing the subject.

"A month ago, I was driving from Boston to my apartment in New York and I had a flat tire on the interstate. I didn't have a spare, so when the tow truck finally came, the driver towed me into Scarborough. While I waited for the tire to be patched, I walked around the town and fell in love with it." She added nonchalantly, "That afternoon I also bought Philander Webb's antiques shop."

"You *bought* the shop? I didn't know he'd sold it."

"I'm going to keep the name. Besides not having to repaint the sign, the name Philander Webb has a venerable New England sound about it, don't you think?"

"Philander has a real eye for quality. I've bought a number of things from him over the years."

"I'm just learning the business," she admitted. "But at least, I can tell majolica from Tupperware."

Jon smiled. "It sounds like you're off to a good start."

"Anyway, I stayed in Scarborough that night at a motel, instead of driving to New York. The next day I visited a realtor, and after looking at a couple houses, bought the one I liked. After that, I got rid of my New York apartment and moved here. Since then, Mr. Webb has been giving me a crash course in antiques. In fact, most people in town didn't even know he'd sold the business, even when he stopped coming to the shop."

"Has anybody asked you why you're there and old Philander isn't?"

"No." She shook her head. "Maybe they just think of me as hired help. Or possibly that I'm his mistress."

Jon laughed. "Philander Webb is eighty-eight; that should get a lot of people talking about him and you."

"Let them." She leaned her head back on the headrest. "Most of my life, I haven't cared what others thought about me, one way or the other."

"Most people would find it very hard to follow that philosophy."

"I'm not most people," she told him.

Obviously not, Jon thought.

Approaching the center of the village, they began passing a number of well-kept Georgian colonials, some built by a prosperous sea captain who had settled in Scarborough more than a century ago.

They arrived at the town green, and Jon slowed for a red light. As they waited, Mrs. Merriwell studied the buildings that surrounded the green.

"It looks so peaceful in the moonlight, doesn't it?" she said.

Jon agreed.

"I already know most of what's around here," she continued, pointing. "That's the town hall, of course. And the Congregational church. There's the Captain Turnbull Inn.

And past it is the drugstore. And the office of the realtor who helped me get my house. I don't remember her name.''

"Madeleine Thoreau," Jon said.

"There's the Scarborough Bank on the other side. I got my mortgage from them.''

"You seem to know a lot about the town.''

"I also know the population, average water table, and the millage. What I really don't know yet are the people. Tonight's party crowd excepted.''

"They're pretty much like people anywhere. A mix," Jon said. "Some commute to New London, or across the border to Rhode Island. There are even a few Yale professors who make the long drive to New Haven. And then there are the farmers, and the fishermen who keep their boats moored in the harbor.''

The traffic light turned green and Jon drove on. Soon the town center was behind them and they were on a country road again.

"Tonight's Harvest Hoedown," she asked him, "was it typical of the entertainment enjoyed by Scarborough's smart set?''

"No telling what goes on in private," Jon acknowledged. "As for public entertainment, yes. Unless you count the spring mud-wrestling competition at Swertfagen's Pig Farm.''

She laughed for the first time. "You're all right, you know.''

"I beg your pardon?''

"I was beginning to think most men in Scarborough were like Gus Schiller. Or your estimable first selectman.''

"Rod Ramsey? You said he was bad news.''

"He came into the shop the third day I was there. He introduced himself and welcomed me to Scarborough. He also gave me a campaign button and said he was up for reelection this year. I told him I was new in Scarborough and couldn't vote. But that didn't seem to stop him. He showed interest in an antique brass bed we had displayed inside the shop. I lied and told him somebody had bought it. I was sure he was going to ask me to demonstrate it for him, if I hadn't.''

"Let's say Rod Ramsey is familiar with a lot of beds in town,'' Jon said. ''But he's handsome and unmarried. He's also what you'd call a 'somebody' in town. In his job, he holds a lot of power locally. Even more behind the scenes, I'm told.''

"It sounds like you don't like him much yourself.''

Jon frowned. ''I don't.''

They drove for several miles, most of it through open farmland. Again, Mrs. Merriwell was silent, peering out the passenger side window at the moonlit fields, harvested and ready for the winter.

Finally, she raised her hand and pointed forward. ''My road is on the left, beyond the bridge.''

Jon slowed the car, passed over a two-lane wooden bridge, and turned onto a dirt road.

"That's mine,'' she said. On the right, a hundred yards ahead, a solitary farmhouse stood.

"You bought the Truitt place? It's charming. Even if it is a little bit remote.''

"That's fine with me.''

Jon stopped the car opposite the flagstone walkway leading to the house. The house was Victorian in style, white with dark-green shutters and lace curtains covering the windows. The porch that faced the road had gingerbread beneath the overhanging roof. To one side of the porch stood an old-fashioned glider; on the other was a huge antique wire birdcage holding dried hydrangea blossoms that were spilling from the sides.

"Thanks for the ride.'' She gave Jon a quick smile and

opened the car door. "Stop by the shop sometime when you're in town."

"I'd like to."

"By the way, you were gracious not to ask me. But there is no Mr. Merriwell. He hit the high road long ago, leaving me with lots of debts and an ironic married name. I didn't marry well at all."

The next moment, she had stepped out of Jon's car and headed toward her house at a brisk walk.

THREE

THE FIELDSTONE structure sat on six acres of a promontory known as Plover Point that jutted into Seal Island Sound. A three-story turret with a pointed, slated roof stood at one end, giving the house a certain castlelike appearance. It had been built in the 1920s by an eccentric millionaire who'd made his fortune in gentlemen's foundation garments. Since then, it had served as a retreat for a religious order, a billet for navy men during World War II, and as a sanitarium for well-heeled alcoholics, who had paid enormous sums of money to dry out while enjoying a water view. Then, early in the 1980s, the owner filed for bankruptcy, and the house fell into disrepair. A year later, a young couple, both of them artists, bought it at a bank foreclosure sale. Repairs had been costly and extensive. But once completed, Jon Wilder and his wife, Joy, had a house both of them truly loved. Two years after that their daughter was born. They named her Suzanne.

ON SUNDAY MORNING, Jon awoke at seven. He showered and dressed, fixed breakfast for himself, refilled the bird feeders outside the house, and was at the drawing table in his studio by eight.

The studio was in the turret on the second floor, and was surrounded by casement windows on three sides. The room faced mostly south and west, affording Jon a sweeping panoramic view. From it, on a clear day he could look due south across twenty miles of open water to Montauk Point, on Long Island's eastern tip. That morning, however, thick fog obscured everything beyond the beach below.

Jon entered his studio, switched on the lights above his drawing board and opened the draperies. He seated himself on a high, rolling chair opposite the drawing board, adjusted the angle of the board, then secured a large sheet of watercolor paper to it. The wooden table to his right was filled with open jars containing pencils and paint brushes. He picked out a pencil, sharpened it, and blew briefly at the tip. Finally, he turned and looked at the small square table to his left.

Staring at him, mounted on a polished rosewood pedestal, was a mature male crow; its feathers black as ebony and iridescent in the light. It was an excellent example of the taxidermist's craft. It was also quite large; almost two feet long, and so natural in its appearance that Jon had to remind himself that it was dead. For this crow, anyway, there would be no more raucous caws, no gathering of grain, no tearing into carrion meat with its powerful hooked bill. A tag hung down from the bird's tail. Family: Corvidae, the tag read. Genus: *Corvus*—Species: *brachyrhynchos* (American or Common Crow). The tag also noted the bird's age as seven years, and the name and address of the taxidermist in New Orleans. Jon removed the tag and pinned it to the corkboard on his wall.

The crow had been the gift of a birder in Louisiana. Rarely did Jon work from models, as earlier bird artists had done, including Audubon. But this crow was so lifelike, it was perfect for the watercolor portrait he had planned.

Jon turned the model to one side and studied it some more. In profile, the downward-curving bill was sinister, and the crow's black gimlet eye stared at him with cold malevolence.

Jon moved the crow to its original position and began making quick light strokes with the pencil on the drawing paper, sketching the outline of the bird. First came the head and bill, and then a circle for the eye. Next, the rounded breast above the abdomen and legs; followed by the neck and slightly raised back, sweeping toward the tail. Last came the under-tail coverts, then the long flat outer feathers of the tail itself. When the portrait was completed, it would be included in an exhibition of Jon's work that a gallery in Sante Fe was planning for next year.

Jon worked until twelve-thirty, unaware of passing time. But when he finally stepped back from the drawing, he was pleased with the results.

The fog had also lifted and sharp sunlight poured into the studio. Jon walked to the windows and looked out. On the sound, small curling whitecaps were beginning to appear. He pulled the curtains to protect the paints and drawing board from the sun, and went downstairs.

He had just started to prepare a bowl of clam chowder for his lunch, when he remembered Arthur Tingley's visit. Tingley was a retired fisherman, now in his seventies, who had recently discovered birding. Although he was not a member of the Friends of Birds, he regularly trooped through the woods and meadows of the area, binoculars in hand, in search of uncommon or rare species. Having gone from fish to fowl, as he was fond of telling Jon, he had become remarkably adept at spotting birds that even long-time birders missed.

Then, two days ago, Tingley had appeared at Jon's house unexpectedly to report the sighting of a Townsend's solitaire; a slim, gray bird of the thrush family that made its home in several western states. A Townsend's solitaire had not been spotted this far east in years. But Arthur Tingley swore he'd seen it in an abandoned cornfield near his home. He'd even gone on to identify its markings. Jon himself had only seen the solitaire in the conifer forests of the Colorado Rockies. Still, Tingley knew his birds better than many, and Jon found the thought of seeing one in Scarborough intriguing.

Finishing his lunch, he went to his study. From a cabinet, he took his Nikon camera, loaded it with a roll of fresh film, and placed it in his camera bag along with several telephoto lenses. From a hall closet leading to the garage, he grabbed a thick wool jacket, then headed out. He opened the garage door, backed the Range Rover into the turnaround, and started up the winding driveway that would take him to the road.

The cornfield Arthur Tingley had described was four miles due east of the village. Jon checked the dashboard clock—one thirty-two. As he approached the town green, he was glad Sunday church services had ended. But the streets around the green were still congested. Tourists always flocked to Scarborough on autumn weekends, and today was no exception. Passing the green, Jon could see a line of people standing on the walkway of the Captain Turnbull Inn. As on most Sundays, they were waiting for admission to the inn's Seafarers' Brunch that was always popular with out-of-towners. Elsewhere around the village, Jon knew visitors would be investigating the antiques and craft shops, photographing the historic houses along Periwinkle Walk, as well as the fishing boats moored in the harbor, and in general soaking up the very real charm the town possessed.

The road that led east passed more fashionable homes of the town's early aristocracy. Two miles beyond, the Range Rover bumped over the grade crossing for the four-track rail line connecting Boston and New York. From there, the road curved gently north, soon bordering flat open fields, which on the old maps of the area were called Walnut Plains. Jon remembered that last year the twenty acres it encompassed had been bought by Gustav Schiller for what the builder boasted at the time would be a community of fine, distinctive homes.

Jon slowed the car and studied Walnut Plains as he drove

past. Since Schiller's ownership, the land had been transformed into something very plain indeed. Not a tree, walnut or otherwise, remained; nor, for that matter, any sort of vegetation. Bulldozers and backhoes had efficiently and permanently raped the land, removing the topsoil, and pockmarking it with the beginnings of foundations for the forty houses Schiller planned to build.

Then, just beyond the shoulder of the road, Jon saw the builder's sign. It had been nailed to the stump of what had once been a huge, venerable maple tree. It bore the logo of a lightning bolt, and the name of Schiller's firm, which he called Action Builders. Certain wags around Scarborough, who thought of Gustav Schiller as a crypto-Nazi, referred to it as Achtung Builders.

Being Sunday, there were no workmen on the property. Near the road, a bulldozer sat beside a mound of broken branches and debris. Where once delicate white pine and wild dogwoods had flourished, there were now carelessly cut stumps resembling the stubble of a derelict. The only evidence of their existence was a blackened mountain of incinerated logs and tree limbs that had been their crematory pyre.

Jon grimaced at the sight. Gus Schiller would be right at home in the Brazilian rain forest, he thought. He increased his speed again and forced his eyes back to the road.

IT WAS THE CROWS Jon was aware of first; he heard their cries before the first of them came into view. Turning into the rutty farm road that gave access to the abandoned field, their loud, hoarse caws were audible. Closer to the cornfield, he observed several dozen darting in and out of the tall hemlocks bordering the field on the other side.

There was a stand of meadow grass between the road and what had once been an entrance to the field. Jon pulled into it and stopped. Looking through the windshield, he could see more crows above him, circling or making passes over the field, before rising up into the trees again. The cornfield itself was small; approximately two acres in size, surrounded by a split-rail fence. Many of the wooden rails had rotted and lay fallen on the ground. The field had obviously not been worked in years. The owner probably had died, and his heirs, or whoever had come into possession of the land, had simply given it back to nature to do with as she wished. Still, year after year, without cultivation or attention, new stalks of corn had grown, producing ears. Those that the birds or foraging animals had not stripped and eaten remained shriveled in their brittle husks.

Jon opened the glove compartment of the Range Rover and withdrew a paperback book, one of his own nature guides. He checked the entry for the Townsend's solitaire. "Similar to the northern mockingbird," it said, "except that it displays a white eye ring, notched tail, darker-gray breast, and buff wing patches." In his description, Jon had also noted, "...a rare or casual visitor east through the Great Lakes to New England." Jon returned the guide to the compartment, picked up his camera bag and stepped out of the car.

Bits of litter were visible along the edge of the road— beer cans and cigarette butts mostly, as well as empty shotgun casings and discarded condom packets. Apparently, both hunters and lovers found this place ideal for their particular activities.

The brightness of the day had dimmed behind high clouds and Jon felt a chill wind at his back. In the cornfield the dead stalks swayed with it, crackling and scraping as they touched.

He walked along the road, stopping every twenty feet or so to look through his binoculars. Tingley's sighting of the solitaire had occurred at the far end of the field near the road; the bird had been hopping among stalks, the man had said. It was also where the crows were concentrated now. Focusing his binoculars on that part of the field, Jon saw them swoop down, then rise again, their shrill cries fracturing the air. What was attracting them was probably some carrion, Jon thought; the remains of a dead rabbit or raccoon. Even if the solitaire had been here several days ago, as Tingley claimed, this noisy commotion would have driven off the smaller bird at once.

He lowered the binoculars. The rails of the fence near where he stood were missing, and between it and the road the weeds were matted down. In the cornfield itself, many of the stalks appeared to have been bent or broken, as if someone or something had gone into the field recently, creating a crude path.

Jon stepped through the open space along the fence and started following the makeshift path, batting away tilted cornstalks as he moved. The path went straight ahead. But to his left, Jon noticed that the ground sloped upward to a modest rise. From it he might get an overview of the entire field and see what was attracting the attention of the crows. He climbed the rise and lifted the binoculars again.

The only thing he saw at first were the tops of more dead cornstalks, greatly magnified. Then, unexpectedly, his eyes caught what seemed to be the top of a straw hat. Jon lowered the binoculars and stared.

Fifty feet away, he saw a scarecrow. Its arms had been stretched out along a piece of wood that formed the horizontal section of crossed stakes. The scarecrow wore a yellow flannel shirt, dark-stained in many spots above the denim overalls. The lower portion of the scarecrow was less visible. But as the dead stalks waved and twisted with the wind, the illusion they created made it seem as if the scarecrow's legs were moving, even dancing, in a kind of *danse macabre*.

Loud caws and a rush of air above Jon startled him. He

looked up as a crow swept over him, then flared its wings and landed on the scarecrow's hat. A second crow came down and lighted on a shoulder. The bird cawed, then started jabbing downward with its beak. It pecked the scarecrow's throat with curiosity, then began poking into the breast pocket of the overalls. After several tries, it caught what it was after and withdrew it. The object was a red bandanna.

Jon came down from the rise and rejoined the path, moving quickly to that part of the field where the scarecrow hung. As he approached, the pair of crows sprang up and, cawing, headed to the safety of the trees.

Ten feet from the figure, Jon stopped. For yards around the cornstalks had been trampled. The piece of wood that had been thrust into the ground to hold the scarecrow's body was a fresh two-by-four, as was the bar on which the scarecrow's arms were stretched. On its feet were black clodhopper shoes. Clothesline rope wrapped several times around the waist secured the figure to the upright wood. Similar rope had been used to lash the arms. With its head slumped downward to one side, the scarecrow had an almost crucifixion pose.

Jon saw that the darkish stains across the chest and upper portion of the overalls were blood that had seeped out from rough gashes in the cloth and dried. Below the farmer's hat, the scarecrow wore the mask Jon remembered from the Harvest Hoedown of the night before—the bulbous nose and great buckteeth above the mouth that was still arcing upward in an oafish grin.

Jon tried to force his eyes away, but he could not. Behind the mask, he knew, there was the face of death—Rod Ramsey's face—the features frozen in an everlasting scream.

FOUR

JON LEANED AGAINST the Range Rover and watched as a policeman played out the spool of yellow tape and a second officer tacked it to the fence posts. Behind him Jon could hear the chatter of the police radio from inside the blue cruiser. The passenger side door was open, and Lieutenant Lydecker continued talking into a handset, mentioning the state police and other matters Jon couldn't make out.

After discovering Rod Ramsey's body, Jon had gone back to the Range Rover, and using his portable cell phone, called 911. Ten minutes later the Scarborough Police, in the person of Lieutenant Lawrence Lydecker and two other officers, arrived, roof lights of their cruisers flashing and sirens splintering the Sunday calm.

Following a hurried conversation among them, it was decided that the entire two-acre field would be designated as the crime scene. Another pair of officers, who had appeared soon after, were now scouring it for any evidence that might be found.

Finally, Lydecker had stationed a single officer and police cruiser at the entrance to the road to discourage visits by the curious who may have picked up the police reports and hastened to the cornfield for a firsthand look.

Since Jon's arrival at the field, the wind had increased, so that the cornstalks swayed continually, their thin brittle crackling a death rattle. Ramsey's body still hung from the stakes. But a short time ago a gust of wind had tilted the stakes backward slightly, at an angle, so that the figure had the appearance of a suppliant appealing to an empty sky.

Lieutenant Lydecker stepped out of the cruiser and

zipped up his gray parka. He was a saturnine man in his late forties, with a fringe of hair on his otherwise bald head. He walked toward Jon, blowing on his hands to keep them warm.

"I hate outdoor crime scenes in cold weather," Lydecker said. "You stand around freezing your butt off. The state crime squad should be here soon, though. I talked to them. They're on their way."

He stood beside Jon and looked in the direction of the field. "And, of course, it had to be Ramsey who screwed up my Sunday afternoon. I could have been home watching a Patriots game. Anyway, the sooner the state and the ME get here, the sooner they can cut down the son of a bitch, and the happier I'll be."

"It sounds like you weren't a fan of Ramsey either," Jon said.

Lydecker shrugged. "A lot of people weren't. Except maybe the ladies around town he was playing bed games with. The guy wasn't nicknamed Ramrod for nothing."

"So who do you think killed him? A jealous husband?"

"Could be, or maybe it was one of the ladies themselves. From what I've heard, enough people around Scarborough wanted Ramsey dead; they could've lined up like in a bakery and taken numbers."

A dark-blue police car appeared along the road, followed by a large ambulance-like vehicle with CONNECTICUT STATE POLICE emblazoned on the side. Below it were the words "Major Crime Squad."

"Here come the experts." Lydecker sighed. He turned from Jon and headed in the direction of the state-police car, as it stopped along the road. The crime-squad van halted behind it.

A state trooper got out of the car, crossed around and opened the passenger side door. What emerged were two beefy hands. One grasped the door; the other, the side mirror. A brown fedora appeared, followed by its wearer, a large man with a florid face. Dressed in a dark coat, he studied the cornfield briefly before lumbering in the direction of Jon and the lieutenant.

"Hello, Dan," Lydecker said to him.

"Hi, Larry." He shook Lydecker's hand, then offered it to Jon. "Foley," he said. "State police."

"Jon Wilder."

"You the one who found the victim?" Foley inclined his head toward the cornfield.

"Yes."

"What time was that?"

"A little before two."

Foley grunted noncommittally. He stepped to the fencing where the yellow tape was strung, and watched as three state policemen made their way into the field. One carried a camera. When the man reached the stakes where Ramsey hung, he began taking photos of the body and the area adjacent to it. The other troopers separated, each studying the ground and cornstalks that stood nearby. Foley grunted for a second time and rejoined Jon and Lydecker.

"How long since your last murder in Scarborough, Larry?"

"Ten years," Lydecker said.

"Was that the society dame who poured brandy over her naked lover and set him on fire?"

"Yes." The lieutenant frowned, remembering the crime.

"What did one of the newspapers call it? L'amour flambé?" asked Foley, chuckling. "I'll say this for your picture-postcard town. Your murder rate is a lot lower than Bridgeport or New Haven, but when you get one, it's a dilly. Who did you say the guy is hanging on the bars?"

"Rod Ramsey is his name," Lydecker said. "He was our first selectman."

The officers around the crime scene waved to Foley, indicating he and the others could enter the cornfield.

Foley turned to Jon and then Lydecker. "Well, what say we go pay our respects to the recently departed Mr. Ramsey."

He walked over to the fence again, held down the tape, and swung one leg across it, then the other. The lieutenant and Jon followed, as Foley batted his way through the cornstalks to the body.

When they reached it, Foley stepped forward until he stood directly in front of the stakes. He peered up and down the body, face impassive.

"What was the guy doing wearing a costume like that in the middle of a cornfield?" he asked of no one in particular. Then he winked at Lydecker. "Is that some sort of strange Scarborough custom, too?"

"There was a Halloween party at the grange last night," Lydecker informed him. "He and some of the others dressed like scarecrows."

Finally, Foley turned and addressed Jon. "Was he leaning back that way when you found him?"

"No," Jon said. "He—Ramsey—and the bars were fairly straight. The wind must have pushed them back."

Foley nodded at Lydecker. "See this, Larry? Lots of puncture wounds around the upper torso, but not all that much blood on him or on the ground. Probably killed somewhere and brought here."

"I'd say that," Lydecker agreed.

"Whoever killed him also probably dragged his body in that way." Foley gestured to the path among the broken stalks.

"I'd say that, too," Lydecker repeated. "And it looks like rigor's just beginning."

"Which means he's been dead at least twelve hours, give

or take. I'll leave that to Forensics.'' Foley looked at Jon. "Were you at this costume party last night?"

Jon nodded.

"And you saw Ramsey dressed like this?"

"Yes."

"What time was that?"

"Between ten and ten-thirty. The dancing scarecrows were the evening's big event," Jon said. "The party ended after that."

Foley grunted once more, but said nothing.

As the three men stood in silence, an old black Buick drove slowly down the road and stopped behind the state police van. Jon knew the car. It belonged to Dr. Norris Monchen, a local GP in his seventies, who also doubled as an assistant medical examiner for the state. Foley, Jon and Lydecker walked back to the road to join him.

The doctor was a small, wizened man with saucer eyes and a high voice, whose name was sometimes mispronounced as Munchkin. He met them at the fence and hands were shaken all around.

"Is it really Ramsey?" the doctor asked, incredulous.

"It is," Lydecker said.

The doctor shook his head. "Ironic. I gave him a physical just last week. He was in perfect health."

"Is that so?" Foley didn't seem to care, but let the doctor ramble on.

"Well, almost perfect," Monchen said. "His blood pressure was a little elevated. It might have been his heavy campaign schedule. But the reading was one-sixty over ninety-two."

Foley pursed his lips and looked down at the doctor. "I think when you examine him today, you'll find that's changed. It's zero over zero now," he said.

ON MONDAY MORNING, at Lieutenant Lydecker's request, Jon went to the headquarters of the Scarborough Police and provided a full statement concerning the discovery of Ramsey's body. When the interview with Lydecker was over, Jon debated with himself whether to return home and resume his work, or take care of some chores in town. He decided on the chores.

Traffic was a good deal lighter than it had been the day before, and activity around the town green was light. Jon made a quick stop at the post office, then walked to Fitch's Pharmacy to pick up a prescription for a lingering sinus problem that the cooler autumn temperatures had aggravated. The pharmacist, Lester Fitch, was nowhere to be seen. It occurred to Jon that Fitch must have been affected, too, by Ramsey's death. He recalled that Lester had been one of the dancing scarecrows at the Harvest Hoedown.

Returning to his car, Jon turned at Harbor Street. He passed Philander Webb's Antiques and briefly thought of stopping in to see what changes Mrs. Merriwell had made. But he admitted to himself that that was an excuse for seeing her again—or she might think so. He decided he would wait.

Across the street and half a block ahead, there was one stop he did intend to make. He pulled into an empty parking space in front of the shop. Approaching the door, he looked up at the beautifully carved sign above it. It read simply:

C. HIGHTOWER
WOODWORKER

Jon peered in through a front window. The shop was brightly lit, although its owner, Colin Hightower, was not in evidence. On a rolltop desk against the wall, a large tortoiseshell cat lifted its head and yawned when it saw Jon.

As he opened the door, the bell above the doorway chimed. Unlike the tinny-sounding bells some shopkeepers used to announce a visitor's arrival, this one gave off a delicate high note, as pure as crystal. The bell was from a Himalayan temple in a remote corner of Bhutan, Colin had once told him. "Unusual," Jon had remarked. But, of course, there was nothing whatsoever about Colin Hightower that he considered usual.

The sound of the bell was replaced by the rising whistle of a teakettle coming to a boil in the rear room of the shop.

"Colin. It's me," Jon called. "Fix your tea first. I'll wait."

"You bloody well *will* wait," a voice boomed out in response. "Do you think I would deny myself the pleasures of a recently arrived Darjeeling without allowing it to steep adequately?"

Jon smiled to himself. Colin Hightower was in familiar crusty form. Jon knew it was a public pose the man assumed against the world to mask a sensitive and vulnerable personality.

"Take your time," Jon said.

The voice from the rear room softened. "Would you like a bit yourself? It came in a new shipment I got yesterday. I'm told it's excellent."

"Don't bother on my account."

"Jonathan, don't bother *me* with wishy-washy answers like 'don't bother.'" The voice had regained its verve. "Would you like a cup of tea or not?"

"Yes. Please."

"That's better. Indulge me for a few more moments. Then I'll pour."

"Fine," Jon said.

He sat down in a large ladderback chair and looked around the shop. The modest occupation of woodworker by which Colin chose to identify himself gave little hint of the man's mastery of the art. A good portion of his business came from the restoration and refinishing of fine antique furniture, not only for private owners, but for collectors, dealers and museums in New England and beyond. Yet, he was also a cabinetmaker and wood sculptor of extraordinary talent, creating everything from chairs and tables that could rival Chippendale to delicate carvings of birds and other animals.

Jon rose and went to inspect an armoire in tiger maple that stood beside the desk. Then he heard the *ting* of a kitchen timer, followed by the step-thump rhythm of Colin walking with his cane. The limping gait continued across the workroom floor. Abruptly, Hightower emerged; a great barrel-chested man in his late sixties, whose salt-and-pepper beard was complemented by an unruly riot of gray hair. For those rude enough to ask about his limp, Colin informed them he had been severely injured as a child, after being dragged into the Kashmiri jungles by a tiger. In fact, his father had served as an assistant to the British viceroy in that region. But the condition had actually been caused by a case of rickets that was misdiagnosed and left untreated for too long.

"Here's yours, dear boy," Colin said.

He handed Jon a Wedgwood cup and saucer that he carried in his free hand, then turned and clumped back to the workroom. When he returned, he shooed the cat off the desk and placed his own cup down on it. He set his cane against the desk, then gently eased himself into a Windsor chair that seemed inadequate for his considerable girth.

"So..." Colin Hightower began, "I gather our first selectman has saved me the trouble of voting against him on Election Day."

Jon pulled up the chair opposite. "You heard about Rod Ramsey then."

"Good news travels fast." Colin raised his teacup. "To more pleasant subjects, try the tea. I value your opinion."

Jon took a sip. "Delicious."

"'Delicious'? Is that all you can say? Surely, you have enough facility with words, Jon, so as to give me a more colorful description. Telling me this Darjeeling is delicious is like appraising a Lafite Rothschild sixty-one as 'tasty.'"

Jon smiled. "Colin, you never change."

Colin Hightower returned the smile. "I do hope not. Thank you for the compliment." He raised his cup again.

"Actually, it was sent to me by one of our worldwide-tea group who lives in Rawalpindi," Colin said. "This is a Darjeeling Mist: its leaves are found above four thousand feet. And mind you, this is not the second flush, whose leaves are picked in June, but the autumnal. It's the very best."

Colin closed his eyes and delicately sipped the tea as if it were the nectar of the gods. Eyes open again, he leaned forward in his chair. "Now tell me all you know about the murder."

"The state police have started their investigation. Autopsy results should take several weeks."

"I make it a rule never to speak ill of the deceased," Colin Hightower said. "But in Roderick Ramsey's case there *are* no good words to be spoken."

"Did you have some sort of disagreement with him?"

Colin cradled the teacup in his hands and gazed idly in the direction of the street, as if choosing his answer carefully. "I once told Ramsey to his face," he said, "that Scarborough would be better off if he were eliminated from our midst.

"But I didn't mean he should be killed," Colin went on. "It was in the heat of argument, that's all. I threatened to sue him over a Sheraton highboy I had refinished for him. He never paid me for the work, except for a deposit. The man was ethically and morally despicable. And I believe most of Scarborough shared my opinion."

"Then why did they keep electing him to office?"

"For the same reasons most politicians are elected," Colin said. "He told people what they wished to hear. He was handsome, charming in an unctuous sort of manner, and articulate. He was also at the center of the power interests in this town, which he controlled very well."

"What's more, he never had much competition for the office," Jon suggested. "Not in this election, anyway."

Colin snorted. "Hardly. Our second selectman, Bernie Benjamin, is a fool. If you were voting, who would you rather have managing the town's affairs—a crooked former lawyer like Ramsey, or a three-hundred-pound simpleton with the mind of a short-order cook, which Benjamin used to be?"

Jon gave Colin a wry look. "Is there anyone in Scarborough you *do* like?"

"Truthfully, not many. You are one."

"Thank you."

"Although you can be tiresomely serious sometimes, Jon."

"Oh?"

"Infrequently, I'm glad to say. Nonetheless, there are those moments when you could enjoy yourself more. What is the phrase?—Lighten up." Colin sipped at his tea. "I also like Madeleine Thoreau. The woman has intelligence and an eye for human foibles, even if that eye is occasionally blurred by alcohol.

"And I'll add someone further to that list," Colin said. "A new arrival. The young woman who bought Philander Webb's Antiques. She's very pretty, bright, and has a wit that's nearly equal to my own."

"That's quite a compliment," Jon said.

"She's quite a woman," Colin answered him. "And having been thrice married, I consider myself as good a connoisseur of women as I am of tea."

Colin pushed himself up from his chair and grasped his

cane. "Apropos of that, how about a touch more of the Darjeeling?"

"Thanks. But I've got work to do." Jon rose as well.

Colin nodded. "As do I. I must apply myself aggressively to Mrs. Burnwell's chest. It's massive." Seeing Jon's expression, Colin smiled. "In this case, I'm speaking of her chest of drawers. I'm giving it a second coat of stain."

They exchanged good-byes. Jon left the shop and crossed the street to the Scarborough Smoke Shop. The place sold newspapers, magazines and candy, as well as cigarettes and other tobacco products. He scanned the front pages of several area newspapers. As expected, news of Ramsey's death was prominently featured. The lead paragraph of one called it a "bizarre killing," and suggested the police were at a loss for clues.

He paid for the newspapers and stepped out into the street, when he felt something brush against his feet. He looked down and saw it was a crumpled piece of paper. As he bent to pick it up to throw in the trash container near the curb, he saw Rod Ramsey's picture and realized it was a discarded campaign circular.

Jon turned around and saw he was standing opposite the storefront that had been the headquarters for the first selectman's reelection campaign. Above the door, across the full length of the building, was a red-white-and-blue sign with the familiar "RRR," and below it, the words were spelled out. Giant posters of the smiling candidate himself remained taped to the windows, urging the electorate of Scarborough to return to office the candidate with "Vision—Integrity—Experience."

Yet on the day before Election Day itself, when Ramsey's headquarters would normally have been bustling with campaign workers, a single young woman sat at a desk, talking on the telephone, her face still mirroring her disbelief at the news of Ramsey's death. After anticipating an easy victory, his supporters now had to confront the awful truth that between last Saturday night and Sunday morning, some unknown person had accosted Roderick Ramsey and, in a few swift moments of violence and horror, cast the one dissenting vote that nullified all polls and predictions of the first selectman's certain reelection.

IT WAS exactly noon as Jon pulled the Range Rover into the garage. As he headed toward the door that led to the rear hall of the house, he heard the muffled ringing of the telephone. He jogged to his study and grabbed up the phone.

"Jon, is that you?" the woman's smoky voice said. He knew immediately who the caller was.

"Hello, Madeleine."

"I've been calling you all morning. Is it true?"

"Is what true?"

"What I heard," she said. "You were the one who found Rod Ramsey's body yesterday? That you were out looking for some bird and found him strung up in a cornfield with his scarecrow costume on?"

"Yes."

"Was it a ghastly sight? Scratch that," she added quickly. "For your sake and mine both, spare the details. Anyway, that's not the reason that I called. Two reasons, actually. The first is to tell you the funeral will be tomorrow at the Congregational church. It's not really a funeral. It's a memorial service."

"Thanks for the information. But he wasn't one of my favorite people. I'd feel like a hypocrite if I went."

"He wasn't the favorite of a lot of people, Jon, but they'll still be at the church."

"Even so—"

"The other reason is, I'd like you to be with me," Madeleine went on. "You may or may not know it, but Rod and I had a brief thing a long time ago. It ended badly, but we sort of, you know, kept in touch. I suspect some of his other castoffs will be there, and probably alone, except the married ones whose husbands never guessed. I don't want to look like just another of the Ramsey Rejects. Will you come with me?"

"Madeleine—"

"The service is at eleven. We can meet at the church and after it's over go our separate ways. I just want somebody to sit with. Please, Jon. As a favor."

"Okay." He sighed. "But don't expect me to offer any platitudes of tribute for the deceased."

"Jon, you're a darling. Tomorrow at eleven at the church. I'll probably be dressed in red, not black. I hate black, it's so—"

"Funereal?"

She laughed. "It is. Besides, red was Rod's favorite color. It's the least I can do for him. See you tomorrow."

He heard a breathy kiss. The phone clicked off.

FIVE

A CHILL November drizzle was falling when Jon parked beside the green and walked to the Congregational church. A line of mourners, all holding umbrellas, were filing slowly through the wide front doors, and Jon regretted he'd brought neither an umbrella nor a hat. Near the street entrance to the church's parking lot, he spotted Madeleine Thoreau. True to her word, she was dressed in a red raincoat and held an umbrella of the same color above her head. She saw Jon and waved.

"I'm glad you didn't have a change of heart," she said as he approached.

"I'm here in body, at least," he told her. "My spirit decided to stay home."

"Thanks again for coming. And the body I'll accept." She gave him a quick kiss. "By the way, you see I'm wearing red."

"You look lovely."

"After we talked, it occurred to me that red is also the devil's color." Madeleine laughed. "Of course, knowing Rod, he's already made a deal with the devil for mineral rights to the brimstone. Shall we go in?" She offered Jon her arm.

He took it and together they joined the others moving up the walkway to the church. Looking at them, Jon still had mixed feelings about coming. Although he knew it was uncharitable, he didn't feel any more kindly toward Rod Ramsey now that the man was dead. On the other hand, he was glad he could provide Madeleine with an escort. And he admitted to himself that he was frankly curious about

who might be in attendance at the service. Or who wouldn'
be.

Reading the morning newspaper earlier, he'd learned ad
ditional details of the crime. After the discovery of th
body, the police had visited the first selectman's house, :
stylish contemporary three miles from the center of th
town. There were no neighbors within half a mile. Whe
the police arrived, they found Ramsey's sports car parke
in the driveway. On the walk leading to the house, ther
was considerable blood. The speculation was that Ramse
had not bothered to put the car in the garage after returnin
from the Harvest Hoedown. Instead, as he was walkin
from his car to the house, still dressed in his scarecrov
costume, he'd been accosted by the murderer and stabbe
to death. The killer had then transported the body to th
cornfield, where it had been tied up on the stakes.

As Jon and Madeleine stepped into the nave, he saw th
church was crowded. But the last pew on the right remaine
unoccupied and they slid into it. The pews in front of them
were filled and ushers were busily setting up folding chair
along the aisles on both sides. The doleful chords of
church organ droned lugubriously on. The organist, wh
was also the town's undertaker, seemed to perform best a
moments such as this.

Because this was a memorial service and not a funeral
there was no casket visible. The body was, in fact, still th
property of the state medical examiner, undergoing an au
topsy and other tests. Jon wondered why the organizers o
this service, whoever they were, had chosen to hold it onl
three days after Ramsey's death. Perhaps because it wa
Election Day, and since the first selectman regrettably coul
not attend the celebration of his reelection victory, thi
event, at least, would honor him.

Here and there among the mourners Jon could see hand
kerchiefs and tissues held to eyes. In every case, the perso

was a woman. For their part, the men sat stony-faced. Beside him, Madeleine Thoreau was also studying the crowd. He remembered her remark the night before about the Ramsey Rejects, and he wondered just how many were sitting here in church today. In his first political campaign for local office, Ramsey had vowed that, if elected, he would show "a mastery of town affairs." Few knew at the time how determinedly he would fulfill that vow.

Quietly, at the far end of the pew, another figure entered and sat down. It was Lieutenant Lydecker. After a brief show of reverence, he, too, began studying the mourners. Jon saw him pull a hymnal from the rack in front of him, open it, place a small pad inside the open book and surreptitiously begin making notes.

The organ music ceased. From the rear, along the center aisle, four figures in dark suits marched single-file to the front of the church and moved into the left-hand pew. As they turned to sit, Jon saw their faces. They were Bernie Benjamin, Justin Kittridge, Aaron Peabody, and Lester Fitch.

Now down the aisle came a handsome silver-haired man with a deep tan. "Rod's father," Madeleine whispered at Jon's shoulder. "He lives in Florida."

The man was followed by a slim woman in black silk, her face shrouded in a veil. Beside her moved a pale, awkward boy of about eleven in a ill-fitting dark suit. Jon remembered hearing once that Ramsey had been married years ago. Was this the former wife? And could the boy be their son? The woman and the boy joined the silver-haired man in the first pew to the right.

Suddenly, from a door behind the altar, the Reverend Chester Rill appeared in his white vestments, his fleshy face gazing beatifically at the assemblage. He lifted up his arms, as if ready to take flight.

"All rise," he announced, in a high and slightly nasal

voice. "Let us sing together hymn number sixty-nine, 'Abide With Me.'" Amid the shuffling of feet, the congregation stood. The organ sounded out the introduction. People coughed. The hymn began.

The service followed a familiar form. At the conclusion of the hymn, Rill offered a brief prayer, there was another hymn, then a psalm was read. Jon noted that the psalm was number 102. He knew it well. "I watch and am as a sparrow alone on a house top," one of the lines went. Again, casting his eyes across the sea of mourners in the church, Jon realized he had become a watcher also, hoping that, through some sort of clue or gesture, he would spot the person who had ended Ramsey's life. He was surprised, then, when he glanced to the far end of the aisle where he sat, and saw Lieutenant Lydecker watching *him.*

The Reverend Rill stepped to the pulpit and bestowed his smarmy smile on the congregation once again. "Roderick Ramsey—Rod, as we all called him—was a friend of mine," the minister began. "Just as he was of every one of you who gather here today to pay him tribute for a final time. We mourn his death. But it is his life I wish to celebrate…"

What came next was a tedious chronology of Ramsey's life: his childhood and youth in Massachusetts, his college years spent at some small school in Vermont, his law degree earned on the West Coast. Nowhere in the minister's remarks was there a reference to marriage or a child. Instead, most of what was said focused on the public figure, from the time he came to Scarborough six years ago, established a law practice, and involved himself in local politics.

The reverend had begun rhapsodizing on Ramsey's contributions to town government, when Jon noticed a young woman in the pew a row ahead of him. He couldn't see her face. But her hair was luxuriantly black and spilled over the collar of the thin beige raincoat that she wore. He also saw her head was bowed and that her shoulders seemed to shake with silent sobs.

"Good night, sweet prince..." the minister intoned, ending his remarks with Horatio's eulogy to the dead Hamlet. Given the adenoidal monotone in which it was delivered, it had a somewhat comic quality. Jon heard several snickers from the crowd, and nearby a man whispered, "Good riddance is more like it."

The service drew to its conclusion. Another hymn was sung, the Lord's Prayer recited, a benediction pronounced. What surprised Jon was that at no time did the Reverend Rill ask any member of the congregation to offer personal memories of the deceased. Whatever private thoughts or recollections each might have, it was apparent they would stay that way.

The chords of the recessional began. Robes flowing, Rill swept up the center aisle. In the front pew, the veiled woman stood and led the boy up the aisle with her, followed by the silver-haired man. In the pew opposite, the four black-suited figures also stood, their heads downcast, and headed toward the rear.

Then, as a group, the other mourners rose and the church began to empty. Jon and Madeleine waited for their chance to step into the aisle. Among those attending the service, Jon now saw several young women weeping softly to themselves. Of the older men and women, most appeared expressionless, except for two men who, incongruously, were grinning.

In the vestibule of the church, only the Reverend Rill was there to greet the mourners as they left. The silver-haired man, the veiled woman and the boy were nowhere to be seen. As Madeleine approached the minister, he seized her hands and kissed her on both cheeks.

"Dear Madeleine, how good of you to come," he oozed.

"I wouldn't have missed it for the world, Chester," Madeleine said.

Rill grabbed Jon's hands next, pumping them. "Jon Wilder... Bless you, too, for being here. Such a great loss to our town. Rod was an extraordinary man."

The Reverend withdrew his hands and waved over Jon's shoulder to someone in the crowd. Jon took the opportunity to move on without responding.

Outside, the rain had become steadier. Jon looked down from the top step at the crowd of people spilling out along the sidewalk and around the cars parked on the street. In spite of the rain, many lingered, talking in small groups, umbrellas raised above their heads. Somewhat separated from the rest and sharing a single umbrella were Bernie Benjamin, Aaron Peabody, Lester Fitch and Justin Kittridge. Abruptly, the four separated, each man walking briskly in a different direction.

Jon and Madeleine came down the steps of the church. At the sidewalk, she paused and took Jon's hands. "Thanks again for coming with me, Jon. It made it easier."

"I'm glad."

"How about lunch at the inn? If you have time."

He shook his head. "I really don't. I've got a lot of work to do at home. And I still should go and vote."

She gave him a regretful glance, then nodded. "Sure."

"Where's your car?" he asked. "I'll walk with you."

"Don't bother. It's in the parking lot behind the church." She reached and gave him a quick kiss on the cheek, then turned again and walked briskly to the driveway of the church parking lot.

Jon started for his car. What caused him to glance up at a leafless sycamore beside the church, he didn't know. But sitting in its branches, untroubled by the milling crowd of mourners, he saw a single crow facing the church.

It did not stir. Studying it, Jon recalled that certain ancient tribes considered it a fearful omen if a crow was present at a person's death. The bird was thought to be an emissary of the Evil Spirit, who on death would seize the soul in its rapier-sharp talons and fly with it to the world of the damned.

IN THE YEARS since the Scarborough Middle School was built, its gymnasium had been used for everything from physical-education classes and school assemblies to adult-fitness classes and quilting contests sponsored by the PTA. But several times a year, voting machines were rolled onto the hardwood floor, and the citizens of Scarborough had the opportunity to vote yea or nay on the town budget, bond issues, and prospective candidates for a variety of local offices.

Jon found a space in the school parking lot opposite an old white Chevy van. He switched off the wipers, turned up his coat collar, and prepared to step out into the rain. At the same time, he noticed several of the cars around him still had bumper stickers urging Ramsey's reelection. It was to be expected, Jon supposed; this soon after the man's death, few had taken time to scrape the stickers off. In fact, Ramsey might still gather some votes in memoriam from his most staunch supporters. But it amused Jon to consider that for Ramsey to remain as first selectman, he would have to stage the most miraculous political comeback since the return of Lazarus.

Just then Jon saw a figure coming toward him. Although the windshield of the Range Rover was streaked with rain, he recognized the man as Oren Bellkirk. Dressed in a gray coat and rain-soaked cap pulled forward on his head, the owlish face was visible, as well as the large, bulging eyes, made even larger by the thick-lensed glasses Bellkirk wore.

A hardscrabble farmer with a small spread north of town, he raised chickens and sold eggs along with his farm produce. He used the van to make deliveries around the area. In his late sixties, Bellkirk was considered an "odd bird" by many; appropriately, Jon thought, since in addition to his chickens, he also provided ducks and turkeys on request. Although Jon had once been an infrequent customer, he hardly knew the man. Yet he felt a certain pity for him, too. Both he and Jon had lost their wives in the same year. Since then, Bellkirk had remained unmarried, and had hired no one to assist him with the chores, stubbornly determined to maintain the farm alone.

Bellkirk approached the van, reached into a pocket, and with arthritic fingers fumbled to insert the door key in the lock. That task accomplished, he climbed into the van. At last, the engine gave a throaty cough and came to life. Slowly, the van backed out of the parking spot. Finally it swung around and started forward, joining the other vehicles that were exiting the lot.

It was then that Jon noticed the sun visor on the passenger side of the van had been turned downward. Pinned to it was a large white button with the initials "RRR." Likely, Ramsey had handed out a number of them at some senior-citizen campaign stop, asking the recipients to wear them, or display them on the visors of their cars. Bellkirk probably had stuck it up there after receiving it, and since it wasn't visible inside the van, forgotten it.

Jon stepped out of the Range Rover and walked quickly in the direction of the school. When he entered the gymnasium, he was pleased to see the number of people lined up before the voting booths was not as great as he had feared. At the registrars' table two ladies sat—one small, the other a large lump of a woman with a face the texture of unkneaded dough. The large woman greeted Jon and asked his name. Using a ruler, she scanned down a list of eligible voters, then tapped it with her pencil.

"Wilder, Jonathan M." she recited, looking at the page. "You're still on Plover Point Road?"

"That's correct."

"Machine three, please. At the far end."

Jon thanked her and walked to the end of the gymnasium, where six people stood in a line leading to the voting booth. The curtains of the booth were closed. A moment later, they parted, and a man stepped out. Jon saw it was Lester Fitch.

He also noticed Jon and appeared startled. Fitch seemed eager to walk on, but stopped instead.

"Uh, Jon, how are you?" Fitch's sallow face seemed drawn; the eyes behind the wire-frame glasses tired. As he spoke, Fitch ran his tongue around his lips. "Listen, I'm sorry I wasn't in the pharmacy yesterday when you came in. The desk calendar refill you ordered—it arrived."

"Good. I'll get it the next time I'm there."

"I should've mentioned it to the assistant pharmacist," Fitch said. "But these past three days have been very upsetting for business. With Rod's death and all."

Jon wanted to ask how Ramsey's death had affected business at the pharmacy, but Lester Fitch continued on. "A tragic waste to lose a man like that before his time. He was my lawyer, you know."

"I didn't."

"Oh, yes. Anyway, stop by. I'll make sure you get the calendar."

"I will, thanks. Give my best to Muriel."

"Indeed, indeed," Fitch said, and headed for the door of the gymnasium.

Three people now remained ahead of Jon to cast their votes. In the waiting line leading to the booth beside his own, Jon saw the owner of the lumberyard. While those around him chatted amiably, Aaron Peabody remained dour and aloof, the figure of New England rectitude.

When it was Jon's turn, he stepped into the booth and threw over the lever that closed the curtains and activated the machine. Scanning the list of candidates, Jon saw Roderick Ramsey's name was still featured on the ballot. Below it was the name of Bernard Benjamin, who by default would automatically succeed Ramsey in the first selectman's post. Jon voted for neither man, but instead clicked down the ballot marker for an able and no-nonsense older woman, who was running as an independent candidate.

There were also a dozen candidates for various lesser offices in the town government. Mrs. Constance Milbauer, who had occupied the office of town clerk for thirty years, was running unopposed. Jon also saw the name of Lester Fitch listed as a candidate for a seat on the town's planning and zoning board. Then he remembered Fitch had been appointed to the board last year by Ramsey after an opening occurred. Jon voted for him. Although he considered Lester Fitch rather weak-willed and pliable, he liked him and believed Fitch had the town's interests at heart.

He had just voted his approval of two local charter issues, when he heard loud shouting in the gymnasium, followed by voices advocating quiet in more reasonable tones.

Jon opened the curtains of the booth and stepped out. As he started back across the floor, he saw Gus Schiller pounding on the table of the registrars and heaping expletives on the two women who sat there. Schiller seemed resoundingly and incorrigibly drunk.

The large woman was no longer smiling, but instead pored over the voter lists. The small woman was regarding Schiller stonily.

Jon heard Schiller mention Ramsey's name, followed by more expletives.

The small woman now rose and hurried to an exit door. At the same time, several men in the crowd had begun surrounding Schiller, trying to calm him. Schiller punched one in the chest.

As more men attempted to restrain him, Schiller shoved the men aside and stormed in the direction of the exit door. Simultaneously, the door opened and a policeman entered, followed by the small woman. The officer attempted to grab Schiller's arm. Jon anticipated trouble. He didn't want to be a part of it, and headed quickly for another door.

Hurrying across the parking lot, he climbed into the Range Rover, set the windshield wipers to full, and merged into the long line of vehicles trying without much success to exit. The police officer who'd been directing traffic earlier was inside the gym now, dealing with Gus Schiller. As a result, cars entering and leaving the lot were at a standstill. Horns were leaned on, headlights flashed.

Suddenly, behind him, Jon heard tires squealing. He looked in the side mirror. Parallel the line of cars where Jon and the others sat, he saw Schiller's pickup truck coming at high speed. Confronting the congestion at the entrance to the lot, the pickup swerved across the lawn, roared through a muddy flower bed and lurched onto the road.

As it turned, Jon saw the tailgate was down and lengths of lumber stuck out from the rear. The boards were two-by-fours.

"THE PRICE IS as the tag suggests..." Colin was saying to a well-dressed younger couple, as Jon entered the woodworking shop the next morning. In contrast to them, Colin wore a varnish-spattered work shirt and his woodworker's apron, with awls and chisels visible. In his hands, Colin held a carving of a black-billed magpie.

Colin nodded fleetingly at Jon, then peered over his half-glasses at the couple. "Why do I ask this price for the bird carving?" he continued. "I will tell you. First, because the bird is carved in walnut, which is an extremely hard wood to sculpt. Second, because my birds are works of art. If you desire a crude duck decoy hacked out of pine, there are any number of amateur wood carvers in the area.''

''It's beautiful,'' the woman said, showing her embarrassment.

''What kind of bird is it?'' the man asked grudgingly. ''It looks like a blue jay.''

''It is a magpie,'' Colin told him. ''Blue jays have a crest.''

''Okay, we'll take it,'' the man said. He reached beneath his cashmere coat and took out a money clip. He peeled off some bills and handed them to Colin, along with a business card.

Colin placed them in a pocket of his apron and carried the carving to the rear room of the shop. He returned with it nesting in tissue paper in an open box. He handed the box to the woman, then looked at the man.

''May I ask you a question, sir?'' Colin said to him. ''Why, of all my sculpted birds, did you choose the magpie?''

''I didn't. My wife did,'' the man answered.

''Then it is you I compliment on your discerning taste, madam,'' Colin told her.

The woman smiled quickly, but said nothing.

''Let's go.'' The man took the woman by the arm and steered her toward the door.

Colin watched as the couple stepped into a Jaguar parked beside the curb, then looked at Jon. ''Ironically appropriate that fellow should have bought my magpie.''

''Why?''

''Because, as you well know, the magpie is an ill-tempered creature, notorious for stealing the eggs of other birds. From the man's business card, it seems he is a money manager for wealthy clients. How many of *their* nest eggs has he plundered, do you think?''

Colin gave an amused laugh. "Now to what do I owe the pleasure of your company today, dear Jon?"

"I wondered if you're free for lunch."

"A splendid thought. It's almost noon and I'm in the mood for a good hamburger. In spite of what I think of Bernie Benjamin, would you be agreeable to dining at his restaurant? We can congratulate him on his ascension to the post of first selectman yesterday."

"Fine."

"Good." Colin hung a "Closed" sign on the inside of the door, seized his cane and gestured with a flourish toward the door.

BERNIE'S BAR B-Q BARN was located three miles north of the village, close to the interstate, making it continually popular with both travelers and local residents. The restaurant was a lively, cheerful place located in a wooden building that had been converted from a former dairy barn. It retained the wide plank floor and barnwood walls, but the bar stood where the hayloft once had been, and wooden tables and chairs had replaced the cow stalls. Indeed, the only cows found in Bernie's Bar B-Q Barn nowadays appeared in ground form, grilled to varying degrees of doneness. In keeping with the restaurant's rustic origins, the waitresses were dressed as milkmaids, with halter tops and skirts cut well above the knees.

When Jon and Colin arrived, the front parking lot looked filled. Painting of the building's exterior was underway, and ladders and scaffolding blocked several of the spots. Jon was about to drive around to the rear lot, when he saw a space and pulled in. At the front door, they were greeted by a hostess in a low-cut calico sundress, who escorted them to a table. The menu was inscribed on the side of a small milk pail, which she set in front of them. Colin sat down, picked up the milk pail and studied it.

"Yes, a hamburger it shall be," he said. "I'll have what's called on the menu 'Bernie's Triple B.' That's a burger with bacon and blue cheese."

"I thought you were watching your weight," Jon said.

"I am. At the moment I'm watching it go up."

He patted his considerably ample stomach. "I'm a believer in acquiring an extra layer of fat to live on in the winter, like the hibernating bear."

A waitress suddenly appeared beside their table. "Drinks, guys?" she asked.

Colin raised an eyebrow. "Tell me—what are the house wines?"

"Red and white."

Colin sighed. "A diet soft drink then."

"The same for me," Jon said.

The waitress scribbled on her pad and went away.

"A diet soda with a Triple B?" Jon said. "Isn't that inconsistent?"

"Consistency is the curse of the prosaic mind." Colin withdrew the pair of half-glasses from beneath his jacket and studied the milk-pail menu for a second time. "Perhaps I'll have a salad, too."

"Well, if it isn't two of Scarborough's most famous VIPs. Welcome to the Barn," a voice boomed above them. It had a decided Boston accent; *bahn* for *barn*.

Jon and Colin looked up at the enormous grinning man who hovered over them, wearing an oversized white Stetson hat. Bernie Benjamin was more than six feet tall and only a recent doctor-imposed diet had got his weight below three hundred pounds. Still, his wattles spilled over the collar of his red turtleneck sweater in cascading folds. He offered Jon his hand. "How are you, Mr. Wilder?"

"Fine, Bernie. Congratulations." Jon shook the hand.

"First Selectman Benjamin, at last," said Colin.

"Thanks, thanks, both of you." Bernie Benjamin's grin

faded. "I'm just sorry for the way I got the job. But I mean, hey, it's the town charter. If the first selectman dies, the second selectman steps into his shoes. Even so, it was a tragedy." He shook his head, the wattles swinging back and forth.

The next moment his joviality returned. "So what'll it be?" he asked. "The spare ribs are on special today. And there's great barbecue chicken. I got a new supplier now."

"I'm having your incomparable Triple B," Colin replied.

"You'll never go wrong there," Bernie assured him. "It's the best."

The waitress arrived with Jon's and Colin's soft drinks. "Doreen, take good care of these gentlemen," Benjamin instructed her. "They're friends of mine."

She nodded nervously and took out her pad, as Bernie gave her a quick wink and moved on to the next table. Jon ordered a plain hamburger, medium; Colin, the Triple B, rare, with a salad on the side.

When they were alone again, Colin leaned back in his chair and cast his eyes over the lunchtime crowd.

"So…" Colin began. "You told me you attended Ramsey's funeral. Did you make any interesting observations while you were there?"

At that moment, Jon glanced toward the entrance door. He saw the hostess escorting Aaron Peabody and Justin Kittridge to a table on the far side of the room.

"As a matter of fact," Jon said, "four of the men who performed with Ramsey at the hoedown sat in the front row of the church. Two of them just came in. Kittridge and Peabody."

Colin stared at them over the half-glasses. "Thick as thieves as always. And I assume the other two were Bernie Benjamin and Lester Fitch?"

"And of course Chester Rill officiated at the service."

Jon added, "Frankly, I wondered if one of *them* might have killed Ramsey."

"They were supposed to be his friends."

"I know, but…"

Colin shook his head. "Perhaps. But I consider it unlikely."

"So who killed Ramsey?" Jon asked.

"Who killed Ramsey?" Colin repeated it slowly, savoring the words in his sonorous way. "Given the legions who disliked the man, it might be half the people in this restaurant. It could be that child in the booster seat." He nodded toward a family at a nearby table. "Or that old fellow with the walker, shuffling across the floor."

The waitress reappeared and put their lunches down in front of them. Colin seized her arm. "Or the killer may have been our lovely serving lass, Doreen. Tell me, Doreen, did you kill Roderick Ramsey?"

"Huh?" Doreen looked startled.

"Never mind, my dear. I find you innocent." Colin released her and the waitress left at once.

"Seriously," Jon went on, "I have an idea who the killer was."

"You do? Who?"

"Gus Schiller."

"The builder?"

"Yes."

"No, you're wrong," Colin responded. "The man may be a drunkard and a fool, but he doesn't have the soul of a murderer."

"When I was voting at the Middle School yesterday," Jon told him, "Schiller came in drunk. He was shouting something about Ramsey. Then, as he was leaving the parking lot, I saw he had some two-by-four boards in his pickup truck. The same kind that Ramsey's body had been tied to after he was killed."

Colin picked up his Triple B and took a massive bite.

"Look," Jon continued. "I also saw Schiller at the hoedown the night Ramsey died. He was drunk then. Suppose Schiller had a grudge against Ramsey for some reason, surprised him at his house and stabbed him in a rage."

"Delicious," Colin said. "The Triple B, I mean." He took a second bite, then ran a forefinger around the bun to catch some melting cheese.

"Listen," Jon went on, "the murderer was probably a man. To kill Ramsey, carry him into the cornfield, and lift him up onto the stakes, he'd have to be strong."

Colin finished his hamburger in three more bites, then started on his salad, saying nothing.

"We know the crime was brutal," Jon persisted. "And Schiller is a brutal man. Somebody should go to the police before the evidence gets cold."

"What's getting cold is your hamburger. Do eat."

"Colin, hear *me* out."

"Jon, hear me out. Please."

Colin put his salad to one side and regarded Jon with a fixed gaze. "You are the best friend I have in Scarborough, Jonathan. Perhaps my only one. You're a respected ornithologist, albeit self-taught, and a renowned painter of birds. You are also a competent musician, and an unrelenting tennis player, when you put aside your manners and decide to win. In sum, you are an all-round splendid man."

The pale blue eyes blinked once, but remained on Jon.

"What you are *not* is a detective, nor should you aspire to become one. Eschew such fanciful pursuits in which you have not the least bit of expertise. Stay home and paint your birds, and leave the world of mayhem and murder to those who claim to understand such madness. Am I making myself clear?"

"Very," Jon answered.

"Good." Colin appeared pleased.

"You're right about something else, too. My hamburger is cold," Jon said, picking up the bun.

"Well, while you finish it, I'll have some dessert."

Colin caught the waitress's attention as she passed, and ordered a peach cobbler.

Twenty minutes later, after coffee and a jovial good-bye at the door from Bernie Benjamin, Jon and Colin left the restaurant. The road leading back to the center of town wound through open fields and farmland, with wooded areas and occasional small ponds. As they crested a hill, Colin gestured at the scene. "That's one of the charms of Scarborough," he said. "The open land, that is."

He chuckled to himself. "Of course, our local Native American tribe will probably claim it's theirs by ancient treaty. Still, if it ever changes hands, I'd prefer tepees to tract housing."

Colin pointed to a field full of pumpkins. "Now there's a true picture of autumn in New England. Pumpkins in a field."

"Seeing them reminds me Thanksgiving is three weeks from tomorrow," Jon said. "Do you have any plans?"

"None at all."

"Then why don't you come over to the house. The last few Thanksgivings I was traveling. This year it'd be nice to have some people in."

"Who else have you thought of asking?"

"Mrs. Merriwell."

"A fine choice." Colin brightened. "I visited her shop yesterday. We had a lovely chat. Anybody else?"

"No. Just the three of us. When I get home I'll call old Bellkirk and order one of his dressed turkeys."

"Then let me bring the champagne. Or, as a champion of birds, would you prefer cold duck?"

"I'll have some wine. Just bring yourself."

"No, I insist. Champagne it is. What time would you like me there?"

"How's three? We'll have cocktails and hors d'oeuvres first."

"Fine," said Colin. "And despite the fact that I have recently consumed a Triple B, a salad, a peach cobbler and coffee, the prospect of your dinner stirs my appetite. I accept your invitation with great pleasure."

For the remainder of the ride, Colin was uncharacteristically silent, except for burping several times.

"Please do excuse me," he said to Jon at last. He put a hand to his midsection. "After eating one of Bernie's Triple Bs, I've concluded that I should have asked him for another B. Bicarbonate." He burped again.

"Maybe that's how Ramsey died," Jon ventured. "He overdosed on Triple Bs."

"My friend," Colin said, in his stentorian bass voice, "let it go. As much as Ramsey's death intrigues you, give it up. The crime will eventually be solved by the police, not by you. Involve yourself, and you could be the victim of a great deal of harm, which, as your friend, would make me very sad. So I repeat, Jon, *let it go.*"

SIX

JON REACHED INTO the container of watercolor brushes, choosing one among them, a Kolinsky sable. He wet it, then dipped it to the palette for the shade of paint he sought and made long even strokes, filling the area of the crow's upper back…

Evidence. These were stab wounds in the body. The weapon had to be a knife. Have the police found it? If so, have they run tests on it? On the stakes Ramsey's body was tied to?… Suppose they match the two-by-fours I saw in Schiller's truck?

The smooth watercolor paper took the paint exactly as Jon wished…

Opportunity. After the Harvest Hoedown, the murderer surprised Ramsey outside the first selectman's house… Schiller was alone then. Did he follow Ramsey home?

Jon painted in the underfeathers, giving them a somewhat lighter tone. He glanced briefly at the model of the crow beside him on the table. In the late-morning light, the feathers of the model glistened with a purplish-black sheen. Jon took more paint onto the brush, and started on the undertail next…

Motive. The killer hated Ramsey for a reason… Schiller obviously did—considering his outburst against Ramsey on Election Day.

Jon leaned forward at the drawing board, studying what he had done so far. The sharp angle of the November sun was distorting the true shading of the colors now. It was time for a break anyway. He cleaned and pointed the brushes and hung them up to dry. He'd fix his lunch, then drive to the post office in town, and return to the crow painting in the afternoon.

IT WAS A SURE SIGN the holidays were coming. Collecting items from his postal box, he counted eight flyers advertising Christmas sales, plus four appeals from charities for contributions. He discarded the flyers, put the appeals in the pocket of his coat and left the post office. As he started down the steps, he saw Arthur Tingley coming toward him, dressed in the familiar yellow slicker he had kept from those days when he'd been the captain of a fishing boat.

"How do, Mr. Wilder," he said, as they shook hands. "Did you ever see the Townsend's solitaire I called about?"

"No," Jon said. "Actually, the cornfield you mentioned was the place where Ramsey's body was discovered."

"That so?" Tingley gave a shrug. "The missus told me something about the murder, but I didn't get where he was at." He shrugged again, as if dismissing the subject from his mind.

"By the way, I was going to give you a call later," Tingley went on. "Today I saw a pair of yellowthroats along the shore near Ketchem's Creek. Migrating late, I guess. I thought if you were down that ways, you might want to take a look."

"Thanks. I'll keep it in mind."

Tingley reached under his slicker and produced a pack of unfiltered Camel cigarettes. He lit one, inhaled deeply, coughed, then waved the air between himself and Jon.

"Emma's always after me to give these up. Can't do it. It'll be my death. My doctor told me that last spring. Of course, as you can see, I'm still alive."

He gave a rasping laugh, then seized Jon's hand and shook it for a second time. "Well, good to see you, Mr. Wilder. Take care."

"You, too," Jon said. He watched Tingley walk toward a vintage Dodge Dart parked nearby.

It was then Jon remembered: Tingley had once mentioned that his property adjoined the land where Gus Schiller lived.

A short time later, the Range Rover lurched and bumped along the driveway leading to the yellow saltbox that was the home of Emmaline and Arthur Tingley. As he approached, Jon noticed at least half a dozen bird feeders hanging from the trees. Others of various designs and shapes perched on stout poles encircling the house.

The Dodge Dart was idling in front of a detached garage. He saw Tingley to one side of the garage, opening the doors. Jon pulled up behind the Dart. Tingley turned and looked at him, surprised.

"Sorry, Arthur," Jon said, getting out of the Range Rover. "But there was something I meant to ask you when I saw you earlier."

"What's that? Hold it. Let me switch the motor." Tingley returned to the Dart, reached in and turned off the car's engine.

"You once told me Gus Schiller owned the property next door," Jon said. "I mean, his house is up there, isn't it?" He waved at a row of hemlocks separating Tingley's driveway from a dirt road that led up a hill.

"Yep." The man nodded. "He's still there, I regret to say."

"Would you remember if he came home late last Saturday night? Or early the next morning?"

"Wouldn't know. I'm a pretty heavy sleeper," Tingley said.

Looking beyond him now, Jon saw Mrs. Tingley coming around the corner of the house carrying a large Mason jar. Like her husband, she was in her sixties, but short and rounded with a sweet, cherubic face.

"Mr. Wilder," she chirped, approaching them. "You're just in time to see what I was fixing for the birds."

She unscrewed the lid of the Mason jar and showed Jon the contents. "Peanut butter, with ground corn, shortening and flour mixed together. The birds love it. Care to try some?"

"No, thank you."

"Emma, the reason Mr. Wilder is here," her husband said, "is on account he wants to know about our neighbor."

"Mr. Schiller?" she asked Jon.

"Yes."

"Less said the better." Emma Tingley frowned and capped the Mason jar.

"I was just wondering if you heard him going up his driveway late Saturday night," Jon asked. "Or maybe the next morning."

"Didn't have to hear," she said. "I saw."

"You saw Gus Schiller coming home?"

"It was nine-thirty in the morning, Sunday. He wasn't much to look at neither, with the blood."

Jon caught his breath. "There was blood on him?"

"Plenty. I was on my way to church; the service starts at ten. I was about to turn onto the road, when he comes barreling along, not in his pickup truck this time, but in the Olds. He doesn't even stop. Instead, he turns and guns it up his drive to beat the band."

"But what about the blood? How was he dressed?"

"He had on a white shirt and some kind of leather thing with straps across the top. His face was cut and there was bloodstains on his front. It looked like he'd been in a fight and lost."

Jon looked toward Schiller's driveway for a second time. If it's the fight I'm thinking of, he told himself, it was the other man who lost.

THE OFFICES OF the Scarborough Police Department were in a gray, stucco-covered building at the upper end of Harbor Street. As Jon arrived, he saw a pair of police cruisers parked in front. A month ago the first two letters of the word POLICE had been painted out by vandals with a spray can, leading to a number of jokes among those for whom the reputation of the Scarborough Police was not particularly high.

Entering the building, Jon saw Lieutenant Lydecker's office door was partly open. He knocked briefly and began to open it.

"Larry, it's Jon, I—"

"Don't talk; don't move," Lydecker commanded. He was standing on the far side of his desk, his bald head gleaming under the fluorescent ceiling light. One hand was behind his back; the other, with a finger extended, pointed straight at Jon. Jon froze.

Slowly, the hand behind Lydecker came forward, rising gradually above the surface of the desk. Gripped in it was a flyswatter. Lydecker glanced briefly at some papers spread out on the desk. Then, in a lightning-fast move, he brought the swatter down on top of them.

"Got you!" Lydecker reached down, picked up the dead fly and dropped it in a wastebasket beside the desk.

"Would you believe, a week into November and I've still got flies. But one less than I had yesterday. Come in."

He waved Jon into the office with the flyswatter and sat down behind his desk. "So what can I do for you, Jon?"

Jon shut the door and sat in a wooden chair facing him across the desk. "I want to talk to you about the Ramsey case."

Lydecker's eyebrows rose. "Is that a fact?"

"Do you have time?"

"My time is your time, as Rudy Vallee used to say."

He opened the top drawer of the desk and tossed in the flyswatter. "What's on your mind?"

"I think I know who killed Rod Ramsey."

"Oh?"

"I wasn't sure how far along you were. I mean, I haven't heard of any suspects yet."

"There are suspects. At least one, possibly," Lydecker said. "Hold on, let me get the file."

The lieutenant reached into a lower drawer and brought up a manila folder with a rubber band around it. He removed the rubber band and placed it to one side, then spread the folder open on the desk.

"We're making progress slowly," Lydecker continued. "But *slowly* is the operative word. So anything that you can add is welcome."

"You may want to write this down," Jon said. He pointed to a yellow legal pad at one side of the desk.

Lydecker nodded. "Good idea."

The lieutenant picked up the pad and the wooden pencil next to it. He swung around in his chair, shoved the pencil into the electric sharpener behind him on the window ledge. After a loud whirring from the sharpener, Lydecker withdrew the pencil, swung around toward Jon again, and put the point of the pencil to the pad.

"Okay," Lydecker said. "You talk. I'll write. Tell me who killed Rod Ramsey."

"Gus Schiller. The builder."

As Jon anticipated, Lydecker's face registered surprise. "Well, well—imagine that," he said. "You're sure."

"I'm sure." Jon pulled his chair closer to the desk. "It comes together."

"How?" Lydecker laid the pencil to one side.

"I'll take it chronologically," Jon said.

"Whatever."

"Halloween night, the night of the Harvest Hoedown, Schiller brought a date."

"Who?"

"Mrs. Merriwell."

"The blonde who bought Philander Webb's Antiques?"

"Yes."

Lydecker gave a long low whistle. "Schiller's got good taste in women, at least. I'll give him that."

"But that night he was drunk," Jon said. "So drunk, in fact, that she refused to leave with him. I took her home instead."

Jon noticed the lieutenant had written nothing so far on the yellow pad. "Don't you want to make some notes?" he asked.

"Don't worry, I've got a good memory." Instead, Lydecker picked up the rubber band that had been around the folder and began playing with it in his hand.

"Then on Election Day," continued Jon, "while I was voting at the Middle School, Schiller showed up drunk again, and started cursing Ramsey. For what reason, I don't know."

"Schiller blamed Ramsey for getting the P and Z to fine him for some zoning violations," Lydecker said flatly. "Even threatened him. We know about that." Lydecker started a cat's cradle with the rubber band.

"Anyway, the police officer on duty outside the school had to be called." Jon said. "Schiller broke away and when he drove off, I saw he had some two-by-four boards in his truck; the same as those the killer used to tie Ramsey's body to. And get this—"

Jon pulled his chair to the near side of the lieutenant's desk. "I discovered *Schiller wasn't home at all the night that Ramsey died.* A neighbor saw him the next morning. He was still wearing his costume from the hoedown. And there was blood on it!"

The lieutenant remained silent, studying the rubber band he had now wound around his thumb. "I know," Lydecker said.

"You *know?*"

"I know Gus Schiller wasn't home that night. I know he was still in his costume Sunday morning. And I know it had blood on it. Shall I tell you what great detective work led us to that knowledge?"

Jon leaned back in his chair. "Please, I'd like to hear."

"Gus Schiller spent the night with us in the town lockup. Want to hear more?"

Jon didn't, but he nodded.

"The evening of the Harvest Hoedown we had a man directing traffic at the intersection of the highway and the grange-hall road. Schiller was waiting to turn. The officer noticed the left headlight of Schiller's car was out and waved him over to the side. Instead, Schiller ignores him, turns and speeds off down the road, straddling the center line. You with me so far, Jon?"

"Yes." Jon guessed where this was leading. He wished he could get up, apologize for taking the lieutenant's time and go.

"So," Lydecker continued, "the officer calls in and alerts us to a probable DWI. Another cruiser happened to be on the highway on patrol. The officer caught up with Schiller, hit the siren and the lights, and forced him off the road. When he asked Schiller to get out of the car, the guy was so wacked, he fell down on the gravel shoulder of the road and cut his head. The officer got him into the backseat of the cruiser, bleeding like a pig, and brought him here. We kept him in the drunk tank overnight. Sunday morning he had an industrial-strength hangover, but he was sober and could drive. So we took him back to where his car was parked. He drove home from there, I guess, still dressed in his costume with the blood on it."

"I see."

"I'm sorry." Lydecker unwound the rubber band. "I wasn't going to tell you the whole story. But you were so sure Schiller was the murderer, I had to."

Jon sighed. "I guess that puts you back to square one, doesn't it?"

"What do you mean?"

"I mean, I heard you don't have anything to go on yet in finding out who Ramsey's killer was."

"Not quite," Lydecker said. "I told you we have one possible suspect." He stretched the rubber band between his hands. "We found a piece of evidence a couple days ago."

"You did? What was it?"

"A knife. We kept searching the cornfield, and one of the fellows found it down there in the broken stalks."

"Was it the murder weapon?"

"Hard to tell. Forensics's running tests. It had blood on it, though."

"What about fingerprints?"

"Some."

"Whose were they? Do you know?"

The lieutenant nodded. "First, we tried a match with those we had on file here. No go. The state also came up with nothing. So we sent them to Washington. The FBI can cast a wide net. Did you know it can call up the fingerprints of anybody who's been in the military, or who even worked for the government in some sort of official way?"

"And did they find out who the fingerprints belong to?"

"Yep."

"Well, is it somebody in Scarborough?" Jon asked. "Or is that privileged information?"

"It is. But I'll tell you, anyway." Lydecker steepled his hands to his chin, the rubber band enclosing them.

He stared across the desk at Jon, then stretched the rubber band apart until it snapped.

"I'm sorry, Jon. The fingerprints are yours."

"That's impossible!"

"Improbable," Lydecker corrected. "Not impossible."

"For God's sake, do you think I killed Ramsey?"

"No. But on the other hand, I can't explain the knife."

"How could somebody get one of my knives?"

"You tell me." The lieutenant picked up the broken strand of rubber band and dropped it in an ashtray at the corner of his desk.

"My guess," Lydecker went on, "is it was someone who had access to your home. When you think about it, most of us have strangers or semi-strangers visiting our places all the time."

"You mean delivery people?"

"Delivery people, repairmen, household help, even kids who do odd jobs. How often do unfamiliar people show up at your door, wanting directions or asking for a contribution to a charity?"

"Last week I had a package deliveryman in the house," Jon said, remembering. "He told me it was his last trip of the day, and he asked if he could use my phone to call his girlfriend."

Lydecker sat back and gave an open-handed gesture. "See what I mean?"

"What kind of knife was it?"

"Long and pointed. And reasonably dull."

"And were my fingerprints the only ones found on it?"

"It appears that way. According to the state police."

Jon shook his head and took a long deep breath.

"Are you okay?" Lydecker asked. "You want a drink of water?"

"Yes." Jon took another breath to fill his lungs. "I guess the whole thing is just hitting me. I could use some water."

"Sure." Lydecker rose and left the room.

Jon closed his eyes and gripped the cold arms of the chair. He tried to swallow, but discovered that his mouth and throat were absolutely dry. He knew his pulse was racing; he could hear it pounding in his head.

After a minute, Lieutenant Lydecker returned carrying a paper cup. He closed the door and offered Jon the cup.

Jon drank it down. "Thanks."

Lydecker stood over him. "More?"

"No." Jon crushed the cup and tossed it into the waste-basket. "Look, I'm prepared to take a lie-detector test—"

"Relax." Lydecker started back around his desk.

"How can I when you said—"

"I said they found a knife near Ramsey's body with your prints on it, that's all."

"That's *plenty.*"

Lydecker sat, picked up the legal pad and pencil and wrote something. "So what do you think," he asked Jon, without looking up, "who's going to win next Sunday— the Patriots or Colts?"

"Damn it, I'm a suspect in a murder and you're asking me about a football game? Why don't you read me my Miranda rights and get it over with!"

"That's only at the time of the arrest," Lydecker answered matter-of-factly.

"Great. Thanks for telling me!" Jon felt his anger flaring now.

"I also told you to relax. It's not a help to you or me for you to go ballistic." Lydecker paused. "I'd like to ask you a few questions. That okay?"

Jon nodded. "Go ahead."

"Do you want an attorney present? You're entitled to have one, you know."

"My regular attorney passed away last year," Jon said. "I never got around to finding a new one."

Lieutenant Lydecker pushed the pad aside. "It's against procedures, but in that case, I'll consider this little chat off the record. If you don't feel like answering me, don't."

"I don't have anything to hide."

Lydecker looked at him. "Good. So, first, how come your fingerprints are on file with the feds? Were you in military service?"

"No," Jon said. "But in the late eighties, I researched a nature guide of Central American birds. I was in countries like El Salvador and Nicaragua. Back then, the administration was suspicious of any Americans who wanted to spend time in that region. So they fingerprinted everyone who sought a visa—nuns, priests, doctors, aid workers. And environmentalists."

"Even guys who painted birds." Lydecker shook his head. "Okay. Let's do a quick review. The night that Ramsey died, where were you?"

"I told you. After the Harvest Hoedown, I drove Mrs. Merriwell back to her house."

"Then?"

"Then I went home."

"Alone?" Lydecker asked.

"Of course, alone."

"Too bad."

"Larry, I just met her that night."

The lieutenant picked the broken rubber band out of the ashtray and began wrapping it around his index finger. "What I meant was, it's too bad she can't confirm your whereabouts later that night. If she could, you'd have an alibi."

"She can't, and I don't have one," Jon said.

"After you dropped her off, what time did you get back to your house?"

"Before midnight, I think. I don't remember."

Lydecker made a notation on the pad. "The next morning, why did you go to the abandoned cornfield? You never said.''

"One of the birding people in town called me. He said he'd seen a Townsend's solitaire in the cornfield.''

"Is that a bird?''

"It lives in the western part of the United States," Jon told him. "It's uncommon to find them in New England.''

"And did you see the bird?'' Lydecker asked.

"No.''

"Instead, you found the body of our first selectman.''

"Yes. Look, if I'd killed Ramsey, and left him in the field, why would I go back there and report I'd found him?''

The lieutenant shrugged. "Some murderers think it makes them appear innocent. Others get their kicks returning to the murder scene and watching the police go through their work.''

"But I am not the murderer. Call Arthur Tingley. He's the one who saw the bird and told me.''

"Spell his name.''

Jon did and provided Tingley's phone number, while Lydecker wrote the information on the pad. He put down the pencil, looking at Jon suddenly. "How did you feel about Ramsey?''

"I didn't like him much.''

"Why not?''

"I thought he was dishonest," Jon said. "I thought he was using his elected office for his own ends.''

"Did you ever have any disputes with him?''

"No.''

"None?'' The lieutenant's eyebrows rose. "That's not what Ramsey's secretary says.''

"Well, there was one," Jon admitted.

"Want to tell me?''

Jon paused. "It was the day before he died.''

"What happened?"

"I was doing a bird-painting class that morning on the beach at Mullet's Bay. While we were there a hunter came out of the reeds and killed two ducks while they were still on the water."

"Ramsey was the hunter?"

"Yes. I'm sure of it," Jon said. "After the group left, I took a walk to that end of the beach and saw Ramsey's car parked in the trees. Later, I went to town hall and confronted him about it."

"You must have been pretty steamed," Lydecker suggested. "His secretary said you shouted something about murder."

Jon recalled the moment and of seeing the girl at the office door. "I guess I did use the word 'murder,'" Jon acknowledged. "But I was talking about the murder of the ducks."

"So you disliked Ramsey and had a dispute with him just before he died," Lydecker said. The implication of what remained unsaid hung in the stale office air.

"A lot of people disliked Ramsey. You know that as well as I do."

Lydecker leaned back in his desk chair. "Give me some names of people you think might've wanted to kill him."

"I can't." Jon shook his head, regretting now he'd said it. "But Rod Ramsey had a private law practice on the side. For all I know, it could have been an angry client. Or the jealous husband of a woman Ramsey was romancing. Even Bernie Benjamin."

The lieutenant made a notation on the pad. Casually, he asked, "Why Benjamin?"

"He wanted Ramsey's job," Jon answered. "He says they were great friends, but he was a political opponent. They'd run against each other twice for first selectman."

"And now Rod Ramsey's dead and Bernie has the job."
Lydecker pursed his lips and added something on the pad.

"Look, Larry—I did *not* kill Ramsey! Somebody else
did. And that person took a knife of mine and left it in the
cornfield for you to find."

"Who would want to do that to you, Jon?"

"Who, I don't know; why, I don't know. The truth is,
the more I hear about this case, the less I understand. What
I *do* know is I'm *not* the murderer."

"Do you do any sailing, Jon? Boating? Anything like
that?" Lydecker asked him.

"No."

"Have you ever?"

"Not for a long time. Joy and I had a small sailboat
when we first came here. Why?"

"The knots the killer used to tie Ramsey to the stakes
were the kind sailors sometimes use," Lydecker said. "But
so do a lot of other people. I just thought I'd ask."

"Is that it then?"

"Are you going to be around town for a while?" Lydecker inquired.

"I have a lecture in New Haven next week," Jon told
him. "The week after that, I was planning to go into New
York City to have dinner with a friend. Otherwise, I expect
to be here."

"Good."

Lydecker stood up. Jon took it as the signal that the
interview was done. He stood as well.

"Just stay in touch," Lydecker told him. "Or I'll stay
in touch with you."

I bet you will, Jon thought.

"One other thing," Lydecker added, almost as an after-
thought. "You said you don't have a personal attorney at
the present time."

"That's right. I don't."

"I'd get one," Lydecker advised.

SEVEN

JON LEFT Lydecker's office and walked out of the building, angry and confused. His thoughts were in a turmoil; he had to sort them, or at least talk them out with Colin Hightower. Leaving the Range Rover parked where it was, he started along Harbor Street toward Colin's shop. As he approached he saw the "Closed" sign hanging on the door.

He turned and started to retrace his steps. Opposite Philander Webb's Antiques, he stopped and looked across the street. Near a front window Lorelei was standing on a step stool dusting glassware on a shelf.

Jon wasn't in the mood for social conversation. Neither did he want to burden her by recounting his conversation with Lydecker. He started to walk on. But as he did, she turned and saw him. She rapped several times against the window, and when he glanced again, she waved to him to come in. He hesitated, then acknowledged her and crossed the street.

"It's my first full day working in the shop without Mr. Webb's help," she told Jon as he came through the door.

She put the dust rag in a pocket of her smock and came down from the stool. "So how do you think everything looks now?" she asked him.

"Very nice," Jon said. "And a lot cleaner. Philander had some great antiques, but you could hardly see them under all the dust."

Lorelei laughed. "You're right. I think I've removed about a century's worth of antique dust since I've been here."

Jon smiled fleetingly. "I'm sure."

She studied him. "I have no right to ask you—but are you okay? Is something wrong?"

"A few things on my mind, that's all."

"Well, you look like the worry bird," Lorelei said. "Which reminds me. Do you have a minute?"

"Yes."

"Wait here."

She went quickly to the office in the back and returned carrying a set of four framed pictures and placed them on a table side by side. Jon leaned over the table and studied them. The frames were inexpensive; plain wood molding with a mahogany stain. But it was what was inside them that absorbed Jon's interest. Each was a watercolor painting of a different bird.

"Where did you get these?" he asked Lorelei.

"At a flea market in Ledyard."

"How much did you pay for them? If I may ask."

"The seller had them priced at fifty dollars each," she said. "But it was late in the day and he was packing up to leave; he let them go for thirty-five."

"You got a bargain," Jon informed her. "The watercolors are worth at least a thousand times that much."

"What do you mean?"

"These are originals by Alexander Wilson. He was a Scotsman who immigrated here about two hundred years ago. He was so charmed by the birds, he traveled west into the wilderness to draw them. In 1810, he stopped in a small Ohio River town, where he tried to sell some of his bird sketches to a storekeeper. The storekeeper's partner looked at them and told Wilson he drew even better birds himself. The partner's name was John James Audubon."

She looked at Jon, impressed. "What kind of birds are they?"

"The small yellow birds are pine warblers. The others are an osprey, a white-eyed vireo and a passenger pigeon.

Passenger pigeons are extinct now. But they were once so numerous, hunters killed them by the thousands on a single day. The last one, a female, died in 1914 in the Cincinnati Zoo.''

"How did you learn all this?" Lorelei asked him. "About birds, I mean."

"By studying everything about them I could find. In the beginning I hardly knew an evening grosbeak from a purple finch."

"And do you go bird-watching a lot?"

"When I'm not painting, yes," Jon said. "And some people call it 'birding.'"

"Would you take me some time? *Birding?*" She emphasized the word.

"I thought I'd go on Sunday morning. You're welcome to come along."

"Sunday morning would be fine."

"Then come to my house first," he suggested. "The driveway is the last on Plover Point Road. How's eight o'clock?"

"On Sunday morning?" She laughed at herself. "You may be a morning lark, but I confess I'm a night owl. Could we say nine?"

"Sure. Nine will be fine."

"And should I bring along some birdseed to attract them?"

The thought amused him. "No. And no salt either to sprinkle on their tails. But dress warmly and wear boots. And bring binoculars, if you have them."

"I have opera glasses."

"They're all right, but they don't have much power. I have an extra pair of eight by forty-twos you can use."

"It sounds like fun," she said.

Lorelei looked at him, as if she was about to say something more, when the door of the shop opened and two elderly women entered.

"Customers," Jon said. He began moving toward the door.

"Thanks for telling me about the paintings," Lorelei called after him. "I'll be there at nine on Sunday."

"I'm looking forward to it," Jon said. "See you then."

He left the antiques shop and started back along the street to where his car was parked. Passing Colin's shop, he saw it was still closed. As much as Jon needed the support and counsel of his friend now, it would have to wait.

THERE WERE ONLY three houses along the dead-end road that led to Plover Point. Beyond Jon's driveway entrance the road abruptly halted in a cul-de-sac surrounded by evergreens and sumac trees. He checked the roadside box for mail, then turned into the narrow drive and negotiated the half mile of rough gravel that ended finally at the paved turnaround of his garage.

He opened the garage door with the remote control clipped to the sun visor above him, but left the Range Rover parked in the turnaround and climbed out. Looking briefly at the sky, he noticed that the clouds were lowering and thickening. They matched his mood exactly.

He continued around the corner of the house to the stone terrace that provided an expansive view of Seal Island Sound. Beyond the terrace was a width of lawn that gave way, finally, to beach grass, and beyond it, the beach itself. To one side of the lawn was a path of broken oyster and clamshells that meandered downward to the sand.

Years ago, in a plot of fertile ground between the terrace and the lawn, his wife and young daughter had cultivated a small garden. Suzy's Garden, it was called. In the spring after their deaths Jon had been unable to tend it—indeed, he'd had no heart for such a task. Eventually, he'd had the soil tilled and grass seed sown. But each spring tiny sprouts appeared, reminders of the much-too-brief time the three of them had lived together as a family.

Jon's thoughts were interrupted by a throaty bark. Turning, he saw Jake, the old retriever, loping toward him from the woods. At sixteen the dog showed his age. Many of the hairs around his head were white and a cataract covered part of his left eye. Jake belonged to a young couple who lived on the far side of the point. But Jon had befriended Jake, or vice versa, and the two of them had become great companions.

The dog sat on his haunches at Jon's feet and barked again.

"Is it a late lunch or an early dinner you want, Jake?" asked Jon.

Jake gave a responsive whine, which indicated he would take whatever Jon was offering.

Jon went into the house and to the kitchen and prepared a bowl of dog food. He carried it out to the turnaround and put down the bowl for the dog. He returned through the garage again, this time closing the garage door as he went. Hanging up his jacket in the hall, he went into the kitchen for a second time to rinse the dog-food can and add it to the items for recycling.

He had just done so when the thought came to him. From somewhere in the house a knife that had belonged to Jon was missing. He checked the knife holder above the kitchen cutting board. Eight knives generally hung from it. He counted them. All eight were there. He pulled out the drawers below the countertop. In one, he kept a bread knife and four carving knives. Looking down, he saw they nestled in their holder, undisturbed.

It was then Jon heard the sound. It came from somewhere above him, the second floor. Ordinarily, he would have dismissed it as one of the chorus of odd noises produced by an old house—the beams groaning, pipes contracting, windows rattling against the wind.

But this sound had been different. This had been a solid thump, as if a piece of furniture had momentarily come into contact with a wall.

Jon listened. Silence. He began to cross the kitchen— when he heard the sound again. Someone else was in the house.

He reopened the knife drawer and took out the long ser-rated knife he used for cutting bread. Gripping it in his right hand, he eased out of the kitchen, moving slowly and as quietly as possible in the direction of the stairway leading to the second floor. The steps were broad, of wide-board oak, with a single landing halfway up. Keeping to their edge next to the wall, Jon began to climb them one by one.

A central hallway ran the full length of the second floor, with rooms on either side. Jon moved along it, one foot following the other, still staying near the wall. The master bedroom where he slept was closest to him on his left. The door was open and he glanced in as he passed. The room was empty. Farther on, the doors of other rooms—the guest rooms, sitting room, and the solarium—stood open, just as Jon remembered them.

One room remained. His studio. The door faced squarely on the hall. It had been open when he'd left the house that morning.

Now the door was closed.

Back pressed against the wall, Jon moved to the door. He lifted his right hand that held the knife. With his left, he grasped the knob. He turned it—slowly, slowly—until he felt the bolt retract into the lock. Then, with the full force of his arm, he flung the door aside.

There was a shriek.

Jon jumped into the open doorway, the knife raised above his head.

"Dear Jesus! Mr. Wilder!"

Facing him, a tiny woman stood against the wall, eyes blinking, terrified, mouth wide in disbelief. She held the vacuum-cleaner hose in front of her in self-defense.

Jon lowered the knife. "Mrs. Epsom—I'm very sorry. I didn't know anyone was here."

The woman's eyes ceased blinking: now she simply stared. "Last week—I asked if I could change my day to Friday. You said yes."

"You're right. I totally forgot," he said apologetically. "Again, I'm sorry to have scared you. But I heard a sound. I thought there was an intruder in the house."

He stepped into the room. Automatically, she backed away from him, keeping at a distance. She was a small, thin woman in her sixties with sparse hair as colorless as the cleaning dress she wore.

Jon put the bread knife on a table to the side. "The fact is, I didn't see your car outside. That's why it must have slipped my mind."

"The car's in the shop. My husband drove me. Walter." She added quickly, "He'll be picking me up soon."

"Well, I'll let you get back to work. And again, I'm very sorry that I startled you."

"I'm done now, anyhow." Keeping the vacuum-cleaner hose in front of her, she trundled the machine into the hall, storing it in a closet near the stairs.

Jon followed her. "Will you be back to Thursday next week, as usual?" he asked her.

Mrs. Epsom closed the closet door. "I plan to." She regarded him uncertainly. "You won't forget."

"I promise I won't," he assured the woman.

From the driveway below, a horn sounded.

"That's Walter. I better go." She gave a furtive glance in the direction of the turnaround.

"Of course." He followed her along the hall and down the stairs.

"By the way," he asked, as they continued through the hall to the garage, "you mentioned once your husband planned to paint the first selectman's house. Did he?"

"Nope. Mr. Ramsey changed his mind. Got someone else." The woman took a gray coat from the closet and put it on. From the shelf, she drew a black brimless hat and placed it on her head. With her gray coat, dark hat and sharply pointed nose, she reminded Jon of a small, nervous chickadee.

Another blast of a horn sounded from the driveway, then a third.

"I'll let you out through the garage." Jon said to her. "That'll be quicker."

They went into the garage and Jon pressed the button to raise the door. As it slid upward, Jon saw first the wheels, then the body of a battered yellow van with the words, EPSOM PAINTING and underneath: "Residential and Commercial."

Behind the steering wheel sat a large beefy man, a Dutch Boy paint cap on his head. A hand with a lit cigarette dangled from the open driver's window. He was about to blow the horn again when he saw Jon and his wife.

Mrs. Epsom scurried to the far side of the van and got into the passenger seat. Jon approached the van. Walter Epsom took a final puff, then flicked the cigarette onto the turnaround.

"How are you, Walter?" Jon asked him.

"Couldn't be better, Mr. Wilder. You?"

"All right. But I'm afraid I scared your wife a little while ago."

"What happened?"

"She'll explain. I'd forgotten she was coming to clean today and I didn't see her car."

"It's in the shop."

"She told me." Jon noticed the man's gaze was directed past him toward the house.

"Need any painting done?" Walter Epsom asked. "Interiors, I mean. Winter is the time I do interiors."

"Thanks, but I don't think so."

"If you do, let me know," Epsom said.

"I will."

The man nodded, raised the window and threw the van in gear. Jon watched as it accelerated up the driveway, taking the turns faster than it should.

Jon liked Mrs. Epsom. He'd hired her six years ago to clean the house each week, and keep an eye on it while he was traveling. She was a conscientious worker, and honest enough to be entrusted with a set of house keys. He'd also given her the number of the security code to the house, so that she could enter it without setting off the alarm system.

Walter Epsom was another matter. As a painting contractor, he'd built up a successful business in Scarborough. But there was something in his manner that made Jon uncomfortable. He turned and started back to the garage. Just inside, he was about to press the button that would lower the garage door, closing it.

His hand reached for the button, but halted in midair. Opposite him was a wooden workbench set against the wall. Jon used it for occasional odd jobs around the house. At one end of the workbench was a vise. Above it, Jon had placed nails in the wall from which he had hung saws, hammers, pliers, screwdrivers and wrenches. Next to the wrenches there was also a magnetized metal bar about ten inches long, and attached to the bar were a variety of knives. Dulled from years of wear and no longer worth resharpening, Jon kept them for prosaic household uses such as cutting tape and twine. The bar had space enough for seven knives.

Now there were six.

EIGHT

Darkness.

It was what Jon disliked most about November. Lying in bed in the darkness of a Sunday morning, he remembered the lines of the old poem: "No fruits, no flowers, no leaves, no birds—November." Well, there were still birds and a few leaves on the trees. Otherwise, it was a gray, depressing month best gotten through as soon as possible.

He rose, showered, and dressed in wool slacks and a heavy flannel shirt. Cold rain had been predicted for late morning. It wasn't a good day for birding, and he was tempted to call Lorelei and postpone their outing. But he also thought she would be disappointed if he did.

Going downstairs to the kitchen, he fixed himself breakfast: an omelet made with an egg substitute. Then, leaning back against the countertop, he poured himself a second mug of coffee and looked out the kitchen windows in the direction of the sound. Under the low, seamless line of clouds, the calm water had the color and appearance of dull stone. On the horizon only a single boat was visible, a lone trawler heading south.

Nearer the house, in a tall shadbush just beyond the windows, birds were lighting and departing from a feeder hanging on a branch. Jon counted a dozen birds of differing varieties—purple finches, chickadees, nuthatches, even a male downy woodpecker, the red patch on its head bobbing with the staccato pecking of its bill. On a high branch of the shad, a blue jay suddenly swept in and rasped a warning to the other birds that the Big Guy had arrived. Watching the birds' quickness and vivacity, Jon wished he had his sketchpad close at hand to draw them as they fed.

"Stay home and paint your birds," Colin Hightower had advised him. Recalling the events of the last week, Jon wondered if he should have heeded that advice. For someone as removed as he was from what Colin also called the world of madness and mayhem, what was it that made Jon believe he could single-handedly solve Ramsey's murder?

His first mistake, he realized, was in seizing on the obvious and trying to build a case. From Gus Schiller's words and actions, the man was obviously guilty. Schiller was a hothead and a drunk; he'd had a grudge against the first selectman and denounced him in public. If it walks like a duck, it must be a duck, the adage went. But as an ornithologist Jon knew that ducks weren't the only birds with a web-footed waddle. Geese walked like ducks, and so did swans and gulls and other seabirds.

But Jon had learned his lesson, as embarrassing as it had been. The police would continue to investigate and the real killer would eventually be caught. At last, Jon was well out of the whole troubling affair.

Or was he?

In spite of Lydecker's assurances, the thought gnawed at him that the police still considered him a suspect, or at least of having some connection with the crime. More than that, and far more worrying, whoever had killed Ramsey had done so with a knife taken from his house. Even if it was discovered not to be the murder weapon, it had been planted near enough the body so as to involve Jon in the first selectman's death.

Why?

Was there some grudge the killer nurtured toward him? Jon set the mug down on the countertop and looked out at the bird feeder again. Not a single bird was visible; all of them had fled. Then he saw the reason. Above the beach a hawk was circling in search of prey.

And Jon?

Had he himself become prey to some unknown killer who had struck once, suddenly and brutally, and could do so again?

Maybe the police would find the killer. Maybe not. And their investigation could take months.

Jon felt no such luxury of time. What he felt instead was fear and the urgency to find the killer soon, as if his life depended on it.

It just might.

THE WATERCOLOR painting of the crow was almost done. He rolled the chair back from the drawing table and stood up. He had just finished pointing his brushes when he heard a car pull into the driveway turnaround and stop. He went down to the rear hall, put on a mackinaw and brown Irish tweed hat he sometimes wore on rainy days, and headed out to the garage.

As he raised the garage door, Lorelei was standing facing him, her arms outspread.

"How do I look?" she asked him brightly. "The way I'm dressed, I mean."

"Terrific."

"I followed your advice about the weather. I put on boots and this old lumber jacket and wool slacks. The red beret was my idea." She pointed to the hat sitting at a rakish angle on her head.

Lorelei turned and studied the facade of the house. "So this is Castle Wilder. I had no idea it was so enormous."

"Actually, it's smaller than it looks from the outside," Jon said, a little embarrassed.

"Well, if you need help furnishing it, I can recommend a wonderful antiques shop in Scarborough."

They began walking back toward the open door of the garage. Jon climbed into the Range Rover and backed it out into the turnaround. Lorelei joined him on the passenger side. Moments later, they were moving up the driveway toward the road.

They drove through Scarborough and headed north into open countryside again. In her company Jon felt relaxed and comfortable. They chatted easily about the weather and about some of the customers who had come into the antiques shop that week. Business was picking up in general, she told him, after the shock some locals felt when they learned the proprietor was no longer a mumbling octogenarian, but an attractive woman in her thirties.

Finally she reached into a pocket of her jacket and pulled out a softcover book. "I also wanted you to know," she said, "that in preparation for today I went to the bookstore in town and bought *Wilder's Guide to Eastern Birds*."

"For which the author and the publisher are grateful," Jon said, smiling.

"Naturally, the first thing I looked at was the note about the author."

She opened the book. "It reads—and I quote—'Jonathan McNicol Wilder is an acclaimed ornithologist and bird portraitist. He has traveled around the world several times and visited every continent. His nature guides of birds have sold millions of copies, and his paintings have been exhibited in major museums and art galleries. He is the recipient of numerous awards from ornithological and environmental groups.'"

Lorelei closed the book. "Is all that true?"

"I guess so. Yes."

"Tell me," she asked, "if you could be any kind of bird at all, what would you be? An eagle, I'll bet."

"I doubt if I'd want to be an eagle," Jon replied. "In

spite of their resolute profiles and official status as the symbol of our country, eagles can have rather nasty tempers."

"What bird then?"

"Probably a petrel. They're oceanic birds. I love the way they seem to ride the winds, like nomads always on the move. I think of them as the freest of all birds."

"Aren't they lonely?" Lorelei suggested.

"Maybe. But it's the price they pay for freedom."

He glanced over at her. "What about you? What kind of bird would you be, if you could?"

"An exotic one," she answered. "Or at least colorful— a bluebird or a painted bunting, I suppose. On the other hand, I'm not sure birds are nearly as well off as we like to think they are. They don't get frequent-flyer miles for all the traveling they do; they have to live on things like seeds and insects, even worms. Lots of them look awful in the summer when they molt. And some of them only have sex a few weeks every year, which leads to lumpy eggs they have to sit on in a scratchy nest for days before the chicks are hatched."

Lorelei shook her head. "In fact, the more I think about what kind of bird I'd be, the more I'm glad that I'm a woman."

Looking at her, it occurred to Jon that he was very glad as well.

"Where are we going birding, by the way?" she asked.

"It's called the Hundred-Acre Wood," Jon said. "At least, I call it that after the forest in the Winnie-the-Pooh books. I used to read them to my daughter."

"Is it town property?"

Jon shook his head. "The owner is an elderly gentleman named Loomis Haverman. The land is actually about a hundred acres overall, and very natural with huge old-growth trees, grassy meadows, streams, and even a few ponds."

"Sounds wonderful."

"It is. We, my wife and daughter and I, used to picnic there."

"This is a new part of town for me," she said. "What road are we on?"

"It's called Cemetery Road. A short way ahead is the original town graveyard. Some of the headstones date back several hundred years."

They crested a hill. Beyond it to the right was a low wrought-iron fence enclosing a small field with what appeared to be randomly placed tombstones. Most were small and lichen-stained, and so defaced by time that the names, dates and whatever epitaphs had been carved into them were barely visible. But there were some newer stones as well, which Lorelei pointed to as they passed by.

"I see the name of Stives," Lorelei said. "I've heard that name a lot since I've been here."

"The Stives were one of the founding families," Jon explained. "In the eighteenth century they owned more than half the land in town. Abigail Stives is almost the last of the line, although she has a son. All the property on the right for the next mile and a half is hers. Her house is on the hill beyond the trees."

"I also saw the name Parrish," Lorelei said.

Jon nodded. "Another early family. There aren't many of them left now either. But they don't have the money Abigail Stives has. Mrs. Epsom—the woman who does housecleaning for me—her maiden name is Parrish. After she married Walter Epsom, she inherited some good farmland. They tried to make a go of it themselves and failed. Finally, they sold it off to pay their debts. He became a housepainter and she took jobs cleaning for people around town."

He nodded to the left. "Their house is the small blue one close to the road."

They drove on in silence for some moments. The road

continued to meander among open land that gradually became less fertile and more rocky. At a sharp bend in the road, along the right, a grove of pines and cedars stood. Beyond it the road was bordered by a barbed-wire fence, its strands occasionally rusted through, that marked the boundary of a field. The fence was interrupted by a wooden gate. A dirt drive went up from it to a weather-beaten white farmhouse. Behind the house were an unpainted barn and a long, low building that was also white.

"Look! A farm stand!" Lorelei said. "Now I know I'm in the country."

She nodded to a wooden shed that stood beside the gate. Hinged shutters had been drawn down across the upper half. Below were the words BELLKIRK'S FARM. Below them, in smaller letters, it said "Eggs—Poultry—Native Corn—Vegetables." Another word had been taped over.

"The farm belongs to Oren Bellkirk," Jon told her. "He's what you might call the local butter-and-egg man. He raises chickens and grows vegetables in season. In the summer he sells things from the roadside stand. His wife also made pies, but she died some years ago. I used to order my Thanksgiving turkey from him.

"Come to think of it," he added, "if you don't have any plans for this Thanksgiving, would you like to come for dinner at the house? Colin Hightower is coming. It'll be just the three of us."

"I'd love to," Lorelei said. "My first New England Thanksgiving. Thank you. I accept."

At last, Jon slowed the Range Rover, then eased it to the shoulder of the road, bumping along in the tall grass before he stopped.

"This has to be the Hundred-Acre Wood," Lorelei said, looking out the window to her right. "It's like something out of a fairy tale."

Jon agreed. Even under low, glowering skies, the woods

had the allure and mystery of an enchanted forest. Many of the trees were massive, old, and greatly gnarled, with branches that bent low to the ground. Natural paths were covered with pine needles and dry leaves, as if promising some magical encounter that awaited deep within the forest.

Jon climbed out, put on his tweed hat, and turned up the collar of his mackinaw against the raw wind that had begun to blow. Everything was just as he remembered it.

Then he saw the stakes.

They were about two feet tall: thin wooden strips placed in a line at regular intervals parallel to the road. Tied around their tops was bright-orange plastic tape that fluttered as the wind lifted it.

Jon knelt at the stake nearest him. Turning it, he saw numbers had been written on the side.

"Is something wrong?" Lorelei asked, joining him.

"I'm not sure." He pointed at the row of stakes. "It looks like the property was recently surveyed. The numbers on the stakes and how they're placed. They look like boundary markers for construction lots."

"They do to me, too," she agreed.

"Except the owner always said he'd leave the property just as it was. He'd even willed it as a wildlife preserve after he died."

"Maybe he changed his mind."

"Maybe." Jon studied the stakes again, then stood. "Anyway, let's get on with our birding before it starts to rain. I'll get the binoculars."

He returned to the Range Rover and came back carrying the field glasses in each hand, one pair of which he gave to her.

"So what do I do, just scan the branches?" Lorelei asked.

"The branches, tree trunks, even the ground. If you see

movement, stop and focus in. More likely than not you'll find a bird.''

Lorelei lifted the glasses to her eyes and slowly began panning across the lower branches of a large white pine. She halted, then ever so gradually fingered the focusing wheel between the scopes.

"It's a small bird," she whispered, "with a red breast and—let's see—two white wing bars…and a cross-tipped bill. It's a pine grosbeak. A male. The female is gray, with a dull yellow rump and crown."

"Very good," Jon said, impressed. "I can tell you've been studying. Let me know what other birds you see."

She raised the binoculars again and aimed them at the trees, repeating the routine. "Oh, this one's easy. A small bird with a gray top, white underside and outer tail feathers. It's a dark-eyed junco. I can't tell the sex; they're both alike."

Jon was about to compliment her for a second time, when she turned and aimed the glasses toward a growth of young fir trees farther down the road. "Imagine that—here comes a barrel-bellied baldie."

"A what?"

"And behind him is a large-beaked sourpuss."

Jon lifted his binoculars and focused in the direction Lorelei's were fixed. From around the firs, he saw Bernie Benjamin emerging, followed by Aaron Peabody. After a moment Lester Fitch appeared. Each man wore the same black raincoat Jon recalled from Ramsey's memorial service. In one hand, Bernie Benjamin grasped his white Stetson hat. Binoculars hung from a strap around his neck. Aaron Peabody was carrying a camera. Lester Fitch held a small blue notebook with a metal spiral binding.

In unison, the three men turned, saw Jon and Lorelei, and stared.

Then Benjamin and Fitch said something to Peabody, who shook his head.

Fitch tried to slip the notebook inside the pocket of his raincoat, but missed the opening and the pad fell to the ground. He picked it up at once.

Peabody now turned away and spoke briefly to Bernie Benjamin. The big man shrugged and put the Stetson on his head.

Finally, the three men moved together to the road and began to walk along it side by side toward Jon and Lorelei.

"Well, well, well," Bernie Benjamin said, as they approached. His bonhomie was obviously forced. "Jon Wilder and Mrs. Merriwell. What brings you good people out here on a Sunday morning?"

"We're birding," Jon said. "What about you?"

"Same for us. See? We got a camera and binoculars." Bernie Benjamin laughed; Peabody and Fitch did not.

Aaron Peabody regarded Jon, his gray eyes expressionless above the hawklike nose. "We were helping Lester check the property," Peabody said. "As you may know, Lester was elected to the zoning board again this year."

"Why check the property?"

"Because the land's been sold."

"Loomis Haverman was going to leave it to the town," Jon said. "He wanted it kept natural."

"Apparently, he decided otherwise," Peabody said.

Jon turned to Lester Fitch, who had endeavored to be inconspicuous. "Is that true, Lester?"

"Jon—"

"Is it?"

Fitch ran his tongue around his lips. He nodded. "Yes. The property's been sold. But—"

"Anyway, we gotta go, folks," Benjamin broke in. "Enjoy looking at your birds." He bent toward Lorelei and raised the Stetson briefly.

The three men turned and started quickly back along the road. When they were some distance away, their pace quickened into a near trot.

Beyond, they disappeared into a dense thicket of trees, shrubs and wild vines. Moments later, a dark-blue Buick swung out from the thicket, scattering dry leaves in its wake. It accelerated up the road.

"That was strange," Lorelei said, when the car was out of sight.

Jon didn't answer.

Lorelei glanced up at the sky. "It's starting to rain."

Around them large drops were dappling the roadway. The sound of the rain whispered on the forest floor.

Jon turned down the brim of his hat. "I'm afraid that washes out our birding for today," he said.

"Do I get a rain check?"

"Sure." His mind was obviously not on birds. "We better go before we get too wet."

He took her arm and together they ran for the car.

RAIN WAS falling now in torrents; rivulets streamed down the windows. Holding the coffee mug, Lorelei gestured to the small bird on the feeder.

"That bird with the red cap. It's either a swamp sparrow or a chipping sparrow, but I can't remember which is which."

Jon peered over her shoulder. "A swamp sparrow. The two are similar. But the chipping sparrow has a white stripe over its eyes."

"We could have gone birding right here in your kitchen. It's much cozier."

She drained the mug and set it in the sink. "Thanks for the coffee. Now I really should get back to the shop. I'm opening at one." She looked at him. "I have a question, though, before I go."

"What's that?"

"Could I have a quick tour of the house?"

"Of course. Follow me."

He put down his mug also and guided her out of the kitchen. Leading the way, he showed her his study. Next, they walked on to the living room. Entering it, Lorelei halted and stared up at the beamed ceiling. Moving her eyes downward, she studied the massive fireplace, then scanned the row of two-story-high Tudor windows with panels of stained glass set among the panes.

"The house is beautiful," she said. "It really is."

"It's more than I need," Jon admitted. "Several times I could have sold it. But I guess I'm too attached to it. It has a lot of happy memories."

"What's upstairs?"

"Bedrooms, mostly. A solarium. Plus my painting studio. Would you like to see what I'm working on now?"

"You mean, come up and see your etchings?" She gave him a quick smile.

He returned it. "No etchings. What's there now are watercolors. And some oils."

"Then I'm safe." She started up the broad staircase and Jon followed her.

On the second floor they walked down the hall, with Jon pointing out the rooms on either side. At last, he gestured to the open door that faced them at the far end of the hall.

"My studio's through there."

"The artist's atelier. May I have a look?"

"Go ahead."

Lorelei went eagerly into the studio. "What a view you have," she said. "You must—" There was a cry. "My God!"

He sprang into the studio. Lorelei was backed against the windows, staring at the model of the crow.

"It's real!" She looked terrified.

"It's real, but it's not alive." He lifted the model by the base and placed it on a cabinet in the far corner of the room.

"I was using it to draw from," he explained, indicating the watercolor of the crow on the drawing table that was near completion.

"It—the bird surprised me, that's all." Her arms were folded tight across her chest. "It's stupid. But I have a thing about crows."

He saw that she was trembling and led her from the studio. "It's almost noon. Would you like something to eat before you go?"

Lorelei walked quickly down the hall ahead of him. "Thanks. But I'm not hungry, really. I should get to the shop."

"I understand," Jon told her, as they started down the stairs.

But he was not at all sure he did.

HE WAITED UNTIL he saw Lorelei's car heading up the driveway, then he went to his study. He looked up the telephone number for Bellkirk's Farm, called, and when Oren Bellkirk answered, Jon ordered a turkey for Thanksgiving. Bellkirk added that he had someone again this year who baked pies, so Jon requested two: a pumpkin and a mince. The man confirmed the order and said he would deliver everything to Jon the day before the holiday. That done, Jon picked up the phone again and tapped out a number that he knew from memory.

The phone rang only once before a woman's voice answered. "Scarborough Realty."

"Madeleine?"

"Jon—how nice to hear from you. Is this a social call, I hope, or business?"

"I'd like to talk with you."

"I'd like that, too," Madeleine Thoreau said. "Your place or mine?"

"Let's make it tomorrow morning at your office. Say eleven?"

There was a pause. "All right. Eleven at my office. May I ask what it's about?"

"The Haverman property on Cemetery Road."

"What about it?" Her voice had a cautious edge.

"I'll talk to you tomorrow."

"Jon—"

"Yes?"

"Nothing. Good-bye, Jon."

NINE

NO ONE SAT at either of the office desks. No lights were lit. The blinds across the door of Scarborough Realty had been drawn down. Jon tried the door, although he was sure it would be locked. It was.

He checked his watch. Ten fifty-nine. Cupping a hand over his eyes, he peered past the photographs of listed houses displayed in a front window to see if there was a light showing from the room in the rear. There wasn't.

Jon reminded himself that something may have come up for Madeleine Thoreau since they had talked the day before. But knowing her, she would have called him if it had, or seen to it that her assistant did. In fact, where was the young woman who maintained the office when Madeleine was out?

He thought again about their phone conversation yesterday. When Jon mentioned the Haverman property, she'd sounded wary. Why? If the property had been sold, as Jon suspected, what more did she know?

Jon's car was parked opposite the real estate office on a street that bordered the town green. He started toward it—when something caught his eye. In a front window of Fitch's Pharmacy two doors away, Timmy, the stock boy, was pasting paper Santa Clauses on the inside of the glass. Walking to the pharmacy, Jon stood for several moments looking at the decorations that were already displayed. Plastic snowflakes hung from the red and green apothecary jars, and tiny Christmas lights in a variety of colors blinked around the edges of both windows.

Jon went inside. A woman and a child stood at the

counter at the rear, concluding a sale. Otherwise, the pharmacy was empty. Behind the counter, Lester Fitch was ringing up the total on a vintage cash register he cranked by hand. Jon moved to a side aisle, selecting some small items of his own. Finally, Fitch handed the woman her change, bagged the merchandise and wished her a good day. When the woman and the child left the counter, Jon walked to it.

"Good morning, Lester." Jon placed what he'd selected on the countertop.

"Morning, Jon," Fitch answered. The eyes blinked through the glasses. "What can I do for you?"

"Just these," Jon said, pointing.

"Let's see what we have here." Fitch began separating the items one by one, ringing them up on the cash register as he did.

"Aspirin...shampoo...razor blades...toothpaste. There's a special on toothpaste this week. A dollar ninety-five." He tapped the register keys and the price popped up on little metal tabs inside the glassed-in section at the top of the machine.

"I'm surprised you don't have one of those computerized cash registers, Lester. The hand-operated models are becoming pretty rare."

Lester Fitch gave a thin smile. "I guess I'm old-fashioned. But I'm sort of used to it after all these years. Will that be it?"

Jon nodded.

"The total comes to eighteen eighty-seven. Should I put that on your account?"

"I have the cash."

Jon handed him a twenty-dollar bill. Fitch rang up the sale. The drawer of the cash register flew open and the pharmacist began scooping out the change.

"A dollar thirteen cents is what you get." Fitch put the bill and coins on the counter.

Jon pocketed the change, as Fitch gathered the purchases and placed them in a paper bag.

"Good seeing you, Jon."

"Oh, Lester, there is one other thing," Jon said.

"I know. The calendar. It's right here with your name on it." Fitch reached under the counter and brought up a desk calendar refill wrapped in cellophane. "You already paid for it, as I remember."

"Yes. But that wasn't what I meant."

Fitch looked at him. "Oh?"

"I'd like to know the story on the Haverman land. The real story. Can you tell me?"

Fitch blinked and the tongue flicked quickly at the lips.

"Well, sure," Fitch offered. "Like Aaron Peabody said yesterday, the property was sold. And as a member of the zoning board, I wanted to look it over to decide if I approved of the use the new owner is proposing for it."

"But Peabody and Benjamin aren't members of the board."

"They came along for company."

"When will your planning and zoning group vote on it?" Jon asked him.

Fitch took a little breath. "They did."

"The board already voted? When was that?"

"Last night," Fitch admitted.

"You met on Sunday night? Where?" Jon's surprise was obvious.

"My house."

"How did the members cast their ballots?"

"It was unanimous," Fitch said.

"But what about a public hearing?"

"It was open to the public. Nobody showed up."

"Because nobody knew about it. Lester, that property

had already been subdivided when I saw it yesterday. Whoever bought it didn't even bother waiting for a vote. They must have known the outcome in advance."

"Jon, look, excuse me, but I'm very busy—"

"There's no one in the store but us and Timmy. And he can't hear us," Jon said.

"I mean I'm busy in the back. The Christmas items are beginning to come in. The inventory—"

"Lester—wait a minute. Listen." Jon put his hands on the counter and leaned across at Fitch. "We go back a long time, don't we?"

The man nodded, but was mute.

"When Joy and I moved to Scarborough, you and Muriel were one of the first to welcome us. Our wives worked together as hospital volunteers. After the accident, when I was in the wheelchair at home, you and Muriel stopped by once a week to see how I was doing. Do you remember all that, Lester?"

Fitch bowed his head. "Yes."

"We've always been direct with one another, haven't we?"

A nod.

"Then why can't you be honest with me now?"

"Jon, I—Jon, I'm really busy."

"I know," Jon said. "The inventory. Thanks for this."

Jon grabbed up the paper bag and walked out of the store.

TRAFFIC ON Harbor Street was light and few cars were parked beside the green. One was Oren Bellkirk's old white van, which sat directly opposite the bank. Jon wondered if the man was making deliveries in town, or was in the bank appealing for a loan to enlarge his henhouse, as he had once told Jon he wished to do.

Jon continued on to the woodworking shop. As he entered, he saw Colin seated at his desk in animated conversation on the telephone. The tortoiseshell cat, Vishnu, was stretched out along the desktop.

"Remarkable—remarkable!" Colin exclaimed into the phone. He noticed Jon and waved him in, then returned to the receiver. "One moment, Roger. Please hold on."

Colin put his hand over the mouthpiece. "It's one of our tea group. He's just come into possession of a spectacular Formosan Jewel."

"I just wanted to know if you had time for lunch," Jon asked.

"Certainly. Bernie's Barn again?"

Jon shook his head. "I'd rather not. I saw Bernie yesterday up at the Hundred-Acre Wood. That's part of what I want to talk about."

"Indeed. Shall we say Jonah's then?" Colin regarded the wall clock. "It's eleven-twenty now. How's noon?"

"That's fine."

"I'll meet you there." Colin returned to the telephone. "Yes, Roger, I'm still here. Forgive the interruption. Please go on about the tea. You say the shipment's coming to you via Singapore..."

Jon let himself out of the shop.

It was five minutes after twelve when Jon entered Jonah's Restaurant. Colin was nowhere to be seen, so he went to an empty table near the rear and sat down to wait.

The restaurant was comprised of one large room with windows facing out on Harbor Street. Globe lights hung from the white corrugated-metal ceiling, as did a large fan whose blades turned slowly over diners' heads. The dark-stained plank floors had been made darker by a patina of grease smoke that had built up over half a century. The walls were decorated with the sailing schedules of the packet boats that had once plied the waters between Boston and New York, making stops at Scarborough en route.

A moment later, Colin came through the door, a newspaper tucked under his arm. He leaned his cane against the wall, took off his coat and sat down in the chair opposite Jon.

"Forgive me, dear boy," he apologized. "Have you been waiting long?"

"I just arrived," Jon said. "I had a stop to make at Peabody's lumberyard to get molding for some picture frames."

"And I took time to buy the newspaper." Colin placed it, folded, on the table. "I was curious to read it. It appears the police are hinting at a suspect in the Ramsey case."

A chill passed over Jon. "Did they give any names?"

"Oh, no. They never do until they're sure. They merely hint. Suggest. Their 'suggestion,' if I read correctly, is that the murderer is someone local, someone with whom Ramsey had an argument before he died."

"Shall we order?" Jon asked him, changing the subject.

"By all means." Colin scanned the blackboard on the wall where specials for the day were listed. "The cod looks good," he ventured. "But so does the scrod. Cod or scrod, that is the question."

Colin leaned back in his chair, and cast his eyes around the room. "You know why the original owner of the restaurant called it Jonah's, don't you?" he asked Jon.

"No."

"Not because his wife had the proportions of a whale— which she did—but because he was a deeply religious man. He first thought of calling the place Noah's, but decided if he did that, he'd have to serve his patrons two by two."

A young waiter arrived, wearing jeans and a green sweatshirt with the restaurant's name emblazoned on the front.

"Splendid timing," Colin said to the waiter. "To begin,

I'll have a glass of the domestic chardonnay. As for the entree, I've decided on the codfish special.''

"The same for me," Jon said.

"Cod be with us both," Colin intoned.

The waiter wrote the order on his pad and left.

"Or should I say, in cod we trust?" Colin went on. He paused, then looked at Jon. "Come, come, Jonathan—something's on your mind. Generally, you laugh at my atrocious puns, if only out of courtesy. What's wrong?''

"I know who the police suspect of killing Ramsey," Jon said.

"Do you?" Colin paused and pursed his lips. "And who is that?''

"Me.''

"*You!* But that's impossible!''

"Improbable, but not impossible, according to Lieutenant Lydecker.''

"I still don't believe it." Colin harrumphed mightly. "Has the Scarborough constabulary become so incompetent as to believe you could commit such an outrageous act?''

"Apparently," Jon said. "They found a knife at the murder scene. The fingerprints on it were mine.''

In a low voice, Jon related his visit to the police station and his conversation with Lieutenant Lydecker. Except for occasional mutterings that were unintelligible, Colin remained silent; something he very rarely was. When Jon had finished, Colin shook his head.

"Impossible," he said again.

"Whoever stole my knife did it for two reasons. Either they happened to be visiting my house, came through the garage, and took the knife with the idea of leaving it in the cornfield to confuse the police. That's the scenario I'd like to believe. Or they took the knife deliberately to frame me.

Why? Because they have a grudge against me about something."

"Dear God! The thought terrifies me. What are you going to do?"

"I don't know yet."

"Have you contacted your attorney?"

"Simon Weems was my attorney. I haven't bothered looking for a new one since he died. But even if I did, I doubt there's much that he could do."

"What about police protection?"

"They'd think I was paranoid. Lydecker would, anyway. In this, I'm on my own." Jon paused. "I have a few ideas, though."

"Such as?"

"Such as, I think there's a connection between Ramsey's death and whatever the Scarecrows are involved in."

"The who?"

"At least, that's what I call them," Jon explained. "At the Harvest Hoedown, six of the town's leading citizens dressed up as scarecrows for a comic dance. I told you that."

"Yes, yes—go on."

"Then yesterday, I ran into Peabody, Fitch, and Benjamin checking the Haverman property on Cemetery Road. The land's been sold."

"Nonsense," Colin snorted. "Loomis Haverman would never sell that land. He loves it. Always has."

"Then if he didn't, someone sold it for him," Jon went on. "The property had already been staked for building lots. Mrs. Merriwell and I were there yesterday morning, birding. Suddenly, the three men appeared out of the woods. They were surprised to see us—and uncomfortable about being discovered there. When I mentioned the incident to Lester Fitch this morning, he was very nervous and didn't want to talk. Later, while I was at Peabody's lumberyard, I noticed Peabody observing me from behind his office window. When he realized I'd noticed him he quickly shut the blinds.''

The waiter returned to their table, bearing two wine-glasses on a tray. Colin and Jon said nothing while the young man placed the glasses on the table.

Colin leaned forward. "So you believe these men you call the Scarecrows are in league together?"

"Yes."

"Which could mean that Ramsey was a part of it, and whatever it was he and the others were doing may have got him killed."

"Exactly."

"Jonathan, this whole affair is getting very ugly. If I were you, I would disassociate myself from the whole mess, perhaps even from Scarborough. But of course, I am not you. I also know you well enough not to stand in the way of your inquisitiveness and tenacity. Once you make up your mind to do something, you're like a dog with a bone."

He gave Jon a small smile. "Or should I say a bird with a worm?"

"Thanks." Jon returned the smile.

"Thus I know you will pursue the case no matter what I might advise. In any case, I am prepared to assist you in whatever way I can."

"Thanks for that, too."

"It may be dangerous."

"I know," Jon said. "But I intend to stay alive."

"An understandable priority, dear boy." Colin raised his wineglass, toasting Jon. "To your continued health, my friend."

STEPPING OUT OF Jonah's onto Harbor Street, Colin put the folded newspaper in his left hand that held the cane and offered Jon his right.

"I meant what I said, Jon. I'll do what I can to help."

Jon shook the hand. "I know you will. Come on, I'll walk you to your shop."

Jon took a step, then halted. "Colin—turn around slowly. Take a look."

"What is it?"

"Look toward the antiques shop. There's a girl leaving. Do you see her?"

"The one in the beige raincoat. Yes."

"Do you know who she is?"

"I only got a brief glance. Why do you ask?"

"I saw her at Rod Ramsey's memorial service," Jon told him. "She was very upset."

"Some people are emotional at such events."

"It was more than that. Madeleine and I both commented on how overcome she seemed to be."

The girl disappeared into a side street. Jon and Colin continued on toward Colin's shop.

"She was a pretty thing, as far as I could tell," Colin said, still looking in the direction she had gone. "Now that I think of it, I've seen her before. I'm sure I have. But I can't remember where." He shook his head.

They said good-bye in front of Colin's shop. Jon started to his car, then changed his mind and crossed the street to the antiques shop.

The shop was open, but there was no sign of Lorelei. As Jon stepped through the door, a buzzer sounded in the back and Lorelei appeared.

"Jon, I'm glad you're here, I called your house this morning and left a message on the machine. I wanted to say thanks again for yesterday."

"It was my pleasure. I'm just sorry it was cut short by rain."

She gave him a brief frown. "I'm sorry also for that silly business of the crow. The way I acted, I mean."

"Not everyone likes crows. Somebody once said they look and walk like undertakers enjoying their job."

"So, is this a social call?" she asked. "Or did you decide to get something for the house?"

"Neither, really. It's about the girl who just left your shop. She was wearing a beige raincoat."

Lorelei looked out toward the street, remembering. "Funny you should ask about her. It was strange."

"What was?"

"The whole business. There were a few people in the shop when she came in. That was about half an hour ago. She asked me if there was a rest room. I said there was a small one in the back, next to my office. I told her she was welcome to use it. When she'd been in there about ten minutes, I was worried if she was all right; she'd actually looked faint when she came in. I knocked on the door and asked her if she was okay. She said she was. A few minutes later, she came out to the front of the shop again. Even then, she didn't leave. Instead, she stayed behind a row of shelves pretending to be looking at some stoneware."

"Pretending?"

"She wasn't a buyer, or a browser, either. I could tell. I thought she might be a shoplifter, so I sort of kept an eye on her. Every so often I'd see her glance out through the shelves in the direction of the street. At one point, I tried to make light conversation; I asked her if she lived in town. She said she did. That was about all I could get out of her. She was very nice, though. Extremely pretty also, but quite shy. Finally, she thanked me and left. Since then, I've been trying to figure out why she came in to begin with."

"Have you?" Jon asked.

Lorelei looked at him and nodded. "I think she needed someplace she could hide."

TEN

THE LIGHT VOLUME of traffic pleased Jon as he turned onto the interstate the next morning. It was a holiday, Veterans Day, and the fewer cars on the road would make his drive to New Haven easier.

It was a trip he generally enjoyed. Soon he was moving smoothly along the broad, undulating highway, cresting bridges that hopscotched the tidal inlets leading to Long Island Sound. On the metal poles straddling the road like croquet wickets, he saw the signs for Noank, Niantic and Hammonasset—names that recalled the region's earliest inhabitants, as well as towns like Groton, Lyme and Essex, whose English settlers had sought to preserve memories of the country they had left behind.

Jon took a cassette tape of Vivaldi mandolin concertos from a small box below the dashboard and began to play it, drinking in the sprightly melodies. The day was clear and sunlight glinted off the granite outcroppings he passed along the road.

Still, several matters occupied his mind. His first stop that morning had been to the Scarborough town hall. Only after discovering the doors were locked did he recall it was a holiday. What he sought from the office of the town clerk would have to wait until tomorrow.

There were other questions, too. One was the identity of the young woman he'd seen leaving the antiques shop the day before. Except for speculating on the girl's curious behavior, Lorelei hadn't been able to offer any other information; either what her name might be or where she lived.

And what had been behind Madeleine Thoreau's surprising absence from her office? She'd telephoned last night and apologized profusely for not being there when he'd arrived. Something had come up quite suddenly—she'd had to leave—her assistant was out ill, et cetera, et cetera. It all sounded quite plausible. Jon only wondered if it had been true. To make amends, she had invited him for dinner at her house tonight. When he explained he'd be in New Haven until late afternoon, she'd changed the invitation to tomorrow night. He had accepted with mixed feelings torn between his eagerness to find out what he could about the sale of the Hundred-Acre Wood, and reluctant to reopen any of the past that they had personally shared.

As he continued driving, Jon reviewed his schedule for the day. At one o'clock there was lunch with a friend and former classmate at the Yale School of Art where Jon had spent a summer years ago. The friend owned a gallery on College Street and had offered Jon a one-man show in mid-December. Today, they would finalize plans for the event. At three, he had been invited to address a local chapter of the Audubon Society, illustrating it with slide photos of birds he had taken on his trip to South America last year.

Crossing the bridge over the silty river that formed the eastern boundary of New Haven, Jon was reminded of the contrasting views the city offered. To his left were the acres of oil-storage tanks and mountains of scrap metal. To his right, he saw the cityscape of gleaming corporate high-rises, and beyond them, the Gothic campanile that was Harkness Tower at the center of the university itself.

Exiting at Orange Street, Jon made his way through traffic and parked at a multi-level garage on York Street. From there, he walked up York to Mory's Tavern, where his friend was waiting. Over drinks, they caught up on old news and completed the details for the show. During a lunch of juicy T-bone steaks, the friend supplied similarly juicy gossip about fellow classmates and other artists whom they knew. After lunch, Jon headed west on Whalley Avenue to the building where the Audubon group met.

It was past five when the gathering concluded. Walking back to York, he started south again, passing the residential colleges of Davenport and Branford, past the drama school, the forbidding high stone wall of the undergraduate society called Wolf's Head, and the small building that housed the *Yale Daily News*. Glancing across the street, he saw the lighted windows of the art school and recalled the summer he had spent there.

At the corner of York and Chapel Street, he slowed his steps to allow for the crowd exiting the British Art Center at closing time.

He'd started to walk on, accelerating his pace, when a voice called out: "Jon!"

He turned, startled. Lorelei was coming down the steps of the art center. She hurried toward him. In one hand she was carrying a large-size paper bag.

"What are you doing in New Haven?" she asked, pleased and as surprised as he was.

"I could ask you the same question."

"There's an antiques show at the Coliseum this week," she explained. "I had some time to spare afterward, so I decided to come and see the Turner exhibition at the BAC."

"Did you drive down?"

"I came with the Whittlesey sisters. They have a shop in Mystic and offered me a ride."

"When are you going back?"

"They're supposed to pick me up here any minute," Lorelei said, then made a face. "But I can't say I'm looking forward to the trip. At the show, they bought a bentwood rocker that I'll probably have to share the backseat of their car with on the ride home."

"Why don't you come back with me?"

"May I?"

"My car's nearby, and there's a wonderful Swiss restaurant up the street where we can have dinner first."

"Wonderful. I'd like that—"

She was interrupted by the horn of an old Chrysler Imperial that had pulled in along the curb. A pair of gray-haired women sat in front; a rocking chair was wedged in back.

"Wait here. I'll talk to them," Lorelei said. She went over to the car and spoke through the half-open window on the passenger side. After a few moments, the ladies nodded and the car drove off. Lorelei returned to Jon.

"No problem," she told him. "Let's have dinner."

"Good."

"So how was the antiques show?" Jon inquired, as they began walking along Chapel Street.

"Overwhelming. And exhausting. Everything was on display from A to Z. Agateware to zabaglione spoons."

"I see you managed to buy something." He pointed to the paper bag Lorelei was carrying. "What did you get?"

She gave Jon a sheepish look. "I'm embarrassed to tell you."

"Why?"

"Let's say, it's not something a bird lover would approve. I'll show you at dinner if you promise you won't scold me."

"Why would I do that?"

"Wait and see," she said, and swung the paper bag playfully as they walked on.

The restaurant was three blocks up Chapel Street on the ground floor of an old and somewhat shabby second-class hotel. The facade resembled a Swiss cottage, with latticed windows below which hung window boxes filled with yellow mums. A sign above the plank door identified it as "Oscar's Rathskeller."

As they entered, Jon and Lorelei were greeted by a ruddy-faced man in his mid-sixties with a shock of snow-white hair. Hands the size of bear paws grasped Jon's arms.

"Ach, vat a surprise!" the man enthused. "Velcome, Meester Vilder." He bowed graciously to Lorelei. "And welcome to the beautiful young fräulein, too."

"It's good to see you, Oscar." Jon provided introductions all around. Oscar helped them with their coats and took the coats to be checked.

"I like this man, especially the 'young' part," Lorelei whispered to Jon before their host returned.

Oscar led them to a small corner table covered with a checkered tablecloth. A stubby candle burned inside a copper lantern in the center. Crests of the Swiss cantons were visible against the dark wood-paneled walls.

Oscar handed Jon and Lorelei their menus and recited the dinner specials for the night, most of them traditional Swiss dishes, and asked for their drink orders. Lorelei requested a Pinot Grigio; Jon a Scotch. Oscar noted their requests, then left for the bar.

Lorelei waited until he was gone, then looked at Jon. "Veil, Meester Vilder," she said, "vat do ve recommend tonight?"

"For you, Frau Merrivell," Jon said, matching the accent, "ve haf veasel sautéed in white vine." He pressed his fingers to his lips and kissed them. "Vunderbar!"

Lorelei laughed. "Colin was right. You're not nearly as serious as people think you are."

"Really? Is that what you thought when you first met me?"

"Absolutely. You were Mr. Boy Scout. Straight-arrow. Dudley Do-Right, all the way." She gave an impish glance. "Of course, you're all of that, but more besides."

"What else did Colin say about me? I'm curious."

"Several things I didn't know."

"Such as?"

She touched his hand. "Another time, mein liebchen. Cocktails are here."

A waiter appeared beside them at their table. He put their drinks before them and went off.

Jon raised his glass. "Prosit," he toasted. "I'm not sure of the Swiss-German word, but it's close enough."

Lorelei raised her wineglass also, touching his. "I'll drink to closeness anytime," she said.

"So show me what you bought at the antiques show," Jon said. "The piece you're hiding in the bag."

"All right. But I warned you it's not ornithologically correct."

She reached down and lifted the bag onto the table. From it she withdrew a rectangular tin box a foot long and eight inches wide, and stood it on end. She opened the hinged door to reveal the interior. Two sharp hooks hung down from the top, with a metal grate below.

Lorelei held up the box. "Do you know what it is?"

"I think so. I've seen pictures of them. It's a Colonial bird oven."

"That's it. The dealer who sold it to me thought it some kind of contraption for baking bread."

"Will you sell it in the shop?"

"And ask a good price for it, too," Lorelei said. "I'm told they're rather rare." She smiled. "You're not in the market for one, are you? It should be great for roasting larks and blackbirds."

"Thanks. But I think I'll stick to chickens and turkeys in the kitchen range."

She returned the bird oven to the bag and put it down beside her on the floor. "Now tell me what you were doing in New Haven today."

"I had lunch with a friend." He saw her eyes grow curious and added, "A male friend. He owns a gallery here and he's giving me a show next month. Later in the afternoon I spoke to the local Audubon group about a trip I took to South America. I saw some fairly fascinating birds while I was there.''

"In South America or at the lecture?''

He laughed. "I meant in South America. But since you mention it, there were a few birdlike people at the lecture, too.''

"What do you mean?''

"It was a mixed group—young and old, men and women both. But among them there was this small, what should I say, flock of older women who chattered constantly and flitted around like wrens. What surprised me was that during the question-and-answer session, they were particularly interested in the courting habits of some birds.''

Lorelei seemed interested as well. "What did you tell them?''

"I said courting behavior varied among species. Pigeons, for example, hit their wings together in a clapping sound as they take flight, or bow in front of a prospective mate. Woodpeckers, on the other hand, make a very rapid tapping noise to attract a member of the opposite sex. Males and females both do it.''

"Really? What do they tap on? Tree trunks, old logs, things like that?''

"Yes. Any surface that resounds.''

"You mean like this?'' Lorelei picked up the salt shaker and began drumming it rapidly against the tabletop.

"Like that,'' Jon said.

"I'll keep it in mind,'' she said, smiling at him, as she took another sip of wine.

A SHARP WIND had begun to blow when Jon and Lorelei left the restaurant. They retrieved the Range Rover from the parking garage and headed for the interstate. Reaching the city limits quickly, they were soon into open country-side again.

"Do you mind if I take off my shoes?" Lorelei asked, stretching out her legs.

"Go ahead. I'm sure you did a lot of walking at the show."

"A thousand miles, give or take. At least, it feels like that many." She worked off her shoes one after the other and massaged her toes.

"How about some music while we drive?" Jon suggested.

"Lovely."

"When I was in New York last month, I found a wonderful recording of a Mozart serenade."

"That's fine with me."

Jon reached down, chose the cassette of the *Serenata Notturna,* and inserted it in the tape player.

As the first notes of the piece sounded, Lorelei leaned back, letting the music wash over her. "Amadeus could certainly carry a tune, couldn't he? In fact, I'll make a wild guess and say that Bach and Mozart are your favorite composers. With Vivaldi for occasional variety."

"Did Colin tell you that about me, too?"

"And being an accomplished flutist, you're particularly fond of several of his flute sonatas."

"The two of you must have had quite a conversation."

"Quite," Lorelei confirmed. "He also said you're actually a shy and modest man in spite of being famous."

Jon shook his head. "I'm hardly that. I have a certain reputation in my field. But calling me famous makes me sound like a rock musician. The world has enough celebrities without me joining their ranks."

"You're blushing."

"Probably," he said. "But can you see that in the dark?"

"No," she said. "But it proves Colin's point. You're modest and shy and sometimes maddeningly diffident. Now I'd like to know what was left out."

"Just a lot of uninteresting details."

"Tell me anyway," she said.

"Okay. I grew up in a small town in Maine. My father was a country doctor. He still is. He also hoped I'd follow him in his profession, and while I was growing up, I thought I would. The truth is, I can't stand the smell of medicines. As a child I could hardly bear to go into his office. What I loved most was to draw. So instead of pursuing a degree in medicine after college, I enrolled in the Art Students League in New York. After that it was the National Academy of Design, plus a summer at the Yale School of Art. Early on, I discovered I did portraits pretty well, and through several of my teachers I began receiving some commissions."

"Was your wife a painter also?"

"Yes. We met at the Art Students League. We fell in love immediately, lived together for a while in a loft in Soho, then were married."

"And you continued doing portraits?"

"With a growing reputation, I'm afraid," Jon said. "The more I did, the less I liked my subjects, who, of course, were paying me great sums of money for the portraits of them that I did."

"You mean, they were the rich and famous?"

"Rich and fatuous would be more like it; bloated CEOs and wealthy men who wanted to preserve a likeness of their jowly and rapacious faces for posterity. Then there were the blue-book dowagers who were convinced a Jonathan Wilder portrait of them would ensure them the immortality of the titled ladies Gainsborough had painted."

The Mozart serenade modulated to a minor key. Jon

paused, studying the road ahead of them, breached only by the headlights of the car.

"The money was good. Very good," he went on. "With the commissions I was making, Joy and I bought the house on Plover Point. A few years later, Suzanne was born. Then...something happened."

"The accident?"

Jon nodded, but said nothing.

Lorelei reached across and touched his arm. "I'm sorry. Colin told me some of it. You needn't."

"I can. Now," Jon said. He continued looking at the road. "It was ten years ago. A few weeks before Christmas. The three of us were on a two-lane highway west of town. I was at the wheel. It was dark. A drunk driver came across the center line and hit our car head-on. Joy was beside me; Suzy was sleeping in her car seat in the back. Both of them were killed instantly. I should have been, but wasn't. For months afterward I wished I had. I was in the hospital for quite a while.

"When I came home I wasn't in great shape, physically or otherwise. I couldn't paint. Had no desire to. Commissions came and I ignored them. Instead, I sat up in my studio for hours doing nothing. Staring out at nothing."

"And what changed you?"

"One day in early May, a goldfinch landed on the window ledge. It didn't know what glass was, but it saw its own reflection, and was determined to drive away the 'intruder' from its territory. I watched as it kept dashing at the pane, then fluttering away, but always coming back to fight again. Finally, it was so exhausted, it spent most of the time panting on the ledge and staring desperately into the room. That's when I began to sketch it. At the same time, it occurred to me that if that small bird had the courage not to give up, and to keep on trying, I could do the same."

"So what did you do?"

"First, I closed the door. Then, slowly, I opened a window near where the bird sat. When it saw its reflection again, it went after the intruder from another angle and suddenly found itself inside my studio. It swooped around a few times and flew out. By then I'd already made half a dozen sketches of it on the ledge. That's when I decided to stop doing human portraits and paint birds instead. Of course, they're too lively to sit still for a formal sitting. But there's also something natural and joyful about them that my human subjects never had.

"From then on I did more drawings of the birds along the shore and in the woods around the house. Some I carried into watercolor portraits. I showed them to the owner of a gallery in Essex and he offered me a show. A book publisher visiting the gallery admired them; he called me and suggested that I do a nature guide of birds. The rest, as the expression goes, is history."

"I'm glad you told me," Lorelei said at last. "And they weren't 'uninteresting details.'"

She glanced out the side window at the broad bridge they had begun to cross. "Where are we now?"

"A hundred feet or so over the Connecticut River," Jon told her. "It won't be long before we're home."

"The wind is getting stronger." Lorelei turned up the collar of her coat.

"Are you cold?"

"A little," she admitted.

He increased the heater on the dashboard. "This should help. There's also a car blanket on the backseat. You can put that around you, if you like."

"Thanks, I think I will." She reached behind her, took the blanket and unfolded it around her, tucking her feet under her as she sat. She raised a hand to her face, stifling a yawn.

"Excuse me. It isn't the company. Maybe it's the sooth-ing powers of the music."

"Why don't you take a nap?" Jon suggested.

"Do you mind?"

"Not at all. I'll wake you when we get to Scarborough."

Lorelei allowed a second yawn, then leaned back her head and closed her eyes. A short time later the cassette tape ended and Jon removed it from the player.

The wind was blowing now in fitful gusts. Jon gripped the steering wheel tighter to stay on a steady course. Approaching Mystic, he passed the highway turnout indicated on the sign as "Scenic Overlook" that gave travelers their first glimpse of the restored eighteenth-century village known as Mystic Seaport. Another road sign noted that the exit for Scarborough was four miles ahead.

When he was within a half mile of it, Jon slowed the car, letting the downgrade carry them. Turning at the ramp, he glanced up briefly through the windshield. The night sky had been swept clean of clouds and he marveled at how numerous and bright the stars appeared.

Then something caught his eye. Above the tree line bordering the exit ramp the sky was tinged with red.

Halfway down the ramp, a horn sounded and a car swept past them, a blue light flashing from the dashboard. A second car, also with a flashing blue strobe, came behind it, cutting in front of the Range Rover and turning quickly at the bottom of the ramp.

Lorelei awoke and raised her head. "What's happening?"

"A fire, I think."

"Where?"

"Probably on the road to town," Jon said. "It must have started recently. The volunteer firemen are still arriving."

"Do you know what's burning?"

"I'm not sure. There aren't many buildings in this area." He added, "Except one."

At the base of the ramp Jon stopped and looked in the direction of the fire. Now tips of flames were visible above the trees and embers swirled upward, driven by the wind.

He turned onto the road leading to Scarborough. Even with the windows closed, the acrid smell of burning wood and oil filled the car. Muffled sirens wailed and the Klaxon horns of fire engines filled the night.

Rounding a curve, Jon saw a police cruiser had pulled up on the shoulder of the road, its pulsating roof lights throwing blue and crimson streaks against the trees. Fifty yards beyond, another police car was parked across the road at a right angle, making it impassable.

Two police officers, both wearing reflective orange vests and swinging flashlights, were diverting traffic toward a side road to the left.

"Hold on," Jon said.

"What for?"

"I'm turning right."

He braked and swung the wheel sharply to the right, suddenly bumping along a narrow gravel driveway leading among trees.

Lorelei held tightly to the door handle. "This isn't a road."

"It's the service road to Bernie's Barn. It leads to the rear parking lot."

The trees ended and they emerged into an open area. Jon halted the Range Rover. Both stared out at what they saw.

"My God!" Lorelei said, drawing in a breath. "It's Bernie's Barn!"

On the far side of the parking lot, the building that was once a restaurant had become a barely recognizable inferno. Violent red and orange flames clawed into the night sky, along with roiling clouds of smoke. Four pumper fire engines fought the flames, the streams of water from their hoses arching over one another in glistening cascades. The second story of the structure seemed to have collapsed onto the first. The area Jon knew to be the kitchen had been blown away; probably, he thought, by an explosion of the tanks of propane gas.

Scattered helter-skelter everywhere around the lot itself were fire engines, plus the cars and pickup trucks of the volunteer firemen who had converged there, all with blue emergency lights winking from inside.

Lorelei still looked in horror at the scene. "How many people were inside when it started, do you think?"

"Luckily, it's Tuesday," Jon said. "It's the one night of the week the Barn is closed."

He scanned the parking lot. "I know some of the volunteers. I'll try to find out what I can."

Jon stepped out of the Range Rover. Nearby, a group of firemen were removing air tanks from their backs. Another man, wearing a yellow slicker, was distributing containers of hot coffee from a tray. Jon recognized him. It was Arthur Tingley.

Jon walked toward him. "Arthur, do you have a minute?"

Tingley looked up. "Evening, Mr. Wilder. Want a cup of coffee?"

"No, thanks. Do you know what happened?"

Arthur Tingley put aside the tray and lit a cigarette. "There's not much anybody knows."

"When did the first alarm come in?"

"Twenty minutes ago, maybe," Tingley said. "I don't live too far, you know, so I was one of the first here. Even then, the whole thing was engulfed. Started in the kitchen, probably."

"Does anybody know the cause?"

Tingley took a deep drag on the cigarette and shook his head. ''Not so as I've heard.''

''Has Bernie Benjamin been told?''

''They tried calling him. His wife said he was out.''

Abruptly, shouts came from the side of the building where the kitchen area had been.

Jon and Arthur Tingley watched as one of the firemen ran to an emergency vehicle, took something from it, and rejoined the others. As several of the firemen started to unroll the object, Jon saw what it was. A body bag. Apparently a victim had been discovered in the mass of smoldering debris.

Jon decided there was no need to remain; in fact, a sick feeling had come over him. He had a fairly good idea who the victim was. He also knew what would be found when fire marshals began sifting through the wreckage of the Barn itself.

The charred remnants of a Stetson hat.

ELEVEN

THE AMERICAN and Scarborough town flags were at half-staff and black bunting hung in swags across the portico of the town hall as Jon arrived the next morning. Local newspapers had already announced the death of Scarborough's new first selectman, Bernard Benjamin, with accompanying news accounts about the fire. His body, badly burned, had been discovered in the destroyed kitchen of the restaurant as firemen were battling the flames. Some stories noted it was the second time within a month Scarborough had lost its top official under unusual circumstances.

As he mounted the steps, the door opened and Mrs. Stives appeared, her right hand wrapped in gauze.

"Why, Mr. Wilder, good morning," she said cheerily. "I was going to call you later."

"Oh?"

"The Friends of Birds have been invited to an eagle watch in Newtown in mid-January. Can you join us?"

"I'm sorry, but I have a trip to California planned for then."

"A pity. Have a pleasant day." She waved with her left hand and started down the steps. Jon watched her go. It occurred to him he'd never heard a mention made of any Mr. Stives, although he knew Abigail lived with a grown son, a hulking young man whom townspeople euphemistically termed "slow."

Jon entered the town hall and walked across the lobby to the clerk's office. Mrs. Milbauer, the town clerk, was a short, plump woman in her sixties with frizzed hair and who wore thick bifocals in pink frames. She stood behind a high counter studying a large loose-leaf binder.

"Well, Mr. Wilder," she chirped, closing the book. "I haven't seen you since the Harvest Hoedown."

"Good morning, Mrs. Milbauer."

The woman frowned. "But there's not much good about it, is there? I mean, considering poor Mr. Benjamin and all." She shook her head, as if to strike the matter from her memory. "What can I do for you?"

"I'd like to look at some town records, if I may."

"Certainly. Which did you have in mind?"

"A real estate transaction." He paused. "Specifically, the one regarding the Haverman property on Cemetery Road."

"Now isn't that a coincidence to beat all?"

"What do you mean?"

"I have the book right here." She tapped the loose-leaf binder. "Abigail Stives was just in here looking at it, too. She told me the property was sold."

"I gather it was."

"First I heard about it," Mrs. Milbauer went on. "My assistant must've entered the details. And a big surprise it was. All my life I've lived in Scarborough, and I never thought I'd see that property change hands."

"Was the buyer anybody local, do you know?"

"Not that I remember. But let's take a look." She spread the binder open on the counter and began flipping through the pages. At last, she placed a stubby finger on a page and peered down at it through her bifocals.

"Here it is…October thirtieth. The day before Halloween. Would you like to see the entry?"

"Please."

Mrs. Milbauer turned the open book around and slid it across to Jon. The information at the top concerned the geographic location of the property, its latitudinal and longitudinal coordinates, the roads that bordered it and a brief topographical description.

Following down the page, he saw that the sale of the Hundred-Acre Wood (officially termed "Land in Trust to L. Haverman") had occurred on Friday, October 30. What surprised Jon was that the listed seller of the property was not Loomis Haverman, but someone by the name of M. Brunhill. The seller's address was noted as 989 Fifth Avenue, in New York City. On the lines below it were the name and address of the purchaser: the RKS Corporation, 1520 Broadway, also in New York.

Jon took a pad and pencil from his pocket and copied down the information. Reading further, he noticed that the lines allotted for recording the agents for both the seller and the buyer were blank. He looked up and called over to the clerk, who had gone back to her desk.

"Excuse me, Mrs. Milbauer—but there are no entries for any third parties who might have been associated with the sale."

"I noticed that, too," Mrs. Milbauer said. She returned to the counter and studied the page.

"Isn't that unusual?" he asked.

"Not necessarily. Most of the time, a realtor or an attorney is involved. But there doesn't have to be. Now and then, it's a private transaction between parties—a few legal papers, plus the writing of a check, a handshake, and that's that. Besides, it's cheaper; no one has to pay a broker's fee."

"One more thing," Jon said. "Apparently, the planning and zoning board met recently and voted to approve the sale."

"If they did, we should have minutes of the meeting in our records."

"That's what I was thinking."

"Let me look."

The woman disappeared into an adjacent room. Through the open door, Jon saw rows of file cabinets and floor-to-ceiling metal shelves. He heard loose-leaf binders being moved around, opened, and then closed.

After a few minutes, she called out, "How recent was this meeting of the P and Z?"

"A few days ago," he called back. "Last Sunday night."

More opening and closing of the binders. At last, Mrs. Milbauer reappeared. She came to Jon and shook her head.

"I'm sorry, but there's nothing in the files anywhere about a meeting Sunday night. But that's only three days ago. Maybe no one got around to typing up the minutes yet."

"Maybe," Jon agreed.

More likely, he thought, no one ever would.

THE HOUSE STOOD on a hilltop at the northwest corner of Scarborough, situated at the end of a long driveway and screened by massive white pines lining the road. It had been built a century ago by Loomis Haverman's grandfather, who had also given it the name High Meadows. Observing it now, silhouetted high and dark against the setting sun, Jon thought that for all its stately grandeur it looked to be a cold and lonely place.

He drove up the long driveway and eased the Range Rover into a graveled parking area near the front of the house. On closer view, the house seemed even more impressive. The structure probably had more than forty rooms. Yet few lights burned.

Ever since Jon had lived in Scarborough, stories of the old man's reclusiveness were legion. When Jon had telephoned that afternoon, he anticipated the call would be taken by a servant, and that his request for an audience with Loomis Haverman would be denied. To Jon's surprise, the man answered the telephone himself. Jon asked if he might stop by briefly later in the day, and Haverman seemed genuinely pleased by the request. Jon suggested five o'clock.

Jon stepped out of the Range Rover and walked up the broad stone path toward the front entrance. He noticed that in addition to the dozen steps that led up to the door, a curving ramp had also been installed. Then he remembered hearing that Loomis Haverman had been confined to a wheelchair for several years. Approaching the sizable oak door, he saw a brass knocker that was large enough to encircle a man's arm. He lifted it and rapped three times.

A minute later, the door edged inward and a small, wrinkled face peered out at him.

"Mr. Jonathan Wilder?" the figure asked.

"That's right."

"Mr. Haverman is in the library. Please follow me."

The door swung open and Jon stepped inside. The servant took Jon's raincoat, then guided him through the foyer to a long hall. Walking behind him, Jon guessed the servant was in his seventies. No bigger than a jockey and dressed in a formal dark suit, he looked as if he had been cryogenically preserved since the Edwardian Age. The servant stopped before a set of paneled walnut doors and opened them.

He inclined his head into the room and announced softly, "Sir...Mr. Jonathan Wilder is here."

Jon heard a cough, followed by an indistinct response. The servant moved aside and extended his hand in the direction of the room.

As Jon entered, he saw the library was dimly lit, illuminated only by wall sconces and a birch log fire that leaped and crackled in a huge black marble fireplace. Bookcases stretched across two walls. The other two walls were of rich mahogany, polished to a glowing sheen and on which hung paintings that Jon recognized as the works of Ammi Phillips, Frederick Edwin Church and Thomas Cole.

Near the fireplace was Loomis Haverman. He sat in a high-backed wheelchair, with pillows at both hips and a tartan blanket covering his legs. He wore a green wool Norfolk jacket, a white shirt and an accompanying tie of vivid red. Great dewlaps spilled over the collar of his shirt. His collapsing fleshy face gave him the appearance of a massive melted candle that was moments from extinguishing its flame. The scion of an old New England family that had amassed a fortune in textiles, there were rumors periodically that Loomis Haverman had died. But as Jon approached the man, he saw the rheumy blue eyes had a brightness that belied such talk.

Jon offered out his hand. "How do you do, sir? I'm Jon Wilder."

The old man shook it briefly. Again, the grasp was firmer than Jon would have believed. He waved Jon to a wing chair opposite.

"Wilder. The bird fellow. I've always been particularly fond of birds. Please, do sit down."

Haverman lifted the lid of an inlaid wooden box on a small table next to his wheelchair. "Cigar?" he asked.

"No, thank you."

"Mind if I do?"

Jon shook his head.

Loomis Haverman plucked a panatela from the box, snipped off the end, and lighted it with a wooden match from an antique porcelein striker. He inhaled deeply with great satisfaction.

"A half dozen of my former doctors told me that cigars would kill me," Haverman said. "Now most of *them* are dead and I'll be ninety-one next month. What did you want to talk to me about?"

"First of all, I wanted to thank you for letting me come here."

"My pleasure. I don't get many visitors these days. The truth is, I'll be delighted if you stay and have some dinner with me."

"Thank you," Jon said. "But I have plans."

"A drink, at least. There's a splendid single malt I have shipped to me directly from Dundee."

"Fine."

The man rung a silver bell that was also on the table. The library doors opened and the manservant appeared.

"Two Scotches, Mattley," Haverman said. "And don't ruin them by adding ice the way you sometimes do."

The servant nodded and bowed out, closing the doors.

Jon scanned the room. "It's quite an impressive library you have, if I may say so."

"Two thousand four hundred and eleven volumes, by last count. I love rereading some of them. Although I depend on glasses when I do, my eyes are remarkably good for somebody my age. Otherwise, I'm a shipwreck washed up on the sands of time. Again, thanks to my doctors, I've been subjected to more 'ostomies' and 'ectomies' than any one man should endure. You know what they say about old age. 'Old age is an island surrounded by death.' It was the South American writer, Juan Montalvo, who said that."

Jon smiled. "I'd say your memory is also pretty good."

"It is. My daughter tries to tell me that it's going, but it's not." He exhaled a quantity of cigar smoke, as if to accentuate the point.

"Now tell me why you're here," he said again.

"I'd like to ask about your property on Cemetery Road."

The brightness faded from the old man's eyes. "A wonderful place. We used to take our daughter there when she was small."

Jon nodded. "So did we. My wife and our daughter and I sometimes went there for summer picnics."

"And do the three of you still go?"

"They died some years ago," Jon said. "But I've always thought of it as one of the most beautiful natural places in Scarborough."

"Yes, it was," the other said.

Jon noted the past tense. "At any rate, I was there last Sunday hoping to see birds."

"And did you?" Loomis Haverman asked.

"What I saw were a number of surveyor's stakes." Jon paused. "As if the land had been divided into building lots."

The library doors opened and the servant reentered with two crystal highball glasses on a salver. Jon saw both glasses were liberally filled with the mellow amber liquid. And no ice. Jon took a glass when it was offered; Haverman, the other. The man made a perfunctory gesture in Jon's direction by way of a toast, then sipped.

Jon waited. At last he said, "This morning I learned from the town records that the property's been sold. The buyer lists an address in New York."

He looked across at Haverman, expecting a reaction. But the old eyes simply stared at him through a miasma of cigar smoke.

"Sir—it is my understanding that the land was to be kept natural and deeded to the town. Perhaps as a wildlife preserve."

"It was." Once more, the past tense. "That had been my intention." Haverman said, "Then, several months ago, my daughter came to me—she came with her attorneys, actually—and they convinced me that if I gave the land to her instead, it would reduce the amount of estate taxes she would have to pay after my death."

"Was your attorney present at that meeting?" Jon asked.

"No. I didn't think I needed him. That was a great mistake. When I informed him afterward, he told me my daughter wouldn't have incurred taxes, anyway. That is, if I'd contributed the property to Scarborough before my death—or in my will—as a preserve."

Haverman drank deeply of his Scotch. "But, you see— I'd already given her my word."

"Your daughter. Does she live in Scarborough?"

The other shook his head. "New York. Fifth Avenue. She moved there when she married Wallace Brunhill thirty years ago. They're divorced now, but she kept the apartment. Martha is her name. She knew my intentions for the land. I always meant it to be a nature sanctuary after I was gone. She promised me she'd do that if I gave the land to her. She'd even name it in my honor, Martha said—The Loomis Haverman Preserve."

Jon saw the old man's eyes were wet with tears.

"Then, a week after the papers had been signed," the old man said, "she sold it. All of it."

Loomis Haverman began to weep; short, convulsive spasms that affected his entire bulk. "Excuse me..." He coughed, set down his cigar and withdrew a handkerchief from a side pocket, which he wiped across his face. "I'm sorry...please, excuse me," he repeated.

Jon felt enormous pity for him. "There's no need," he said. "I understand."

"I love birds, too. I told you that," Haverman said finally. "I always meant the woods to be a place for them, where they were safe.

"Once when I was a boy," he went on, "my parents were wintering in Florida. I was ten years old, and as a surprise my father brought me a cockatiel in a cage. It was the most beautiful bird I'd ever seen—crested, with a yellow head and orange patches on its cheeks. I loved it. And I hated that I had to keep it in a cage... So one day, I picked up the cage and carried it outside. When no one was around, I unlatched the wire door and let the bird fly out. I watched as it flew out across the lawn, above the trees, and free into the sky... That was the best thing I have ever done in my entire life. The very best."

The old man looked at Jon. Now tears were flowing freely down his face.

"She sold the land," he said. "My daughter sold the land!"

A moment later, the library doors opened and the servant went at once to the man, bending over him and speaking quietly, as he guided the handkerchief across the ruined face.

Jon stood. "I'll let myself out," he told the servant.

Loomis Haverman was still sobbing, head bowed, as Jon left the room.

JON FOLDED his napkin and placed it on the tablecloth. "The dinner was delicious. And you remembered my weakness for your crêpe suzettes."

"I didn't know you had any weaknesses, Jon," Madeleine said. "Besides, thank you for the wine. A French white burgundy, my favorite. You remembered that."

He smiled. "Yes."

"I can open another bottle for us, if you like."

"Not for me."

"My, my—you're becoming abstemious in your advancing years," Madeleine said. "A tonic before dinner, and only two glasses of wine with it. Do you mind if I pour one for myself?"

"Please, go ahead."

She stood up from the table. "I'll just be a minute. Why don't you make yourself comfortable in the living room?"

Madeleine headed toward the kitchen, carrying her

empty wineglass. Jon moved away from the table and walked into the living room.

Glancing around, it was still very much as he remembered it: the soft cream fabric walls and the abstract art and metal sculptures placed against them, many of them works by one of Madeleine's former husbands, who had been a sculptor. Situated directly on Seal Island Sound, the house provided a spectacular view of the water during the day. Now, draperies had been drawn across the sliding glass doors that led out to the terrace and the swimming pool.

Two large curved sofas faced one another across a massive copper brazier set in the middle of the floor that served as a fireplace. Above it, a broad copper pipe, belled at the bottom, acted as a chimney. The fire had reduced itself to glowing embers, and Jon added a few sticks of driftwood kindling from a basket nearby. He stirred the fire with a poker, then sat down on a sofa.

In the low light of the living room, with the fire starting to flame up before him, Jon leaned back and briefly closed his eyes. As he did, more memories returned of the relationship that he had had with Madeleine Thoreau. In the terrible year following his wife's and daughter's deaths, he had needed someone to assuage his desperate loneliness, to help him to sustain a link with life. Madeleine had served that role. Ten years older, and the victim of three failed marriages, she masked her disappointment with life behind a wry and often rueful wit. They had become lovers gradually and naturally; each maintaining a kind of cautionary wariness, as if both knew it would not, could not last. And yet it had for several years. They had enjoyed one another's company, even traveling together to the Windward Islands of the Caribbean, so that Jon could paint the native birds.

At the same time, both knew they would never marry, and at times of mutual reflection, often before dawn, they candidly admitted it to one another.

Madeleine now reappeared from the direction of the master bedroom carrying a half-filled wineglass in one hand and an open bottle in the other. To Jon's surprise, she had changed out of the black dress she had worn at dinner to a short silk one in green with a slit side that flattered her slim figure.

"Don't look so startled," she told him, sipping at her glass.

"You look lovely."

"When I saw you at the Harvest Hoedown I was dressed as a witch. I wanted to wear something more appropriate for this occasion."

She sat down on the sofa opposite and lifted the wine bottle. "Will you change your mind and have a glass of wine?"

"No, thank you."

She refilled her glass, then lit a cigarette. In the firelight her eyes shone, and Jon was reminded what an extremely attractive woman she still was.

She also looked around the living room. "The place is pretty much as it was when you last saw it. Except I've added a much larger window to my bedroom for the water view." She sipped her wine and looked at him. "You remember that room also, don't you, Jon?"

"Yes." He nodded, but said nothing more.

"So—my dear Jon, I apologize again for not being in my office when you came by Monday morning. But this is a much nicer environment for conversation, wouldn't you agree?"

Again he nodded yes.

"And already tonight, we've discussed the books we've read, the films we've seen, and all sorts of topics that have made the evening as stimulating as it always is with you…"

She paused. "What we have not discussed is the subject

of your call to me the other day. I'll admit, at first I had the fleeting hope that you wanted to renew—what shall I say?—old times.''

''Madeleine...''

''Don't worry.'' She waved her cigarette, dismissing the thought. ''It was wishful thinking on my part. On the other hand, knowing your sense of chivalry, I thought perhaps you wanted to break the news to me directly, and in private, that you were marrying the pretty divorcée who bought Philander Webb's Antiques.''

''I'm not,'' Jon said. ''And that wasn't why I called.''

''But you are attracted to her. Rumors circulate, Jon.'' She waved her wineglass, as if to bestow a blessing. ''Never mind. If that time comes, I will release you from whatever well-intentioned vows you may have made.''

''I did want to talk with you,'' he told her. ''But it has nothing to do with Mrs. Merriwell.''

''What then?''

''When you and I were at Ramsey's service, you said the murderer was probably a jealous husband or boyfriend of a woman Rod had been involved with. Do you still think so?''

She took a long drag on her cigarette. ''It's logical. Who knows what woman—or women—he was bedding recently. The husband or the boyfriend found out, and ended the affair by killing Ramsey. You know, certain men, particularly husbands who've been cuckolded, can have extremely rigid attitudes toward female fidelity.''

''But the same theory doesn't apply to Bernie Benjamin,'' Jon said.

''Maybe, maybe not. In any case, Bernie's death was accidental.''

''The police don't know that. In fact, there's a suspicion the restaurant was deliberately torched.''

Madeleine shrugged. "Bernie could have gone there when he heard about the fire and got trapped inside."

"As you said, maybe, maybe not. Do you remember the night of the Harvest Hoedown when the six men did their scarecrow dance?"

"Of course."

"Now two of them are dead."

She shrugged again. "Coincidence."

"I doubt it. Instead, I think somebody is trying to kill them one by one."

She leaned forward and flicked some cigarette ashes into the fire. "Who?" she asked him finally. "And why?"

"Who it is, I don't know yet," he told her. "As for why, I think it has something to do with the land Loomis Haverman owns on Cemetery Road."

"Really?"

"Last Sunday morning, I went there to do some birding. What I found were stakes along the margin of the property, as if it'd been divided into building lots. While I was there, Bernie Benjamin, Aaron Peabody, and Lester Fitch suddenly came out of the woods. They didn't want to talk and couldn't wait to get away. When I asked Fitch about it later, he admitted that the zoning board had approved the sale of the land. This morning, I went to the town clerk's office and confirmed it. Tonight, before I came here, I also visited with Loomis Haverman, and he confessed that it was true."

"Goodness, Jon." She raised her eyes. "You've been a busy bee. I didn't know you were so interested in local real estate."

"I'm not. But you are," Jon said. "You're the major realtor in town."

She studied the smoke curling upward from her cigarette, then asked, "What else did you learn?"

"That Haverman gave the property to his daughter, and

she turned around and sold it to some group in New York City. There was no broker listed for the sale."

"There's nothing illegal about that," Madeleine said. "You've seen those signs in front of peoples' houses—'For Sale by Owner.' It's the same thing."

"Except you're talking about private homes. I'm talking about a hundred acres of prime property developers would love to get their hands on."

He looked at her, hoping she would answer. When she didn't he went on. "Anyway, I thought you might have heard something...or know something."

She sipped her wine. "No. Not a thing."

In the silence following, a log shifted on the fire. Embers crackled and sparks exploded upward in the air.

She seemed about to speak, but shook her head. "Nothing that I can recall," she said instead.

Jon knew Madeleine Thoreau well enough to know that she was lying. He knew also there was nothing he would gain by saying so.

At last, he nodded and stood up. "Well, thanks again for dinner. But it's getting late. I better go."

She lifted the wine bottle. "Sure you wouldn't like a nightcap?"

"No."

"Suit yourself." She tossed her cigarette into the fire and stood also. "Let me get your coat."

She went quickly to the foyer and returned with his raincoat. She held it open for him to put on.

As he slid his arms into the sleeves, he heard her say, "I'm sorry, Jon."

He turned. "For what?"

"You know for what. The real reason that you came tonight was to get information from me, not because you craved my conversation or my crêpe suzettes. It's my fault, though. I invited you here, you didn't invite yourself."

She smiled up at him. "Of course, I might remember one or two things in the middle of the night."

"If you do, give me a call," Jon said.

Madeleine Thoreau studied him a moment. "Sure," she said, then led him to the door.

She opened it. Looking out into the night, both saw the air was thick with fog, enveloping the porch light and the low lights set along the walk.

Jon leaned and kissed her lightly on the cheek. "Thanks again."

"My pleasure," she said, returning the kiss. "And be careful driving home. There's a sea fog tonight."

"I will."

Suddenly, she reached out and took his hands. "Be careful about many things, Jon. That's strange advice coming from me, isn't it?"

"What do you mean?"

"I mean, I'm a person who's been very careless with her life. I still am. I smoke too much, I drink too much, and I never wear my seat belt when I drive. I've made a royal mess of things. Quite unlike you. You're a careful person, Jon. Watchful, quiet, cautious. Be all those now. Be careful, Jon. Be very careful. Please."

She withdrew her hands, kissed him again, and closed the door.

TWELVE

JON STOOD on Fifth Avenue and looked up at the majestic facade of the Metropolitan Museum of Art. One of the banners hanging from its roof announced an exhibition of the works of Fra Angelico, a painter Jon very much admired, and he hoped he'd be able to see it while he was in New York. Across the avenue the afternoon sun reflected dazzlingly from the topmost floors of the apartment buildings opposite.

Carrying his overnight case, Jon stepped around a flock of pigeons pecking bread crumbs from the sidewalk and made his way across the street to The Stanhope Hotel. He liked The Stanhope for its quiet elegance, as well as for its proximity to the museum. The hotel was also only two short blocks from the apartment of Martha Brunhill.

Jon checked in, went up to his room, showered and changed. He had called Mrs. Brunhill before leaving Scarborough that morning. With obvious reluctance, she had finally agreed to see him—briefly, she emphasized—at four-thirty that afternoon.

When he arrived at the apartment, the doorman noted Jon's name in the register, then spoke briskly into the intercom behind the desk. Acknowledging a confirmation, he directed Jon to a bank of elevators at the far side of the mirrored lobby.

Stepping from the elevator on the penthouse floor, he saw a single door. Jon pressed the bell and waited.

A short time later, the door opened and he found himself facing a deeply tanned young man with dark curly hair and the physique of a body builder. He was dressed in a butler's uniform, but his macho sexuality was so apparent, Jon couldn't help wondering what other services the young man performed for his employer.

Jon gave his name, the young man nodded and repeated it, giving it the Italianate Gian. He led Jon from the front hall and through a wide and beautifully appointed living room. Aubusson carpets stretched across the parquet floor, and a row of French doors opened onto a terrace overlooking Central Park.

The butler conducted Jon into what seemed to be a combination sitting room and study that was smaller than the living room, but no less exquisitely furnished. The room was empty.

"Uno momento," the butler said and bowed out, closing the doors. Jon stepped to the windows and looked out. The sun was already setting, casting the buildings along Central Park West into jagged dark relief.

Behind him, Jon heard the doors of the room open again. "Mr. Wilder?" a voice said.

In the doorway stood an attractive woman in her early sixties wearing an expensive Armani suit in brown and black. Her auburn hair had been recently coiffed and there was a touch of frosting at the sides.

"Yes. I'm Jon Wilder," he said.

"I'm Martha Brunhill. Please sit down." She closed the doors and gestured to a leather club chair near the window. She sat on a settee to his right.

"Would you care for a cocktail?" she asked. "Tonio makes a very good martini."

"No, thank you."

"Let's get directly to the point, then," she said. "I'm leaving soon to join friends. What is it you want?" She ran a hand across her hair, and Jon noticed several of her fingers displayed elaborately jeweled rings.

"Thank you for seeing me," he began.

"Forgo the formalities. I know the reason you're here. I also know it's not to talk about old times in Scarborough. I left there many years ago," she added, "and I have no desire to return."

"As I mentioned to you on the phone," Jon said, "I spoke with your father the other day. Your name came up regarding the property on Cemetery Road. He said he'd given it to you."

"That's true."

"And that you sold it."

"Yes. That's also true. Now may I ask you, Mr. Wilder, what concern is that of yours?"

Jon paused, then went on cautiously. "As you may know—or may remember—Scarborough has a number of wonderful tracts of wooded areas and open land. Because I'm a naturalist of sorts, I'm interested in the preservation of that land."

"In other words, you're an environmentalist—a tree-hugger."

"Specifically, I'm an ornithologist and painter of birds."

"I thought only old ladies or old men with no useful hobbies were interested in birds. You don't seem to fit either of those categories."

He ignored the remark. "It's my understanding," Jon said, "that your father intended to leave the Cemetery Road property in its present natural state, and then, after his death, will it to the town of Scarborough as a wildlife preserve."

Martha Brunhill looked at him without responding.

"Your father told me," Jon continued, "that you convinced him to deed the land to you on the promise you would also keep it as it is now, even name it in his honor when he died. Instead, once the property was yours, you sold it."

"Mr. Wilder," she said at last, "my father is an old man.

His memory is insufficient and selective. He hears and retains only what he wants.''

"According to town records, the purchaser of the property is the RKS Corporation of Manhattan," Jon said. "I tried calling them this morning."

"I know," she said. "They contacted me. They informed me that they told you nothing."

"That's correct."

"And why should they?" she asked him. "I repeat, what concern is it of yours?"

"Because I *am* concerned with the environment," he answered, just as directly. "I thought I might approach them, or the actual buyer whom they may have represented, and encourage them to leave the land just as it is. As you're probably aware, there can be financial advantage to making a donation of a piece of property that size."

The room had darkened swiftly now that the sun had set. The woman reached over to a table lamp and switched it on.

"In the first place, Mr. Wilder," she said, "whoever the buyer or present owner of the property may be, I couldn't be the least interested.

"Second, my father is an elderly, sentimental fool, who spends great amounts of money trying to save the whales or the spotted owl, or whatever animal some group or other has convinced him will become extinct. He's blathered on for years about that property; those hundred acres that he calls his 'virgin land.' Virginity is a myth as far as I'm concerned, whether we're talking about forests or young women."

Martha Brunhill paused. Jon regarded her but didn't answer. His silence obviously annoyed her.

"Mr. Wilder..." she went on, "you see the building where I live. You walked through my apartment. You were enjoying the view when I came in...I also enjoy it. I like the way I live; I like the carpets on the floor, the Baccarat crystal in the cabinets. It's how I *choose* to live. But it takes money. Fortunately, the sale of that property will help me to continue living this way for a long, long time.''

She rose and walked directly to the doors. She opened them. ''Excuse me—but I have a dinner date and tickets for the theater. The Royal Shakespeare Company is in town and I have seats for tonight's performance. Tonio will show you out.''

She turned and left the room, her heels clicking sharply on the parquet floor.

Jon gave a last glance toward the windows of the room. The sun had set and the glowing ribbons of street lamps snaked their way through Central Park.

The woman hadn't mentioned which play would be on the repertory schedule of the Royal Shakespeare Company that evening. Jon hoped it was *King Lear*.

AFTER HURTLING ACROSS Central Park in a dilapidated taxi filled with noxious odors that were all too readily identifiable, Jon climbed out at the corner of Eighty-first Street and Central Park West. He paused to take some breaths. Then, turning, he looked southward past the Hayden Planetarium to the massive gray stone structure that housed the American Museum of Natural History.

He walked south to Seventy-seventh Street, along the front of the museum and turned west, following the drive that led to the museum offices. At the door, he gave his name to the security guard and asked for directions to the office of Dr. Mitchell J. McRae. With his visitor's pass pinned to his lapel, he moved through the labyrinth of hallways until he found the office he was looking for. The plastic nameplate at one side of the door read simply ''M. J. McRae.'' Below it, on a long line, were the words, ''Ornithological Paleontology.'' The two men had met in Tanzania several years ago, when Jon was studying the birds of the Serengeti Plain and Dr. McRae was unearthing the bones of their ancestors. They had remained friends ever since.

Jon knocked on the door. At once, a voice from behind it urged him to come in.

Jon opened the door and found himself staring into the face of a half-bird, half-reptilian creature, baring a set of vicious teeth in its lizardlike jaws. Two feet long, with a broad feathered tail longer than its body and a sizable wing-span, it was a fearsome sight. Sharp, curved claws protruded from the leading edges of both wings.

The creature rested on a pedestal, which in turn sat on a small table. On the far side of the table was a short, balding man peering through thick rimless glasses and dressed in a white lab coat. In one hand, he held a feather; in the other was a pot of glue.

"Good evening, Jon," Dr. McRae said effusively. He gestured toward the table. "You recognize our friend, of course. The archaeopteryx, the first bird in evolutionary history, the forefather of the hundred billion birds who populate the globe today."

"He's a real charmer," Jon said.

"The museum is having a special children's exhibition in the spring," McRae told him, "and Archie here is one of several replicas I'm recreating."

Jon bent and studied the black gimlet eyes. "Actually, he looks like a bird out of mythology—the phoenix, maybe, or the roc from the *Arabian Nights*."

"Except the archaeopteryx really existed in the Jurassic period, say, a hundred fifty million years ago. But unlike the other archosaurs—the dinosaurs and crocodiles—he was the only one that learned to fly."

Dr. McRae put aside the feather and the glue pot and

shook hands. "It's good to see you, Jon. I was delighted when you called. Tell me, are you still free for dinner?"

"Absolutely."

"Good. There's a wonderful French restaurant that's an easy walk from here. It's not far from my apartment either. If you have time, I can introduce you to the newest lodgers in my aviary."

"Fine."

A short time later they left McRae's museum office and walked downtown along Columbus Avenue, then turned east toward the park again. The Fleur de Lis was a tiny bistro, where the aroma of hearty onion soup, escargots with garlic, and fresh bagettes welcomed diners the moment they stepped through the door. Both Jon and McRae ordered cassoulet and split a bottle of Châteauneuf-du-Pape.

After dinner they walked on to West Sixty-eighth Street and the brownstone where McRae had his apartment. The building was an elegant six-story structure dating from the 1900s that had once been a single-family residence. At a rear corner of the lobby, a marble staircase curved upward toward the second floor. Opposite it was a narrow elevator, hardly bigger than a phone booth, and the two men squeezed inside.

"My apartment's on the roof," McRae said, pushing the elevator button for the sixth floor. "It was probably the solarium when one family owned the building. As you'll see, it's definitely not much for space. But it's light and pleasantly breezy in the summer. And the roof surrounding it gives me someplace where I can keep my birds."

"You said you had a few new residents. What are they?"

"You'll see," McRae said.

The elevator shuddered to a halt and they stepped out. McRae unlocked the door of his apartment and went in. Jon followed him. The living room was small but pleasant with bird prints and travel posters hung about the walls, as well as bookshelves filled with books and scientific papers. On one shelf, Jon saw a small skeletal model of another prehistoric creature. McRae observed him looking at it.

"It's a pterodactyl," McRae told him. "A gift from my associates last year. I guess they thought one old fossil deserved another." He gave the skeleton a friendly pat.

McRae stepped into the tiny kitchen, opened the refrigerator and took out a plastic bag. He put the bag in his coat pocket and waved to Jon to follow him. "The aviary is this way."

At the rear of the apartment, McRae unlocked the two locks on a door that led out to the roof. Stepping through the door, Jon saw, set against a brick wall, a row of large wood-and-chicken-wire cages perched on legs.

McRae gestured to the cages. "Lots of people bring me sick or injured birds, you know, and I do what I can to nurse them back to health. This summer I had starlings, owls, even a peregrine falcon with an injured wing. But most of the patients recuperated and flew south in the fall. Right now, I have only a single pair, and they'll be checking out soon."

Jon approached the cages and saw that two were occupied. He looked back at McRae. "They're crows."

"The male is on the left," McRae said. "I've named him Edgar Allen Crow. The other is his mate, Lenore. Both ate poisoned grain somewhere in New Jersey. The two of them were nearly dead when they were brought to me."

Jon moved closer to the cages and the male made a quiet croaking sound.

"It's past their dinnertime," McRae said.

He opened the cage doors briefly, one by one, and took out the feeding pans. He withdrew the plastic bag from his coat pocket, poured some of the contents into each pan, then replaced the pans inside each cage.

"What do you feed them?" Jon asked.

"A combination of mice, cornmeal, and cockroaches."

"You keep dead mice in your refrigerator?" Jon said amused.

"Of course. The superintendent of the building traps them and gives them to me. The cornmeal comes from a pet store on Amsterdam Avenue. The cockroaches I catch myself."

Jon bent close to the cages again. "The mixture must agree with them. They're gobbling it down."

"Oh, they're pretty healthy now. But, of course, crows are extraordinary birds. Extremely intelligent and very gregarious. There's even a growing population of them in the city. Unlike pigeons, they're able to use their bills to slash open trash bags left out on the street. It's driving the sanitation people crazy."

"They really don't have many natural enemies, do they?" Jon asked. "Except owls. And certain hawks."

"Don't forget human beings," McRae said. "They're the worst."

"This may seem like an odd question," Jon said, "but would crows ever kill a human being?"

McRae pondered it, then shook his head. "Virtually impossible. Oh, perhaps under very special circumstances, crows might mob a person who got too close to a nest of young. But kill the person, no. There was an incident some years ago in New Guinea where a cassowary killed a child. But cassowaries are large birds, of course, like emus, and that may have been a protective act also, with the child getting much too near its nest.

"Another thing about crows," McRae added, "they're among the least territorial of birds, with the exception, as I said, of nesting time. At the opposite end of the spectrum is, again, the species Homo sapiens. When it comes to protecting or defending property, man can be the most territorial—and deadly—creature on this earth."

IT WAS WELL AFTER ten o'clock when Jon returned to the hotel. As he entered his room, he saw the message light flashing on the telephone. He called the hotel message center and learned he had received one call. Mr. Colin Hightower had telephoned at seven thirty-five.

Jon hung up the phone and jotted the information on a pad. He debated whether or not he should return Colin's call tonight. But if the message had been urgent, Colin would have indicated that. He also knew his friend retired early; any person calling after 10 p.m. was generally subjected to a torrent of abuse that made certain no similar mistake would ever reoccur. Jon decided he would call back first thing in the morning.

Whatever Colin had to tell him, it would keep till then.

"HIGHTOWER WOODWORKING." Colin's voice rumbled through the telephone.

Jon sat on the edge of the bed, the phone held to his ear. With his other hand, he poured the remainder of the breakfast coffee room service had brought.

"Good morning, Colin. It's Jon."

"Ah, yes—I'm glad you called. Hold on. I'm just preparing morning tea. Before you ask, it's a Chinese green. Very medicinal. I've got a bit of the catarrh."

Jon heard the phone being put down. After some moments, there was the clink of china, followed by the tap of Colin's cane against the floor of the woodworking shop. Another clink as the teacup was set on the desk, then the thump of a great, heavy object plummeting to rest. Colin had sat down.

"In point of fact," Colin resumed, "It was good you waited until now to call. Had we spoken last night, I had one grim but not entirely unexpected bit of information to provide. Now I have another, which is both grim and unexpected."

"Tell me."

"First, I learned late yesterday that the police have a preliminary autopsy on Bernie Benjamin. It was definitely not the fire in the Barn that killed him. He was stabbed to death. Numerous times, apparently."

"Do they know exactly when it happened?"

"Not that I've heard. But speculation is that he was murdered at the restaurant the same evening and that the murderer then set the blaze to cover up the crime."

"Did you get this from Lieutenant Lydecker?" Jor asked him.

"Good heavens, no. The police themselves have been quite mum. But rumors do proliferate. At the moment they're running around Scarborough like mice in an abandoned barn."

"You said there was a second piece of news."

"Yes, I'm afraid so," Colin told him. "Lester Fitch has had a heart attack."

"*What?* When?"

"This morning. About eight o'clock, I'm told."

"Do you know the details?"

There was silence at the other end then, interrupted only by the sound of Colin sipping tea. "A few," he said at last "Apparently, Lester arrived at the pharmacy shortly before eight. Timmy, the stock boy, appeared soon after that. Both went to the office in the back, hung up their coats, and exchanged a few brief words. They returned to the store just as the postman entered with the mail. Lester took it and walked back to the office, sorting through the pieces as he went. The stock boy remained in the store, straightening some shelves. Then, so Timmy says, he heard Lester Fitch cry out. When he ran back to the office, he saw Lester lying on the floor, the mail scattered everywhere. The boy called nine-one-one; the ambulance arrived a short time later and took Lester to the hospital."

"How serious was the attack?"

"Not life-threatening, at least," Colin informed him. "I understand his wife is with him now."

"How's Muriel doing, by the way?"

"I don't know. But I'm sure she'd appreciate hearing from you." Colin added, "Since she and your wife were friends, I mean."

"Thanks for the information. I'll try to stop at the hospital on my way home."

Jon checked his watch. If he left the hotel by ten, he could be in Scarborough by mid-afternoon.

"What about the others?" Jon asked. "Kittridge, Peabody and Reverend Rill?"

"I haven't seen them," Colin told him. "But if I were them, I'd check my will, increase my life insurance, and perhaps get together with a different reverend in prayer."

"Well, thanks again for telling me," Jon said. "I'll call you after I get back."

"Please do. Cheerio." There was a last sip and a click.

Jon hung up and began to pack his overnight case.

THIRTEEN

SCARBOROUGH HOSPITAL was a small, community medical facility with an excellent reputation for an institution of its size. Comprised of a series of low connected buildings, it was located on several dozen landscaped acres and surrounded by tall trees.

Jon drove into the visitors' parking lot and found a space not far from the main doors. As he studied the people going in and out, memories came flooding back. It was here his daughter had been born twelve years ago. That day he and Joy had both given thanks for the beautiful baby girl that had been brought into their lives. It was here also that he and Joy and their daughter had been rushed by ambulance the night of the accident. Following his discharge from the hospital, and except for some outpatient therapy, he had not been back since.

At the information desk in the lobby, he learned the number of Lester Fitch's room. He took the elevator to the floor that ministered to the coronary-care patients and started down the brightly lighted corridor. He paused briefly at the waiting room and glanced in, wondering if he'd find Muriel Fitch there. The room was empty.

He continued through a set of sliding glass doors that parted automatically as he approached. Along both sides, the patients' rooms had glass walls facing the nurses' station in the center of the floor. In some rooms, floor-to-ceiling draperies had been drawn closed; in others, Jon could see men and women lying in beds, all with tubes and wires leading from them to rows of monitoring instruments nearby.

Jon walked to the nurses' station, which was also filled with banks of blinking monitors. A young black woman, the head nurse of the section, was making notations on a patient's chart. She looked up as Jon appeared.

"Excuse me," he said. "My name is Jon Wilder. I was told Lester Fitch is on this floor."

"Yes," the nurse said. "But he's not receiving visitors."

"I understand. But if his wife is here, I'd just like to say hello."

The woman nodded. "Mr. Fitch is in room three-sixteen. It's around the corner to your right. I think his wife is with him now."

Jon thanked her and followed the direction the nurse had given him. Turning the corner, he discovered five additional rooms, also glass-walled. The room numbers on the wall suggested Fitch's room would be the last one on the left.

As he moved toward it, Jon slowed his steps, then stopped. Seated on a folding metal chair outside the room was Aaron Peabody. With his sharp, dour face and arms folded across his chest, he reminded Jon of a bailiff guarding a prison cell.

Peabody turned suddenly, saw Jon and stood up, moving in front of the open door of the room as he did.

"You can't go in there," Peabody announced.

"Hello, Aaron," Jon said, as if not hearing the remark.

"You can't go in," Peabody repeated. "Lester isn't allowed visitors."

"I know that." Jon glanced into the room and saw Muriel Fitch seated in a corner, knitting. "I just wanted to let Muriel know I was here, and ask her if there's something I can do."

"She has enough people doing things for her right now," Peabody told him.

Jon stood his ground. "Are you the judge of who can see her and who can't? My wife and I were good friends of Muriel and Lester years ago. They visited me after Joy died."

Jon looked into Peabody's flint-cold eyes. "I want to tell Muriel I'm here," he said again.

"All right," Peabody allowed. "But be as brief as possible."

"By the way," Jon asked, "does anybody know what may have caused the heart attack? I mean, was Lester exerting himself? Or did he have some sort of shock?"

"Nothing that I know of, no," Peabody said.

The response was almost too immediate, Jon thought.

"I see," he said. "Excuse me."

Jon stepped past Aaron Peabody and into Lester Fitch's room. The room was dim, with only a thin band of light slanting through the closed draperies. Lester seemed to be asleep. A ganglia of tubes and wires led from him to monitoring panels near the bed.

Seeing Jon for the first time, Muriel gave him a sad half-smile and put her knitting to one side. Her white hair had the appearance of spun cotton and her eyes were red behind her glasses. She held out a hand toward Jon.

"Hello, Muriel," he said in a low voice. He kissed her on the cheek, then he pulled up an empty chair and sat beside her in the corner of the room.

"Dear Jon." She grasped his hand and squeezed it. "Thank you for coming."

"Would you rather talk outside?"

She glanced momentarily in the direction of the door. "No. Here is all right. Lester is asleep." Her eyes moved to the figure on the bed.

"How's he doing?"

"Better than we thought at first," she said. "Thank God Timmy was in the store and that the ambulance came as quickly as it did. Otherwise…" She shook her head.

"I won't stay long," Jon said. "I just wanted to ask you if there's anything that I can do."

"Hope and pray. That's all."

"Listen," Jon said, "yesterday, while I was in New York, Mrs. Epsom did one of her wonderful roast chickens for me that she gets from Oren Bellkirk's farm. It's still in the refrigerator. Since you'll be here a lot the next few days, let me bring it to your place tomorrow and you'll have something to eat when you get home."

"That would be very nice. Thank you," Muriel Fitch said.

Jon stood and took her hands again. "And remember to call me if there's anything else I can do for either one of you. I mean that."

"I know. I promise I will."

Jon turned toward the door to leave. Across the corridor he saw Peabody talking with another man whose back was to him. But from the Bible the man held Jon knew it was the Reverend Rill.

"Tell me something, Muriel," Jon asked her quietly. "Have there been many people coming by today? To see you or Lester, I mean?"

"Some. A couple left their names at the information desk downstairs. And some have called, I'm told. A few of his close friends have even come and stayed. They found a chair and sat outside the room."

"Did you think that was a little strange?"

"I did. I told them that they didn't have to. But they said it was to be here if I needed anything. And to protect Lester."

"Protect him? From what?"

"Visitors disturbing him, I guess."

"Who were these friends?" Jon said. "If I may ask."

"Justin Kittridge was here most of the morning. Then

Aaron Peabody came. He told me Reverend Rill would be here later.''

"I think he's already arrived," Jon said. "Good-bye, Muriel. Remember what I told you."

"I will. And thank you again for coming."

What followed was a low guttural sound that came from Lester Fitch himself.

Both Jon and Mrs. Fitch turned toward the bed at once. Lester Fitch's eyes remained closed. But his mouth opened and closed noiselessly several times. The low sound was repeated.

Muriel Fitch moved to her husband's bedside and put her hand on his. "I'm here, dear."

A grunt. Slowly, the eyes opened. They closed, then opened for a second time. For a long while, Fitch stared up at his wife, as if he had difficulty comprehending who she was.

"Muriel…" The voice was a breathy whisper that was barely audible.

"Yes, dear…I'm here." She held his hand. "And Jon Wilder is, too."

Fitch's eyes moved toward the window.

"No, dear—over here," she said. "On the other side."

Fitch slowly turned his head, so that the breathing apparatus at his nostrils became dislodged. His wife quickly readjusted it.

"Jon Wilder?" Fitch blinked several times.

"Hello, Lester," Jon said.

"Jon Wilder," repeated Fitch. He freed his hand from his wife's grasp and seemed to gesture for Jon to come closer.

Jon took a step in the direction of the bed.

Fitch opened his mouth and said something on a single breath that was unintelligible.

"Don't try to talk, dear," his wife cautioned. "Rest."

But Fitch's hand reached out until the fingers touched Jon's sleeve. Jon bent over the bed.

"What is it, Lester?" he asked.

The lips worked. "Feather," said the voice.

"Feather?" Jon repeated the word. He looked down at Lester Fitch. The eyes were closed again.

From the doorway a man's voice spoke. Standing just inside the room was the Reverend Chester Rill. He was dressed in a black coat. The leather-bound Bible was still clutched in his hand. He smiled at the two of them.

"Muriel—Jon—forgive me for interrupting," Rill said. "But I'm sure Lester needs his rest right now."

"I was just going," Jon informed him.

"Yes. I think it's best." Rill smiled for a second time.

Jon gave a nod to Muriel Fitch and left the room. The chair outside the door where Aaron Peabody had sat was empty; presumably to be filled soon by the Reverend Rill.

Jon walked back the way he'd come, past the nurses' station, through the sliding glass doors, past the waiting room, and down the hallway leading to the elevators. And as he walked, the one word Fitch had spoken kept reverberating...

Feather...

Feather...

Feather...

JON LEFT the hospital and made his way across the parking lot. He was halfway to the Range Rover when he saw a police car driving into the lot. It stopped several rows away. Jon watched as Lieutenant Lydecker stepped out and put a gray fedora on his head. Then the detective reached back into the car and withdrew a large bright-yellow toy duck with a polka-dot bill and a pink ribbon tied around its neck.

Jon walked toward the detective. As he did, Lydecker caught sight of him and frowned.

"Hello, Jon," Lydecker said. He put the toy duck under his arm.

"Hi, Larry." Jon looked down at the duck. "I see you're also getting into birds."

Lydecker was visibly embarrassed. "It's not mine. The daughter of one of our officers just had her tonsils out. I'm bringing her a gift."

"The color goes with your blue overcoat," Jon said. "You should wear yellow more often."

"What do you want, Jon?"

"Some information, actually. Or maybe I should call it confirmation. I'm told the autopsy on Bernie Benjamin showed he was stabbed repeatedly before the fire started."

"Where did you hear that?"

"A biplane towed it on a banner past my house. Come on, Larry. It's the latest rumor around town. I also heard the restaurant was probably set on fire to cover up the murder. Is it true?"

"I can't comment on an investigation in progress. You know that?"

"Well, just in case I'm also a suspect in the death of Bernie Benjamin, I have an alibi."

"You're not a suspect." Lydecker looked as if he were somewhat disappointed.

"Does that mean I'm no longer a suspect in Ramsey's death either?"

"Jon, I told you, I can't comment—"

"Damn it, Larry. Am I or am I not? I'd like to know." Lydecker frowned again. "Probably not."

"*Probably* not? You mean, some people—including you—still think I killed Ramsey?"

"I don't think so, no." Lydecker breathed heavily, forming a little cloud of mist in the cold air. "The knife wounds don't match."

"What do you mean?"

"The knife that killed Ramsey and Benjamin apparently had a little curve to it at the tip."

"What sort of a curve?"

"Listen, Jon—I'm due on duty in a half hour. I've got to give the kid this duck and go."

"Okay, but tell me. If I hadn't run into you today, would you have informed me I wasn't a prime suspect anymore?"

"Jon, look—"

"You wouldn't, would you? Instead, you would have left me twisting slowly in the wind."

"Jon, it's a complicated case," Lydecker said impatiently. "Both Ramsey's and Benjamin's. But we've got some evidence and a few leads that look interesting."

"Such as?"

"I told you, I can't discuss it."

"Maybe if you did, you'd get some help," Jon said.

"Are you still trying to play detective?"

"I'm not trying to play anything."

"Because if so, you're wasting time. Let the police handle it."

"Larry, it's been three weeks since Ramsey's murder, and all the police have are a few so-called interesting leads and not much evidence. About the evidence, can you tell me if the police found a white campaign button at the murder site next to his house?"

"You mean the button with the three Rs on it?"

"That's the one."

"No." Lydecker shook his head.

"What about the cornfield?"

"Again, no. There was just—your knife. Why do you want to know?"

"Because Ramsey had a button like that pinned to his scarecrow outfit at the hoedown."

"He probably took it off before he left the grange, or gave it to a prospective voter."

"Maybe," Jon said.

"Look, Jon, I've got to go."

"All right. But let me ask you another question. What do you know about a feather?"

"What feather?"

"I don't know," Jon said.

"Then why did you ask?"

"I heard someone use the word in connection with the case."

"I'll say it one last time, Jon. *Do not get involved.*"

"Okay," Jon said directly. "But since the police are involved, you ought to be aware that something else is going on. And the two murders are just part of it.

"By the way," Jon added, nodding toward the hospital, "I just saw Lester Fitch upstairs. He had a heart attack this morning."

"So I heard."

"It was in the drugstore, right after he picked up the morning mail."

"So?"

"Do you know what was in that mail?"

"No. Do you?"

"No. But I suspect something Lester may have read or found in one of the pieces of mail scared him so much it brought on his heart attack."

"Thanks for telling me. We'll check it. In the meantime, Jon—"

"I know. Be patient. Let the police handle it."

"That's it," Lydecker said.

"The trouble is, there's someone around Scarborough who's getting more impatient all the time. You're running out of scarecrows, Larry. Three down, three to go."

Lydecker glared at him, then turned and marched in the direction of the hospital, clutching the toy duck under his arm.

JON WATCHED the morning sunlight shimmer on the water and he replayed the two messages. He had found them on his answering machine late yesterday after he returned from the hospital. One was from Mrs. Milbauer asking him to stop by the town clerk's office if he had the chance. She had some "curious" information for him, she had said. The other call was from his gallery-owner friend in New Haven, who hoped he could make a quick trip to the gallery next Wednesday concerning the hanging of the paintings for Jon's show. Jon decided that he could, and called his friend to tell him so.

He was leaving the study when he realized there was another call he'd have to make. He looked up the number in the telephone directory and called it.

At the other end, the phone rang a dozen times. Jon started to hang up, when he heard a click. There was a pause, and then a voice. "Yes?"

"Mr. Bellkirk?"

"Who is this?"

"Jon Wilder. I know you were planning to deliver the Thanksgiving turkey and the pies next Wednesday afternoon."

"The day before the holiday. That's right."

"The problem is I have to be in New Haven that day," Jon said. "I wonder if I can swing by your farm on the way back and get them."

"I'll probably be out making deliveries," the man said.

"Well, I'll be having two guests for Thanksgiving dinner. Maybe you could leave the turkey and the pies with one of them."

"Who are they?"

"Mr. Hightower—"

"The woodworking man?"

"That's right. And also Mrs. Merriwell."

"Who?"

"Mrs. Merriwell. She bought Philander Webb's Antiques."

Bellkirk grunted. "Uh. I heard Webb sold the place."

"Anyway, I'll ask them if they'll be in their shops the day before Thanksgiving and call you back."

"Okay," Bellkirk said.

The phone clicked off.

Jon left the study and was heading to the kitchen when he heard a car approaching on the drive. He stopped at a hall window and looked out to see a maroon Chrysler pull into the turnaround. The driver was a woman. A moment later, Muriel Fitch stepped out of the car.

Jon went to the door and opened it as she came up the walk.

"Good morning, Muriel," he said. "This is a pleasant surprise."

"Good morning, Jon." She gave him an apologetic look. "I'm sorry to show up like this. I should have called you first."

"Not at all. Let me take your coat." He helped her off with it. "I was about to pour some coffee. Will you join me?"

"That would be nice. Thank you."

"Why don't you go into my study, we can have it there."

"Fine."

She walked toward the study, holding her purse tightly in both hands. When Jon returned carrying two mugs, he found her seated in a Queen Anne chair, looking small and somehow vulnerable. He handed her a mug and sat down opposite.

"Are you on your way to the hospital?" he asked.

The woman nodded. "Yes."

"How did yesterday go? For Lester, I mean."

"The doctors said he has improved."

"That's good news. You must be relieved."

"Very," Muriel Fitch said. "And thank you again for stopping by. It meant a lot to me."

"Were there other visitors after I left?"

She pursed her lips. "Lieutenant Lydecker of the police."

"Did he talk with Lester?" Jon was curious to know.

"He never came into the room. Reverend Rill stopped him in the corridor and told him Lester was asleep. Lester was awake, though. I don't know why the Reverend said that."

"Did you talk with the lieutenant yourself?"

"No. After Reverend Rill spoke to him, the lieutenant went away." She sipped her coffee, adding nothing more.

"Well, as I told you," Jon went on, "Mrs. Epsom cooked a chicken for me, which you're welcome to. But rather than carry it with you to the hospital, why don't I leave it at your place when I drive into town later."

"If you could, that would be lovely." She paused and set her coffee to one side. "But that's not why I came here today."

"Oh?" He looked at her, then went on cautiously. "Is it about what Lester said to me? When I was there?"

"Yes. But that's not all."

"What do you mean?"

"After I left the hospital last night, I drove to the pharmacy. Timmy had gone home, of course. And the other pharmacist who works with Lester had already locked up. So I let myself in and went to Lester's office in the back. Timmy told me Lester had been opening the mail when the heart attack occurred. After the ambulance took Lester to the hospital, Timmy picked up all the scattered mail on the floor and stacked it on the desk. I brought it home with me.''

''Did you have a chance to look at it?'' Jon asked her.

Muriel Fitch nodded. ''Most were bills. There was a newsletter from the Society of Pharmacists, some sample medicines the drug companies send out. And an envelope with nothing written on it.''

''What sort of envelope?''

''Plain white. The kind that Lester sells in boxes in the store. The long business size; the sort that has a patterned lining, so nobody can see inside. It had been torn open.''

''By Lester?''

''Yes. I'm sure. After what happened when you were in Lester's room, I wanted you to see it.''

She unclasped her purse, reached inside, and drew out a long white envelope. The front was blank, as she had indicated, and there were jagged edges at the top where Lester Fitch had opened it. She handed the envelope to Jon.

Jon took it and felt something inside. He reached in and gently drew it out. The object was a feather, black, about six inches long. Considering its size and iridescent sheen, he was sure it was the wing feather of a crow. But there was something odd about it, suggesting that it hadn't come from the bird naturally. The quill end appeared to be hacked and shortened, as if cut off with a knife. Some of the vanes along the central shaft were bent or missing.

The woman watched as Jon held up the feather to the light.

''I'm certain that's the feather Lester meant when he spoke to you yesterday,'' she said. ''I'm also sure it must have been what caused the heart attack.''

Jon laid the feather on the envelope. ''Why do you say that?'' he asked.

"Because…last week Lester told me Bernie Benjamin got one just like it. Bernie tried to make a joke of it, he said, but Lester knew that he was scared."

"When did Bernie receive it? Do you know that?"

"Yes." She paused. "The day before the restaurant burned. Apparently, it came the same way Lester's did. A plain white envelope shoved through the mail slot of Bernie's Barn."

"Did Lester know why Bernie Benjamin was frightened to receive it?"

The woman looked down at her hands. "He didn't say. But I can guess."

"Why?"

"Because Rod Ramsey also got a feather like it on the day before he died."

FOURTEEN

JON PARKED across the green from the town hall. He'd already decided to put off going to the town clerk's office until after he'd seen Colin. It meant an extra few blocks' walk, but it would help to clear his mind after the visit from Muriel Fitch earlier that morning.

Opening the door of the woodworking shop, he saw Colin chatting with an obviously wealthy couple, who were studying a finely finished dining-room set.

Colin noticed Jon and raised a hand, gesturing to Jon to remain where he was. When the man and woman began to talk between themselves, Colin took the opportunity to excuse himself from them and join Jon.

"You're busy," Jon said. "I can see."

"Rather." Colin bent toward him and whispered. "I don't like to indulge in unhatched chicken counting, generally. But I think I've sold the Regency dining room set, side server and all."

"Congratulations," Jon whispered back. "But I'll be quick. It has to do with Thanksgiving."

"Oh?"

"The day before, on Wednesday, I have to make a trip to New Haven about the gallery show. Mr. Bellkirk wanted to deliver the turkey and the pies that afternoon. But I'm not sure I'll be back in time. I wondered if he could leave them here with you. I'll get them later in the day."

"Oh, dear. That's a problem," Colin said. "Normally, I'd be here. But I'll be in Boston all day Wednesday, and I'd planned to close the shop. Perhaps Mrs. Merriwell could do it."

"I also thought of that," Jon said. "I'll ask her."

Over Colin's shoulder, he saw the husband from the couple come toward Colin with an open checkbook in his hand.

This time it was Jon who leaned to Colin. "By the way, I think your chickens are about to hatch."

Jon left the shop, crossed Harbor Street, and started toward Philander Webb's Antiques. The showroom was empty when Jon entered, but he heard low voices coming from the office at the rear. At last, Lorelei appeared.

"Oh, Jon…it's you." She seemed relieved.

"Were you expecting someone else?"

"Not really. No." She inclined her head in the direction of the office.

In the doorway stood the girl Jon had seen leaving the shop more than a week ago. Now, at close range, she seemed even younger than he'd thought and very pretty. Her skin was alabaster-white, set off by lustrous jet-black hair, and her large pale-blue eyes blinked frequently, like those of a wary animal. She was wearing the beige raincoat Jon remembered.

Lorelei turned and smiled at the girl. "Gina, this is a friend of mine, Jon Wilder."

The girl took a step into the room and nodded cautiously to Jon.

"Jon, this is Gina. She's been looking at some of the old cooking implements. Gina likes to cook."

"Pleased to meet you, Gina," Jon said.

The girl glanced at Lorelei. "I have to go."

"All right," Lorelei said. "But I hope you'll come back again."

"Thank you," the girl said. She clutched her purse, hastened to the door and disappeared into the street.

"At least I know her name now," Jon said, when the girl was gone. "Her first name, anyway."

"She told me she comes from Providence," Lorelei informed him. "But she's been working in Scarborough for a year."

"As what?"

"She never said. An au pair or domestic, probably."

"The last time she was here, you thought she might be hiding from someone," Jon reminded her.

Lorelei nodded. "Yes, that's what I thought. This time I think she wanted somebody to talk with."

"About what?"

"I don't know. She came in a few minutes before you did. She began looking at the old tin cookware. So to make conversation, I asked her if she enjoyed cooking. She said she did. But when I started back into the office she followed me. When I asked if I could help her, she said, 'Yes, please, I need your help.' That was when you came in."

A pair of young blond men suddenly appeared outside the shop windows, pointing here and there at objects through the glass. Both Lorelei and Jon saw them.

"Looks like business," Jon said.

"They're New York decorators who have a house in Scarborough. They've been good customers."

"I should be going, anyway," he said. "The reason I stopped was to ask if you'll be in the shop the day before Thanksgiving."

"I should be. Why?"

"I have to drive down to New Haven. The turkey and the pies I ordered were supposed to be delivered to my house that afternoon. May I ask Mr. Bellkirk to leave them here with you?"

"Of course," Lorelei assured him. "There's an old refrigerator in the basement that came with the shop. I can keep them in that."

"Good. I'll call Bellkirk and tell him. What time do you close?"

"About six."

"I'll be back from New Haven before then and get them."

They said good-bye and Jon started for the door, as the two young men entered from the street.

"Oh," Lorelei said suddenly. "There was one thing I meant to tell you."

"What?" Jon stopped.

"Remember the Colonial bird oven I picked up at the New Haven show? We joked that bird lovers would hate it."

"Yes."

"I sold it yesterday," she told him. "And you'll never guess who bought it...Abigail Stives."

IT WAS AFTER one o'clock when Jon left the town hall. He stood at the top of the stone steps and looked at the two pages of notes he had copied from the records Mrs. Milbauer had shown him. The information hadn't actually surprised him. It was more a confirmation of what he had suspected since discovering the sale of the Hundred-Acre Wood.

He folded the pages, put them in the pocket of his jacket and zipped the pocket shut. Walking down the steps, he crossed the street and continued on across the green. He turned on Harbor Street and went to Jonah's Restaurant. At the small take-out counter, he ordered a tuna-salad sandwich on a roll and a container of black coffee. When they arrived, he paid for his order, took the paper bag that held the sandwich and coffee, and left the restaurant. The weather was exceptionally mild, and Jon decided to eat in a small community park that overlooked Scarborough Harbor. He walked the two blocks to the park.

To his surprise, the park was empty of people, and there were no cars in the graveled parking lot adjacent to the boat-launching ramp. He found a bench near the flagstone walk that ran along the seawall and sat down. There was a gentle breeze from the southwest, and Jon watched a lone sailboat as it tacked back and forth.

He set the paper bag beside him on the bench and opened it. He had just taken out the foil-wrapped sandwich when he felt a hand lightly touch his shoulder.

"May I join you?"

Jon turned, surprised.

"Don't worry," Madeleine Thoreau said. "It's a friend. Do you have a minute?"

"Certainly." He moved over to make room for her on the bench.

"Thanks." Madeleine sat down. She glanced at the sandwich. "I see I'm interrupting your lunch."

"I had business in town," Jon said, "so I picked up something at Jonah's. Since it is a nice day, I came over to the park. What brings you here?"

"You," she said matter-of-factly.

"Me?"

"I saw you as you left Colin's shop to visit the ever-lovely Mrs. Merriwell. When you came out of the town hall I followed you."

She looked around. "I'm glad the park is empty."

"Why?"

"It gives me a chance to say good-bye to you."

"You're going somewhere?"

"Yes. To Florida," Madeleine said. "I have friends in Orlando."

"Well, with winter coming, real estate must be going into a slow period in Scarborough."

She nodded, saying nothing, then lit a cigarette and watched the sailboat, which was now making its way out of the harbor.

"When are you leaving?" Jon asked.

"I have a plane at six."

"Today?"

"Today." She noticed his expression and smiled. "If it weren't for you, I'd be home packing now."

"How long will you be gone?"

"It depends."

"On what?"

"On whether certain local matters are resolved."

"I don't understand."

"Of course you don't." Madeleine turned back to him. "The fact is, my sweet innocent, Scarborough has become a rather nasty place these days."

"Is that why you're going to Orlando?"

"It's not because I have a pass to Disney World...Jon, the night you came to dinner, I told you to be careful. You haven't heeded my advice. You're still asking too many questions about too many matters that don't have anything to do with you."

"Somebody should."

"Maybe. But not you."

"What's going on here, Madeleine? I'd like to know."

"Don't ask me that. The truth is, I'm not sure."

"But you know a few things."

"Yes. A few. Which frighten me." She relit her cigarette and turned to watch the sailboat again.

"Enough to make you leave Scarborough?"

"Yes."

"The men I call the Scarecrows—they're involved in some sort of real estate scam, aren't they?"

"Jon, please...no more questions."

"Then I'll give you some answers. Today, in the town hall, I was checking certain land transactions over the last year. More than a dozen large properties have been sold— woods, fields, wetlands, even farms that have been in the same families for a century or more. Would you like to know the buyers?"

"I can guess…"

"They're faceless corporations like So-and-So Development or the No-Name Realty Consortium. And they're located in places all over the East Coast. I think the Scarecrows are behind those purchases."

Madeleine Thoreau stood up and tossed away her cigarette. "I have to go. My plane's at six."

"Are they, Madeleine?" He reached out, grabbed her hand, and held it. "Tell me."

"All I'll tell you, Jon, is that you can't make scarecrows without straws. And one more thing. It isn't religious conviction that brings Justin Kittridge to Reverend Rill's church every Monday morning about ten."

"What do you mean?"

Madeleine withdrew her hand. "Good-bye, Jon. Enjoy your lunch."

She turned and hurried from the park. Jon leaned back across the bench to watch her go.

It was then he saw the car moving quickly out of the parking lot. He knew it hadn't been there when he'd come into the park. The driver wasn't visible, but the car was the same black Lincoln Continental Jon had often seen parked in its own special spot behind the bank.

It belonged to Justin Kittridge.

THE CLOCK on the steeple of the Congregational church had been a gift of Asa Fordyce, a Scarborough sea captain, when the church was built in 1844, and even now residents swore by its accuracy.

At that moment on Monday morning, it read nine fifty-two. Jon checked his watch against it, then picked up a small pair of binoculars he sometimes used for birding, put them in his jacket pocket and climbed out of the Range Rover. He had parked a block away from the church. Near the corner stood a wooden shelter used by children while they waited for the school bus in bad weather. From it, Jon would be able to see both the front entrance of the church and the rear parking lot.

Jon walked to the shelter and stepped inside. He took the binoculars from his pocket and adjusted the focus until the church and parking lot came sharply into view. There, standing within the dark, rough structure, peering silently through the binoculars, he felt as if he were a hunter hiding in a duck blind waiting for his quarry to appear.

At exactly ten o'clock it did.

The clock on the church steeple was still chiming the hour, as the black Lincoln turned into the rear parking lot. It pulled in beside the only other car parked near the church: the Reverend Rill's white Honda wagon. Jon watched as Justin Kittridge appeared from the Lincoln, struggling with a brown leather attaché case. The banker walked quickly to the rear door of the church and pressed the bell. The door opened at once and Kittridge disappeared inside. Five minutes later, the door opened again and Kittridge reappeared. He strode to his car, tossed in the attaché case—which now seemed a good deal lighter—and got into the driver's seat. The car backed out of the spot, made a U-turn and drove out of the lot.

Jon returned the binoculars to his pocket, left the shelter, and walked to the street bordering the front of the church. Continuing along it, he looked up to the front doors and saw they had been left ajar. He headed up the walkway, climbed the steps and paused before the doors. Then, gradually, he opened one and slipped inside. From the interior of the church, he heard the voices of women. Standing at the doorway that led from the foyer to the nave, he noticed three women near the altar removing vases of flowers that had been placed there for the Sunday services the day before. To one side of the altar, Jon saw an open door. Beyond it, he knew, was a short stairway that connected with the church offices.

He went down the aisle leading to the door. Several of the women turned as he approached and nodded pleasantly. Jon nodded in return. Just before he reached the door, he stopped and studied the small alcove along the exterior wall that served as the church baptistry. The women had resumed their activity around the altar. Jon stepped through the open door and moved down the dozen steps.

At the bottom of the stairway was a door. He noticed it had several locks. Still, when he tried the knob, he found that the door was not locked. Opening it, he discovered he was in a narrow hall that ran the width of the church. At the far end, facing him, he saw the door that went out to the parking lot. It was the one Justin Kittridge had used earlier on his brief visit. What surprised Jon was that the window of the door was covered with steel-wire mesh and a police lock connected the door and doorframe. Beside the frame was a keypad that was presumably part of a security alarm. Considering that the Reverend Rill extolled trust in the innate honesty of his fellowman, he'd gone to a great deal of trouble to protect this section of the church.

Jon started slowly down the hall. There was a door marked ''Sexton'' and another that said ''Choir,'' plus several unmarked doors he guessed were closets. Beyond them was another door, again with a stout lock. It bore no identification, but Jon was sure it was the Reverend Rill's office. It was open several inches. From inside came the soft hum of a computer. Peering through the opening, Jon saw the Reverend Rill's back. The man was seated at the computer, studying a list of names and figures displayed on the computer screen.

Jon stepped back from the door and gave it two sharp taps. ''Reverend Rill?'' he called out.

Startled motion followed. There was the sound of paper

being torn out of the printer, crumpled and discarded, then rapid tapping of the keys.

"One minute," Rill called back. His voice had an anxious edge.

A short time later the minister stepped into the hall, his familiar smile again fixed on his face. Jon saw he was wearing chinos and a bright-red sweater with some sort of school crest.

He grasped Jon's hand. "Jon, what a surprise."

I'll bet, Jon thought.

"The front door of the church was open, so I came in," he said.

"Yes, yes. The ladies of the Altar Guild are working upstairs. Oh, please excuse the way I'm dressed. Not exactly my ecclesiastic vestments, but on Monday mornings I dress down. What can I do for you?"

"I'm sorry to bother you," Jon said. "But last summer you wrote me a note about doing some paintings of birds in the baptistry. You said there was no hurry, and frankly, I'd forgotten about it until the other day."

"Ah, yes—let me see." Obviously, Rill had forgotten it as well. "Ah, yes," he said again, "a member of the board of vestrymen suggested it. That is, for you to paint the Dove of Peace on the ceiling over the baptismal font, perhaps even a whole flock of them, their beaks open, as if smiling down on the infants whom I baptize there. If you could contribute your great talent in that way, the congregation and I would be most grateful."

"Do you know the dimensions of the space?"

Rill paused. "Not really. I could look them up and call you."

"Even better, if you have them in your office, I could jot them down and start on some preliminary sketches."

The Reverend Rill studied him before answering. Finally, he nodded. "I'm sure they're in the files. I can check."

He retreated into the office. Jon followed him.

Rill went to a metal file cabinet against a wall and pulled out a drawer. As he flipped through it, Jon looked around. Against one wall was a table containing the computer and a printer. He noticed the computer was still running, but the screen had been switched off. Beside it, the printer showed a "Ready" light. The rest of the office was as Jon had expected it to be: a wooden desk with a double gilt-edged frame containing some photographs of the minister's family, a small burl-wood crest behind it on the wall, several chairs, and, against another wall, a bookcase filled with books, Bibles in a variety of sizes, and neat piles of religious texts.

Rill plucked a file from the drawer and held it up. "Here we are." He placed the folder on the desk, opened it, and began thumbing through the contents.

"The baptistry...the baptistry... Yes, this is it." He picked up a pair of reading glasses lying next to the computer and scanned the open folder. "It's six feet across and four and a half deep. Floor-to-ceiling, it's eight feet. Let me write those figures down."

Rill took a pad and pencil from the desk and quickly jotted the dimensions of the space. He tore the paper from the pad and handed it to Jon.

As he did, there was a soft knock on the door. "Reverend?" a woman's voice asked.

"What is it, Mrs. Dern?" Rill called.

"Do you have a minute to come upstairs? The ladies and I have some ideas about arrangements for the Thanksgiving service."

"Shortly, Mrs. Dern." He looked at Jon. "Mr. Wilder was just going."

"You know, it occurred to me," Jon said, "I could do some quick sketches while you're upstairs with the women, and leave them here for you to think about."

"You mean, right now?" Rill asked.

"Yes. All I need are a few sheets of paper and a pencil." He added, "To be honest, it would save me time."

The minister regarded him without expression. "All right," he answered. "If it would help you. Otherwise..."

"It would," Jon said.

Rill took some blank computer paper from a box next to the printer and put it on the desk. "I shouldn't be any longer than five minutes," he told Jon.

He went to the door, but hesitated, giving Jon a final glance before he disappeared into the hall. Jon waited, listening. He heard Rill's footsteps going up the stairs, then voices, then more footsteps as Rill and the women walked near the altar area above.

Standing at Rill's desk, Jon took the pencil Rill had used to note the baptistry dimensions and made several rapid free-hand sketches of doves on the computer paper. The sketches took about two minutes. He added a few pencil strokes, then spread them out across the desk. Above, the sound of footsteps and of voices still filtered down.

Jon reached back to the door and eased it closed, making sure to leave it open several inches. Then he went to the computer and turned the switch that lit the screen. It glowed to life, orange against black, while the cursor pulsated in the upper left-hand corner.

On the keyboard, Jon typed HAVERMAN. He pressed "Enter," and waited. After a few seconds INVALID PASSWORD flashed onto the screen. He pressed "Escape." The screen went blank again.

He typed BUYLAND. "Enter." Clicks from the computer. INVALID PASSWORD. And "Escape."

It came to him. He called them by that name. Did they? He typed on the keys: S-C-A-R-E-C-R-O—

He was about to hit the final letter when the screen filled suddenly. He saw at once the name, "M. Brunhill," followed by a slash, followed by the initials "RKS." On the line below it said "11MM"—eleven million, Jon assumed—with lesser figures in parenthesis, and a date in late October of that year. The last line had a single name. The name was "Standish."

Scrolling down, Jon saw more names, all of them familiar from the town hall records he had read. As with the Haverman property, the seller and the buyer were both listed. Following them was a number—presumably the price of sale of the property—as well as smaller figures in parenthesis. Below each entry the name "Standish" had been added.

Jon was about to scroll down again when he heard footsteps on the stairs. He hit the "Escape" key, switched off the computer screen, and turned back to the desk—just as the door swung open and the Reverend Rill reappeared.

As he entered the office, Jon looked over his shoulder at him. "Done," he said.

"Done with what? Oh, yes. The drawings of the doves." He saw the sketches on the desk and joined Jon to look at them.

"Just between us," Rill went on, "I don't have the same fondness for doves most people do. Doves stand for peace, of course, and appear often in the Bible; Noah's olive branch and all of that. But frankly, I've always thought of doves as too naive for their own good, sticking their beaks in places where they shouldn't"

He glanced up at Jon. "Wouldn't you agree?"

"Not really," Jon said.

"No matter." The Reverend Rill gathered up the sketches. "Thank you for doing all these in so short a time."

"Let me know which ones you like."

"I will."

He led Jon to the office door and opened it for Jon to

leave. "The ladies of the Altar Guild are still upstairs. You can go out through the church, if you don't mind."

"Not at all."

"Good. And have a blessed and bountiful Thanksgiving, Jon."

"You, too," Jon said, and started toward the stairs.

The Reverend Rill stood at the office door until he heard Jon reach the upper landing of the stairs. Then he closed the door and locked it. Going to his desk, he tossed down the sketches of the doves and reached across them for the telephone.

AT LAST, the watercolor of the crow was done.

Jon stood up, stretched, and looked down at the drawing board. Since returning from his visit to the church, and except for a quick lunch, he had worked on it all afternoon, painting with a single-minded zeal.

Only when he glanced up at the windows of his studio did he realize how late it had become. The sun would set in less than twenty minutes. But it still left him time for a brief walk along the beach.

He cleaned and pointed his brushes, then closed the draperies and went downstairs. He grabbed his jacket from the hall closet, slipping into it as he walked out through the garage.

He got no farther than the turnaround when he saw Jake coming toward him down the driveway, a large brown oak leaf held between his teeth. He dropped the leaf in front of Jon.

Jon knelt and patted the dog's flank. "How about a walk on the beach, Jake?" The tail began wagging rapidly. "Come on."

Together, they went across the terrace and lawn, along the path of broken shells, and down onto the beach. To the west the sun had already descended through a low deck of

clouds and the light was rapidly diminishing. The water of
the sound was a flat calm and only one boat could be seen,
a fishing trawler anchored well offshore. Fifty yards beyond, a flock of herring gulls were scavenging close to the
tide line; Jon could hear their mewing squeals as they
pecked at the wet sand. Walking just ahead of Jon, the dog
sniffed at a piece of flotsam, then anointed it, leg raised.

Jon picked up another piece of driftwood, got Jake's attention, and lofted the stick. Jake sprinted after it and
caught it in midair. Pleased with himself, he trotted back.

"Good boy," Jon said, patting Jake again. He wrested
the stick out of the dog's jaw and raised his arm to throw
it a second time. Turning his head slightly, he saw a tuft
of sand fly up ten feet from where he stood. Less than a
second after it, a rifle crack reverberated in the air.

Jon stopped. Jake began to whine. *My God! Somebody's
shooting at us!* Jon realized.

"Come on, Jake!" he shouted, sprinting for the line of
beach grass, with Jake running to catch up.

Jon bounded through the grass and headed for the path.
Ahead of him, bits of seashells flew up as a bullet struck
them, followed by the sharp sound of the shot.

Jon fell into a low, running crouch. Jake passed him,
racing toward the open door of the garage. As Jon reached
them, he heard glass shatter in a window of the house.

Inside the garage, Jon leaned against the side of the
Range Rover, trying to catch his breath. Jake had taken
refuge underneath the car itself. Jon started on into the
house, when he remembered the car phone. He opened the
door of the Range Rover, grabbed up the mobile phone and
punched in 911.

The phone range twice. There was a click. "Scarborough
Police," a woman's voice said. "Is this an emergency?"

"You bet it is!"

"Who's calling, please?"

He gasped. "Jon Wilder."

"Sir, you're excited. Please try to relax."

"This is Jon Wilder," he managed between breaths. "I live at Plover Point."

"And what seems to be the problem, sir?"

"Someone's shooting! Someone's trying to kill me!" Struggling for calm, he said, "Is Lieutenant Lydecker there?"

"Just a moment, sir," the woman said.

Jon closed his eyes, trying to breathe evenly, fighting not to give into the panic that was rising in his chest.

Finally, he heard Lydecker's weary voice on the phone. "Hello, Jon. What's the problem now?"

"Larry, I'm being shot at."

"Where are you?"

"In my garage. I'm using the car phone."

"First of all, are you okay?"

"I'm out of breath is all. I wasn't hit."

"Tell me what happened." Lydecker asked.

"I was walking on the beach behind my house when bullets started hitting near me."

"Any idea of the shooter?"

"None," Jon said. "Wait—there was a fishing trawler offshore. The shots came from that direction."

"You're sure it was a trawler. Any name?"

"It was too far away," Jon said. "And getting dark."

"Okay," Lydecker acknowledged. "If the boat is out of Scarborough, I'll have some of the boys welcome her if she comes back to the town pier. I'll also notify the Coast Guard."

There was a pause. "Do you want me to send anybody down to watch the house?"

"No. But thanks," Jon said.

"All right. I'll call you back if I learn anything." Lydecker paused again. "Another thing, Jon…"

"What's that?"

"Don't get too near the windows in the house. Just in case."

JON HEEDED Lydecker's advice, trying at the same time not to acknowledge the fear he felt. He took a flashlight from the car and reentered the darkened house. Keeping the beam directed at the floor, he went from room to room, closing the draperies. Briefly, in his study, he had peered out at the water, wondering if he would see the running lights of boats. But there were none.

An hour passed before the telephone rang. Once more in his study, Jon answered it at once. "Hello?"

"You're still alive, at least," Lydecker said. "Sorry. A bad joke. Are you okay?"

"Shaky, but otherwise all right."

"Good. Listen, you were right. It was the fishing trawler that you saw."

"Tell me."

"The boat's name is the *Dandy D.* The owner is a guy named Willie Trask. He works as an independent; he's not part of the fleet. Besides, he's a lowlife, none of the other fishermen want anything to do with him."

"Tell me what happened."

"I sent a car down to the town pier like I told you. After a while, *Dandy D* comes racing into the harbor at full tilt. When the officers boarded the boat and talked to Trask, he admitted being in the vicinity of Plover Point, but denied knowing anything about a shooting."

"Naturally."

"*But—*" Lydecker's voice was triumphant. "*But* one of the officers found a cartridge casing from a twenty-two lying near the winches at the stern. When he asked Trask about it, Trask said, well, yes, he'd been trying out a rifle he just bought. But he swore he was taking target practice at stuff floating in the water. And he never shot in the direction of the shore.''

"Did you recover the gun?"

"Not exactly," Lydecker admitted.

"What do you mean, not *exactly?*"

"Not at all. Trask said the gun accidentally fell overboard when a wave hit.''

"Larry, the water was dead calm!"

"Maybe. But we still don't have a gun.''

"What will happen to Trask now?"

"He'll—uh—probably be fined.''

"Is that all? Fined for what?"

"Reckless discharge of a firearm near residential property.'' Lydecker sounded sheepish.

"That's ridiculous. He tried to kill me.''

"We don't know that, Jon.''

"*I* do.''

"It's still your word against his.''

"Wonderful," Jon said. "That really makes me feel great.''

"If it's any help to you, I don't believe Trask's story.''

"Good.''

"Jon…'' There was a lengthy silence, which took Jon by surprise. When Lydecker returned, his voice had a seriousness Jon had never heard before.

"Jon,'' the lieutenant repeated. "I'm sorry. You've been right about a lot of things. And I wasn't what you might call sympathetic the first couple times we talked.''

"That's true. But also, thanks for the apology.''

Lydecker grunted. "One more thing. I didn't mention. Trask's fishing boat is heavily in debt.''

"Of course. That's it!''

"That's what?''

"Find out who holds the notes against the debts. Maybe

that'll tell you who's behind the shooting. But I think I know."

"You do? Who?"

"The Scarborough Savings Bank," Jon said. "I'll also bet the loans were personally authorized by Justin Kittridge."

FIFTEEN

COLIN HIGHTOWER came up the front walk, managing his cane with one hand and carrying a large gift-wrapped bottle in the other. He was dressed in a green loden coat; on his head was an English shooting cap against which the rain pelted. Ignoring the dismal nature of the day, he sang lustily to the tune of "Over the River":

> *"From Scarborough green*
> *To Plover Point,*
> *And Jonathan's house I fly!*
> *His Thanksgiving fete*
> *Will be jolly, you bet,*
> *For Colin and Lor-e-lei!*

"Sorry," he confessed to Jon, as he ascended the front steps. "It was a feeble rhyme, but the best I could make up while driving here."

Jon stood at the open door. "Even so, you're the poet laureate of Scarborough."

"A dubious honor if there ever was one." Colin winced.

"At any rate, here's to a festive Thanksgiving," he went on, placing the gift-wrapped bottle in Jon's hand. "A magnum of Roederer Cristal, 1985. It was outrageously expensive. But equal to your culinary skills."

"Thank you." Jon moved aside as Colin stepped into the foyer. He placed his cane in the umbrella stand and took off his hat and coat. "I see from her car out there that the lovely Mrs. Merriwell has arrived."

Looking past Jon, his face brightened. "Ah, here she is now. Happy Thanksgiving, my dear."

Lorelei joined them, a bistro apron tied around her waist. She kissed him lightly on the cheek. "The same to you, Colin. Come into the living room. Jon has a wonderful big fire going in the fireplace."

"Lead me to it. The day has turned exceptionally raw and cold. I predict sleet." He retrieved his cane from the umbrella stand and started toward the living room.

As he entered it, Colin stopped, looked up at the beamed ceiling and swept his cane expansively about. "Behold the great room! Every time I stand in it, I feel I am the lord and master of the manor."

He seated himself in a leather-covered wing chair near the fire and rubbed his hands together. A moment later, Jake trotted in from the direction of the kitchen and lay down at Colin's feet.

"You see? I even have my faithful hound to keep me company." Colin patted the dog's head. Jake yawned and stretched his head between his paws.

"How about a drink?" Jon asked. "The usual?"

"Yes. Bourbon and branch water, if you please."

"Is Wild Turkey all right?"

Colin chuckled. "What other brand would I expect an ornithologist to serve? Particularly on Thanksgiving."

"Bourbon and branch water sounds like you've been Americanized, Colin," teased Lorelei.

"Good God, I hope not," Colin said. "I may be a naturalized citizen, but I haven't been neutralized—or, for that matter, neutered—by you Yanks as yet."

"One Wild Turkey coming up," Jon said, and left the room.

For almost an hour, over cocktails and hors d'oeuvres, the three chatted in the living room, while Jon and Lorelei made periodic visits to the kitchen to check on preparations for the dinner.

At four o'clock they moved into the dining room. Lit by wall sconces and two silver candelabra at each end of the table, the room glowed with a warmth and intimacy that belied its size. The table itself was covered with a damask tablecloth, set with gold-rimmed plates, antique silverware, and delicate crystal champagne flutes and tumblers.

As Colin drew near to the table, he sniffed the air and gave a sigh of sybaritic pleasure. "Ah, there's just the right amount of spices in the oxtail consommé you are about to serve. Furthermore, by lifting my nose thus, I will inform you of what else your splendid dinner promises. Roast turkey, of course, as well as tomato timbales, mashed sweet potatoes, soufflé of Hubbard squash, and Bibb-lettuce salad with Dijon-mustard vinaigrette."

"Colin, you're amazing!" Lorelei said. "That's absolutely right."

"Don't tell me you can smell all those dishes while they're still in the kitchen," Jon protested.

"With an olfactory sensibility as finely tuned as mine, indeed I can." Colin winked. "Also, when you were both in the living room, I happened to peek around the kitchen on my last trip to the loo."

He waved a hand. "So let the feast begin."

Jon poured the champagne, then began to carve the turkey, while Lorelei served the consommé and brought the accompanying dishes. When the three of them were seated, toasts were made. Colin insisted Jon provide a blessing, which Jon gave.

They had been dining leisurely and laughing often, Colin regaling them with stories, when they became conscious of a slight staccato tapping on the windowpanes. As they lingered over coffee, Jon stood, walked to the windows and moved apart the draperies with his hand.

"You were right about the weather, Colin," Jon informed them. "It's starting to sleet."

"Madeleine Thoreau is lucky, at least," Colin said. "I heard she went to Florida last week."

"Really?" Lorelei asked, surprised. "Wasn't it rather sudden?"

Jon said nothing.

"An interesting coincidence," Colin observed. He looked at Jon. "Last night I also heard that Lester Fitch and his wife are leaving Scarborough."

This time it was Jon who was surprised. "Where did you hear that?"

"From the assistant pharmacist," said Colin. "After I closed the shop, I stopped by the drugstore to pick up a few odds and ends. While I was there, I inquired as to how Fitch was getting on. The assistant said that as soon as Lester was well enough to travel, he and Muriel were going to their daughter's place in California."

"Did he say when they'd return?" Lorelei asked.

"Never," Colin said. "Lester plans to put the business up for sale. And their house as well."

Lorelei put down her coffee cup and looked at Jon. "What do you know about this? Anything?"

He shrugged. "Not really."

"Gallant Jon..." Lorelei smiled and patted his hand. "Forgive me, but I think you do. If you're afraid of offending my delicate feminine nature, don't be. Remember, I used to live in New York City. Nothing shocks me anymore."

"Lorelei is right, Jon," Colin agreed. "We're your friends. But neither one of us can be of help to you if you keep the information to yourself."

"I'll tell you this," Jon said. "Lester's heart attack may have been caused by a crow feather someone sent him in the mail."

"A crow feather?" exclaimed Colin. "How bizarre. Was there a note or anything?"

Jon shook his head. "No, nothing. But Ramsey and Benjamin also received one just before they died."

"But why the feather of a crow?" Lorelei asked. "Why not some other bird?"

"Perhaps because scarecrows are the nemesis of crows," mused Colin. "Now the crows are getting their revenge."

"There's something else that I can tell you," Jon admitted. "I saw Madeleine Thoreau the day she left."

"You talked to her that day?" asked Lorelei.

"I was sitting by the water having lunch when she appeared. She told me she was going to Florida that afternoon. She wanted everyone to think it was a vacation. But I know she was afraid."

"Of what?" Colin asked. "Of whom?"

"I don't know," Jon said. "But she made a puzzling remark when I brought up the Scarecrows. She said, 'You can't make scarecrows without straws.'"

"What on earth does that mean?" Colin snorted.

"Go-betweens," Lorelei told them. "My brother used to be in real estate. 'Straws' are the front men, the lawyers or businesses whose names appear in a transaction when the actual buyers of a property don't want their own revealed."

"I have a suggestion," Colin ventured, "that we have a final coffee—and if I may, Jonathan—an after-dinner brandy in the living room, while we continue this most fascinating conversation. Then I will be on my way."

Jon and Lorelei agreed.

Soon, seated again in the wing chair by the fire, with Jake sleeping at his feet, Colin took the brandy snifter Jon had brought to him. Lorelei sat opposite him on the sofa, sipping coffee.

With brandies for the two of them, Jon joined her. "Let me ask you both a question," he said, as he sat down.

"Does the name 'Standish' suggest anything to either one of you?"

"Miles Standish, the Puritan settler," Lorelei volunteered. "Remember the Longfellow poem? It was Miles Standish who was too shy to request Priscilla's hand in marriage. So he asked his friend, John Alden, to speak for him."

Colin nodded. "And being a forthright girl, Priscilla said, 'Speak for yourself, John.' And he did. Except..."

They looked at Colin. His fingers were now poised at his chin. "It just occurred to me that in addition to Priscilla's disappointed swain, there is another Standish I have read about. The Standish Corporation."

"What sort of corporation is it?" Jon inquired.

"It's a New England-based conglomerate that deals in large amounts of property for land development," Colin explained. "They also prefer to let others do the speaking for them, shall we say. Or, in their case, the negotiating. In various communities, where they've bought land, they've hired local citizens to do their dirty work: first, by informing Standish of the biggest and most choice properties; then, through a variety of means, legal and otherwise, pressuring the owners to sell out.

"My guess is Standish also found the straws," Colin added. "They act as signatories when the land purchases are made, so neither Standish nor the Scarecrows' names are ever used."

"All that makes sense," Lorelei agreed. "But that doesn't answer who killed Ramsey and Benjamin, and, in Lester Fitch's case, threatened to. Do you have any ideas, Jon?"

Jon thought of saying that he did. He also thought of a few people who might have a motive. But now wasn't the time to mention it.

Instead, he shook his head. "I really don't."

They sat for several moments, the silence broken only by the patter of the sleet against the windows of the living room.

Finally, Colin gave a massive sigh and hoisted himself up from his chair. "Alas, my friends—I should be on my way. I fear the condition of the country roads with all this sleet. I hope you'll both excuse me."

"Certainly," Jon said.

He and Lorelei rose also and followed Colin to the foyer. While Lorelei helped Colin with his coat and hat, Jon opened the front door. The light that spilled out from the foyer showed the sleet was mixing with light rain again.

Nevertheless, Colin brandished his cane as if challenging the elements. "Onward I go, undaunted by the inclemency of this November night!"

He turned and looked at Lorelei. "As for you, my dear, a wise decision would be to remain here until the morning. Isn't that right, Jon?"

Lorelei laughed. "Colin, you're wicked."

"No. Merely observant," Colin said. "When I see a couple as ideally suited for each other as the two of you, I will do everything I can to foster their conjunction."

Jon glanced at Lorelei and saw that she was blushing. Colin saw it, too, and grinned. He leaned and kissed her on the cheek, then shook Jon's hand.

"Thank you—thank you both," he said. "The dinner and the company were as delicious as I knew they would be."

Giving a final flourish with the cane, Colin started down the steps and made his way along the walk. Lorelei and Jon waited at the door until Colin's car had puttered up the drive and disappeared into the night.

"I should go, too," Lorelei said, when Jon had closed the door. "But first, I'll help you clean up."

"There's nothing much to do. I'll put things in the dishwasher."

"Of course you won't," she scolded him. "We didn't drink Colin's glorious champagne from paper cups. And your plates and crystal ought to be hand-washed and dried."

"Living alone, I guess I've forgotten some of the pleasures of housekeeping," Jon admitted wryly.

"Living alone, I hope those are the only pleasures you've forgotten." Lorelei smiled. "Come on, while we're working in the kitchen we can treat ourselves to the last of the champagne."

AN HOUR LATER, Lorelei untied her apron and looked up at the wall clock. "Almost eight. I really ought to go."

Jon put down the dishtowel and started with her to the foyer.

"Will you be opening the shop tomorrow?" he asked her, as he reached into the front closet for her coat.

"Oh yes. I'm told Thanksgiving weekend is very popular with tourists."

He helped her on with her coat, then took out a jacket and put it on. "Let me go with you to your car."

"Oh, please don't, if it's still sleeting."

"Let's find out." He opened the front door. The sleet had ended and the rain was intermittent, mingling with fog.

"It's warming up," Jon said. "You shouldn't have a problem driving home."

They walked together to her car and Jon opened the driver's door. But instead of getting in, Lorelei lingered.

"Thank you, Jon," she said. "Thank you for tonight— and for a lot of things. When I moved to Scarborough, I felt very much alone. And afraid, too, of where my life was leading me. Among other things, I'm very glad it led me to you."

"So am I."

She put her hands to his face and kissed him. Then she climbed into her car. "Happy Thanksgiving," she called, lowering the window. She waved good-bye and reached down to start the engine.

There was a grinding sound, followed by silence. Lorelei frowned and turned the key again. More grinding. Finally, she stopped.

"I had a problem with it yesterday," she said. "The mechanic said he'd look at it tomorrow."

Jon leaned down to the open window. "Let me drive you home."

"I hate to ask you. Do you mind?"

"Not at all. I can also pick you up tomorrow morning and drive you to the shop," he said. "On my way home, I'll stop at the auto repair place and have them send a tow truck here to get your car."

"That really would help," Lorelei admitted, as she stepped out of her car. "But I'll agree on one condition."

"What's that?"

"Tomorrow morning, when you stop by to pick me up, you'll let me make us breakfast. Deal?"

Jon smiled. "Deal."

THE DRIVE TO Scarborough took longer than both of them expected. The rain and warmer temperatures had washed away some but not all of the patches of ice that had accumulated on the roads. The fog had also become heavier, reducing visibility on the wet, slippery asphalt surfaces. They were approaching the town green when Lorelei looked over.

"Since we're here," she asked, "would you mind making a small detour and drive by the antiques shop?"

"Not at all." Jon made a circuit of the green and turned down Harbor Street.

"At an estate sale last week, I bought a charming antique Victorian breakfast set," Lorelei explained. "I've been wanting you to see it. The pieces all have painted birds; they're mostly English—wood larks, hoopoes, tree creepers, birds like that."

"Yes. Those are English names."

They moved slowly along Harbor Street. The storefronts on both sides were dark. Close to the water, the fog was virtually impenetrable; the streetlights little more than dim pinpoints piercing through thick gauze.

Jon slowed the car. "I'll stop in front of the shop and wait for you. Is that all right?"

"Fine. The breakfast set is in my office closet. I'll get it and be back in a sec."

Leaning forward to the windshield, Jon saw the hanging sign above the door that said "Philander Webb's Antiques." He eased the Range Rover over to the curb and stopped.

"How's this?" he asked.

"Great."

"Would you like a flashlight? The alley leading to the office door looks pretty dark."

"Oh, no, don't take the trouble," she assured him. "I'll turn on the light as soon as I get in."

She jumped out of the car and hurried up the alley that led to the rear door. Jon shifted in his seat to wait, looking idly in the direction of the darkened shop.

A moment later, light shone from the office as Lorelei stepped into it.

Another moment.

Then her screams of terror tore the night apart.

JON BOLTED from the car, raced up the alley, and flung open the door.

The thing came at him at once, ripping a gash in his

scalp. Instinctively, Jon's arm came up to ward off his attacker. It shrieked, swooped away, and caromed off a wall. Jon saw it now—a huge crow, black eyes bright with fear, beak open, ready to tear flesh. Its wings beat wildly in panic, as the bird dashed into one wall, then another. Spread, the wings spanned almost the width of the small room.

"My God! My God! Get it out of here!" Lorelei sobbed. She crouched in a far corner, her hands splayed across her face.

Jon grabbed the nearest object, a newspaper lying on the desk, and swung it, hitting the crow as it came at him again.

The crow flew up and struck the ceiling light, breaking one of the fluorescent tubes, which rained down shards of glass. Diving, the bird's tail hit the corner of a metal cabinet, loosening black feathers that went flying in the air.

Jon swung the newspaper again, and at the same time kicked open the door behind him with his foot.

Sensing freedom, the crow flew at him; Jon jumped away and the bird shot out into the night.

"It's gone," Jon said, struggling for breath.

At once, Lorelei was in his arms, her head pressed hard against his chest.

"It was horrible!"

He held her. She gave way to sobs again.

"It's all right," he told her quietly. "The crow is gone."

"It was so horrible. The moment I turned on the light it flew at me."

"Come on, sit down."

He grabbed the desk chair with one hand and brought it to her. Still shaking, Lorelei sank into it.

"Take a deep breath," he said. "Try to relax."

Lorelei stared up at his face. "You're bleeding!"

"It grazed me with its beak." He touched his forehead,

felt the sticky wetness, and looked at his fingers. They were red with blood.

"Sit there," he instructed. "Let me get you some water."

He stepped into the tiny bathroom, dampened some paper towels, and cleaned and dried the wound. Then he filled a paper cup with water and brought it to Lorelei.

She took it with both hands. "Thank you." As she drank, he saw they were still trembling.

Jon looked around the office. It was chaos. Papers were strewn everywhere. A red-and-yellow coffee mug lay smashed in pieces near the wastebasket. Crow feathers were scattered on the floor and cabinets, from the bird's desperate efforts to escape.

"More water?" Jon asked Lorelei, when he saw the paper cup was empty.

"No." She shook her head. "No, thank you."

"Can you tell me what happened?" he said gently.

She took a long, deep breath. "When I came up the alley, I disarmed the security system, then unlocked the door. As soon as I turned on the light, it flew at me. That's when I screamed."

Jon stepped to the door. One of the two window panels had been broken and glass from it lay on the floor. Lorelei watched as he ran his hand around the opening.

"Did the crow break the glass?" she asked him.

"No." Jon shook his head. "Otherwise, pieces of glass would be in the alley. Whoever did this broke the window from the outside, then probably pushed the bird in through the opening."

"But why?"

"Among other things, they wanted to frighten you."

"They succeeded."

She held up the paper cup. "Maybe I will have some

more water. If you don't mind. Right now, I'm not sure my knees would get me to the sink and back again.''

He nodded, took the cup and refilled it in the bathroom.

When he returned, she was kneeling on the floor, gathering up papers and pieces of the broken coffee mug.

Jon knelt down beside her and also began picking up papers and black feathers from the floor. The papers he formed into a pile, the crow feathers he put into the wastebasket.

Still kneeling, he moved to the area near the door and gingerly collected bits of glass from where the window had been broken. Momentarily, his fingers paused, then closed again. His hand moved to a jacket pocket.

He saw Lorelei watching him and stood. ''Before we do any more cleaning up,'' he said, ''we should report this to the police.''

Lorelei stood also, holding the back of the chair for support. ''What will I tell them? There was a break-in by a bird?''

''Tell them what you told me,'' Jon said. ''After that, I'll put something up to cover the space where the window is missing. Do you have any small pieces of wood I can use?''

''There are some scraps of plywood in the basement. I keep a hammer and some nails in the closet here.''

''Good. After that we're going back to my place. You can have the guest room.''

''Thank you, but I'll be all right once I get home.''

''I don't want you in your house tonight,'' he told her simply. ''And certainly not alone.''

She nodded, then managed a half-smile. ''Considering the circumstances, I accept.''

SIXTEEN

HE WAS AWARE of her presence before she spoke, and knew that she'd been watching him as he took two mugs from the cupboard.

"Good morning," Lorelei said finally.

"Good morning." He held up an empty mug. "How about some coffee to begin the day?"

"Love some." She came into the kitchen wearing a man's green tartan bathrobe, belted at the waist.

Jon filled both mugs and handed one to her. "The mug isn't as pretty as the one you lost last night, but it's the best I can do. How about breakfast?"

"Maybe something. I'm not all that hungry, honestly."

"Grapefruit juice and a bran muffin?"

"Fine." She held the mug up to her lips and sipped from it slowly.

Jon found two glasses for the juice, took a quart container from the refrigerator and filled them.

"Were you able to sleep at all last night?" he asked.

"Yes. But my dreams were terrible."

"I'm not surprised."

"The room was very comfortable, though. It's so light and airy. Thank you for letting me have it. Also, that tranquilizer you left for me really knocked me out."

She gave a brief, ironic smile. "Here we are, cohabiting, as Colin would say, and I'm out like a light."

Jon smiled also. "So—would you like one muffin or two?"

"One's plenty."

He nodded, put the muffins on a plate, and placed them

in the microwave. Lorelei leaned against the countertop and watched him as he worked.

"About last night," Lorelei said, "I'm sorry for what happened at the shop."

"There's nothing to be sorry for."

"I mean, for getting so—what shall I say—over-wrought."

"You had a right to be upset. It must have been a terrifying moment, having the crow come at you like that."

"There's something I didn't tell you," she said after a moment. "I thought of it the day you showed me your watercolor painting of the crow."

"Oh?"

"When I was five years old, I had a wonderful white kitten that I loved so much. One day, while I was playing with her on the lawn, she found an opening in the fence. She got through it and began to run. My father heard me crying and calling the cat's name; he came out of the house and we started searching for her everywhere…

"We finally found her on the road a short way from our house. A car had killed her, probably, and other cars… Anyway, when we arrived, crows were all around her body, tearing, picking, pulling…"

Lorelei paused and bowed her head. "So you see, crows and I are not the best of friends."

The microwave sounded. Without a word, she carried the juice glasses to the breakfast room beside the kitchen, while Jon distributed the muffins on the plates.

As they sat down at the table, he said, "Yesterday, you mentioned you had friends in New York City who've been after you to spend a weekend."

"Yes. They've suggested going to the theater, or out to dinner, things like that."

"What about calling them and asking if you can come

today?'' Jon asked. ''And maybe stay with them a few days after that.''

''I'm sure they wouldn't mind, they've been great friends, but—''

''After what happened last night, I think you're safer out of Scarborough for a while.''

Lorelei nodded. ''Actually, the idea occurred to me. The more I thought about last night, the more afraid I am of being in my house alone, or even in the shop. But yesterday, I also promised you I'd help you any way I could.''

''It'll help me most to know you're not in danger here.''

''But I also thought maybe last night was a prank.''

''It was no prank. Somebody went to a great deal of trouble to put that crow inside your office.''

''Who?''

''My guess is it's the same person who killed Rod Ramsey and Bernie Benjamin.''

''But I'm not one of the Scarecrows. Why should I suddenly be a target?''

''That's what I don't understand. Is there somebody you've angered? A shop customer or anyone?''

''No one I can think of.''

''But the crow is the connection.''

''What do you mean?''

''Frankly, I'm not sure.''

He rose, picked up his coffee mug and gestured toward hers. ''How about more coffee? While I'm getting it, you can give your New York friends a call.''

''All right.'' She reluctantly agreed.

Lorelei went to the telephone as Jon refilled both mugs. From what he overheard of her end of the conversation, her friends were pleased to have her visit them. Returning to the table, Lorelei confirmed it.

''They were delighted,'' she said as she sat down. ''But what about my car?''

"First thing this morning, I called the mechanic. The tow truck will be here about nine-thirty. They'll hold on to the car until you're back."

"Is there a train I can take to New York later?"

"There's an express that stops in Scarborough at noon," Jon said. "After breakfast, I'll drive you to your house, so you can change and pack some things. And don't worry about the shop. The police will keep an eye on the shop and your house both, and I'll get a glazier to replace the broken window in the door."

"Thank you," Lorelei said. "Again, thank you for so much."

She looked at him curiously. "About last night. When you were picking up things near the door, you hesitated over something. Then you put it in your pocket. What was it?"

Jon took a sip of coffee. "Oh, just another feather."

"More feathers?" she asked.

"Yes."

From the driveway turnaround came the noise of a vehicle arriving. Jon looked at his watch.

"Nine-thirty," he said. "That must be the tow truck. You finish your coffee. I'll go and talk with them."

He drained his mug, then rose and left the room.

JON WALKED UP the alley that extended the length of Lorelei's shop. The piece of plywood he had nailed to the door the night before was still in place. He tapped in the code numbers on the security keypad. When the green light came on, he unlocked the door.

Although the day was bright with sunshine, the office itself was dark; it gave Jon a malevolent foreboding, as if something were about to spring at him in the same way the crow had surprised Lorelei last night. He switched on the overhead light. It added little to the gloom, until he looked

up and remembered the bird had smashed one of the fluorescent tubes.

He locked the door to the alley, then opened the other
door that led out to the showroom. Everything was just as
Jon remembered it. The shelves, the display cases, and the
larger antique pieces—all seemed undisturbed.

Jon turned back to the office and went to Lorelei's desk.
He looked up the number of the local glazier and made an
appointment for two o'clock that afternoon. The second call
was to the security company that monitored the shop's
alarm system. He explained that he wanted to install sen-
sors on all the windows of the shop, so that they would
react to sounds of a forced entry, such as breaking glass.

Scanning the floor, the desktop, bookcase and file cabinets, he saw bits of paper still scattered here and there.
Between the bookcase and the wall he found, rolled up, a
wall calendar, with each month displaying prettified New
England scenes. The calendar had been sent compliments
of the Scarborough Savings Bank. Below the bank's name
were the words "Welcome to Serenity."

Jon moved into the showroom and saw two elderly
women standing on the sidewalk staring in. At the sight of
him, they started for the door. He shook his head, mouthing
the word "Closed," and pointed to the hanging sign. Both
women gave a disappointed look and walked away.

Now Jon began a slow circuit of the room. In a rear
corner, he finally found what he was looking for: a set of
shelves displaying cooking implements. On the top shelf,
set on edge, were a half dozen tin pie pans. One in particular caught his attention. He took it from the shelf and
studied it. In the center of the pie tin were the words "Table
Talk—Flaky Crust Pie." The tin probably dated from the
1930s or 1940s. Strictly speaking, it wasn't an antique, but
it would be sufficient for his purposes.

He turned it over and saw a small white sticker with the

price. Carrying the pie tin into the office, he wrote out a check for the amount, folded it, and tucked it in the corner of the desk blotter, along with the price sticker and a short note to Lorelei saying he'd purchased the tin. In the office closet he found a stack of folded paper bags, took one, opened it and put the tin inside.

He closed and locked the door to the showroom, then glanced around the office one last time. The glazier would be there at two, the service technician from the alarm company an hour later. Rather than returning home, he decided he would stay in town, visit Colin, and then come back to Lorelei's shop to meet with the repairmen. Later, after he got home, Jon would devise a plan of what exactly needed to be done. Today was Friday, the day after Thanksgiving. All local and state government offices were closed. That frustrated him. He would have to wait three days, until Monday, before he could take the next necessary steps.

Still carrying the pie tin in the paper bag, Jon left the office and stepped into the alley. He locked the door and reset the security alarm, then walked down the alley to the street and turned toward the woodworking shop.

Colin was working at his rolltop desk when Jon arrived. As Jon opened the door, Colin reacted to the sound of the bell.

"Thank God, it's you. I was afraid it might be Abigail Stives." The man gave a deep sigh of relief.

"I gather you're not looking forward to seeing her."

"Indeed not," Colin said. "Over the years she's been a reasonably good customer. But she's becoming more eccentric every day. And I might add, more macabre. This morning she called and asked if she could come and talk to me about refurbishing what she refers to as a 'family piece.'"

"Did she say what the piece was?"

"A coffin. She told me a great-uncle had had it made

for himself to spare his family the expense after he died. The trouble was, he was a passenger on the *Titanic* when the ship went down and the poor man's body was never found."

"How does Mrs. Stives intend to use it?" Jon asked him.

"Who knows? A coffee-table base. A planter box in her solarium. Perhaps she plans to sleep in it herself.

"To a more pleasant subject," Colin went on. "I was about to call you to reiterate my gratitude for yesterday's Thanksgiving dinner."

He peered at Jon over his half-glasses with an impish look. "And I hope Mrs. Merriwell took my advice about last night."

"She spent the night," Jon said. "But in the guest room, and not for the reasons that you think."

Briefly, he told Colin about driving Lorelei to the antiques shop later, and of her confrontation with the crow.

When he was finished, Colin shook his head. "Outrageous. And Lorelei? How is she today?"

"She has friends in New York City, so I suggested she go and stay with them for a few days."

"I'm glad you did." Colin removed his glasses and began wiping them with a tissue, meditatively.

"It's an execrable situation," he resumed. "A mad killer runs amok in Scarborough, and no one, not the police, nor anyone, has the least notion who it is."

"On the contrary," Jon said, "I think I do."

"You *do?*"

"But I need to learn a few more things before I'm sure."

"Don't tell me it's Gus Schiller after all."

"It's not Gus Schiller."

"Who then?" Colin lifted his cane and tapped the floor with it impatiently. "Tell me, at least, do you have any clues, or is this just surmise?"

"I have a clue."

"*One* clue?"

"Several, actually."

"Yet on that meager basis, you are suggesting you can solve the murders of two men, as well as all the other nastiness that's going on."

"Yes."

"Forgive me, dear boy, but remember what I said last week about counting chickens before they hatch."

Jon gave Colin a wry look. "Ironic you should mention chickens," he told his friend.

"One other thing," said Colin. "I remembered where I first saw that pretty dark-haired girl who was leaving the antiques shop."

"Oh?"

"She was one of this year's help who worked the roadside stand at Bellkirk's farm."

"GOOD MORNING Mr. Wilder," said Mrs. Milbauer. "Did you have a good Thanksgiving?"

"Yes, fine," Jon said. "And yours?"

"Wonderful. Our grandchildren were with us. They call it Turkey Day. Did you know Ben Franklin wanted to make the turkey the national bird of the United States?"

Jon nodded quickly, eager to get to the reason for his visit. But the woman burbled on.

"My husband says if such a thing had happened, we'd all be eating eagle for Thanksgiving now." Her high-pitched laughter rippled through the office. "I think that's just so funny, don't you? Eagle for Thanksgiving."

"Yes," Jon answered pleasantly. "Now I wonder if you'd help me check some additional town records."

Mrs. Milbauer adjusted her glasses and assumed a businesslike demeanor. "Yes, indeed. What do you want to look at this time?"

"Several things. Again, the list of land sales over the

past year. The town property map that includes Cemetery Road. Also, an application that may have been made to the Buildings Department to add on to an existing structure.''

''Any original copy would be in the department offices upstairs,'' Mrs. Milbauer informed him. ''But I can have them fax a duplicate here if it exists. Do you have a date?''

''Sometime this year, I'd say. But I can give you the name of the applicant.''

''Yes. That would help.''

Jon took a piece of paper from a scratch pad on the counter, wrote a name, and gave the paper to her.

Mrs. Milbauer looked at it, and raised her eyes in recognition. ''I'll call over with this name and see if they have anything.''

''Thank you.''

''Meantime, come into the Records Room and I'll get the other things you want.''

He did as she suggested and followed her into the large adjacent room filled with file cabinets and floor-to-ceiling metal shelves. While Jon settled himself at a wooden table, Mrs. Milbauer moved about the room, now and then climbing a step stool to pull loose-leaf binders from the shelves.

When everything Jon had requested had been placed on the table in front of him, he unfolded the property map for the section of Scarborough that showed Cemetery Road. Mounted on thick cardboard, the map was an enlargement of an aerial photograph, with each property outlined in black. Within the boundary lines the name of the owner was printed in block letters, which were also black. Jon picked up the list of recent land sales and read down it, at the same time cross-checking them with the information on the map. As he suspected, several large tracts of land surrounding one existing piece of property had been sold off during the year. On the other hand, that single *unsold* property bore the name of the same owner it had had for years.

Looking down at it on the map, the land appeared to Jon a threatened yet defiant island in a sea of change.

"Yoo hoo, Mr. Wilder." Waving a sheet of paper, Mrs. Milbauer called to him from the doorway of the room. "Here's a fax of the building application that you asked about. You were right. It had to do with adding an extension to a building."

She brought the copy of the application to him and Jon read it through. The official stamp of the department and the building inspector's signature below it showed that the application had been approved on June 12 of that year. Three days later, the approval had been reversed and the application denied. The denial had been by executive order of the town's first selectman—Roderick Ramsey. The denial had been upheld on appeal by the zoning board.

It was almost noon when Jon rose stiffly from the chair. He organized the material Mrs. Milbauer had given him, then walked out of the Records Room. In the outer office, he waited until the clerk had completed filling out a marriage license for a young couple, who stood gazing moonily at one another.

When the couple left, Jon moved toward the door, thanking Mrs. Milbauer as he went.

"Anytime," she warbled back.

He halted. "Come to think of it, there's another question that I meant to ask. Do you have official records concerning the restaurants in Scarborough?"

"I have some, yes," the woman said. "The town sanitarian inspects them every year, of course. Otherwise, the state Department of Health Services has the responsibility for licenses and all. Those records would be up in Hartford. I can give you the address."

"That would help," Jon said.

She wrote the information on a pad, tore off the paper, and handed it to Jon.

He took it, thanked her again, and quickly left the office.

FROM THE glove compartment of the Range Rover, Jon took a road map of Connecticut. He unfolded it and ran his index finger along the route to the state capital. It was the broad and little-used Route 9 that went north from the turnpike, connecting with another interstate that led directly into Hartford. When he had time to spare, Jon preferred the old road that meandered along the west bank of the Connecticut River, passing towns like Tylerville and Higganum. But this was not a day for leisurely sightseeing.

An hour later, driving faster than the speed limit allowed, Jon reached the Hartford city line. He rounded Lafayette Circle and made his way along the edge of Bushnell Park, until he found the street he had been looking for.

It was located in what had been one of the city's fashionable neighborhoods a century ago. In those years, Hartford's most wealthy and respected citizens lived in the great houses, many of them Victorian in style, that graced both sides of the thoroughfare. Since then, the city had endured hard times and many changes. No longer did carriages glide underneath the canopy of sycamores that lined the street. Hitching posts had been replaced by parking meters.

Many of the homes had been demolished to make room for apartment complexes and shopping malls. Some that had survived had been converted into office buildings for the state. While a few maintained a vestige of their elegant exterior, their insides had been gutted and replaced by a labyrinth of small, cubicle-like rooms bearing bureaucratic names, such as "The Department of Health Services, Food Hygiene—Commercial."

It was this office that Jon sought.

He found a parking space opposite the building, crossed the street and headed up the cracking concrete walk. Inside, he discovered that the once-spacious rooms and broad, high-ceilinged halls had been converted into a maze of offices hardly bigger than large closets, and linked by barren, twisting corridors. Jon paused in the small foyer and studied the directory. The office he was looking for was on the second floor. The small elevator just beyond the foyer had a hand-printed "Out of Order" sign taped against the door. So he walked up the stairs.

He found the office down the hall and went inside. The room was windowless and claustrophobic, made even smaller by the rows of cardboard file boxes stacked against one wall. The furnishings were standard governmental issue: a metal desk and chair, two metal armchairs facing it, and a metal table to one side. Two metal trays marked "In" and "Out" sat on the desk. "Out" seemed almost empty; "In" was overflowing with a pile of papers, folders and inter-office memos that appeared in danger of imminent collapse.

No one was in the office, but a gray polyester jacket hung over the back of the desk chair. Jon sat down opposite the desk to wait.

A moment later, a short, balding man in his mid-fifties entered, sipping on a plastic cup. Jon's presence caught him by surprise.

"Oh, sorry," the man said quickly. "I didn't know somebody was here."

He went behind the desk and sat down. "You're the salesman about the file cabinets, yes?"

"No," Jon said.

"Too bad." The man waved the cup in the direction of the boxes piled at the wall. "I'm up to my keister in old files and no place to store them. If I had my way, I'd burn 'em all."

He sipped again and looked at Jon. "So tell me who you are and what you want."

"My name is Jon Wilder."

"Wilemer?"

"Wilder." Jon spelled it. "And I'd like some information."

"Are you a lawyer or a reporter?"

"No."

"Good. That helps. Go on."

"I'd like to know if a certain restaurant owner filed a complaint this year against one of his food suppliers. Would that information be on file here?"

"It's not about that botulism case in Bethel, is it?"

"No. The restaurant's in Scarborough. The complaint was probably filed sometime in the fall."

"You got the name of the complainant and the restaurant?"

"Bernard Benjamin. The restaurant was called Bernie's Bar B-Q Barn."

"And the name of the accused?"

Jon reached in his pocket. "It's written on that piece of paper," he answered, passing it across the desk.

The man read it. "Okay. I'll see what I can find. If it's on file and you want a photocopy, it'll cost ten dollars."

"Yes, I would."

The man left the office. He returned ten minutes later, carrying a sheet of paper, which he gave to Jon.

"You were right," the man said. "The complaint was filed on the first day of October. We sent an inspector down to check out the food supplier's business and his product. To find out if what he sold the restaurant was contaminated, things like that."

"And what were the results?"

"Zilch. Nothing. There were no grounds for a complaint, as far as our inspector found. Why the restaurant owner filed it in the first place, I can't understand."

He pointed to the paper he had given Jon. "It's all in the report."

"Thanks," Jon said. He took out his wallet and produced a ten-dollar bill.

The man took it. "I'll give you a receipt."

The money disappeared below the desk and the man began to write out a receipt in triplicate, stamping each copy as he did.

"Bernie's Bar B-Q Barn, Scarborough," the man said, as he stamped. "Come to think of it, my wife and I stopped there for lunch last summer on our way up to Rhode Island. The owner was a fat guy, big, with a white hat."

"That's right."

"I remember he was a real character, glad-handing everybody in the place." The man shook his head and separated the receipt forms, handing Jon the yellow copy.

"So is it still as popular as it was then?" he went on. "People were lined up at the door."

"Not anymore," Jon said. "The restaurant burned down a couple weeks ago."

"You mean the whole place was charbroiled?" He laughed at his own joke.

"So what about the owner, Bernie What's-his-name?" the man asked Jon. "Will he rebuild?"

"Bernie Benjamin died in the fire," Jon said simply.

The man still looked at Jon, but remained silent. Jon thanked him, put the copy of the receipt and the complaint report into his pocket, and left the office.

Crossing the street to where the Range Rover was parked, he checked his watch. It was two-fifteen.

There was one final stop Jon had to make that afternoon and he wanted to be certain it was made in daylight. That gave him about two hours.

He reached into the pocket of his trousers, took out the car keys and started to unlock the door. To his surprise, he saw the hand that held the keys was trembling.

DRIVING BACK to Scarborough, Jon asked himself a dozen times if what he'd done—and, more important, what he was about to do—was right. He knew the murderer's identity. Now he was sure of it. The next step, therefore, was to act as a responsible citizen *should* act under the circumstances: contact the police, lay out the evidence, and withdraw in safety while the designated representatives of law and order did their job.

But he would not.

Once before he'd gone to the police with certainty, he thought, of who the killer was. He had been wrong.

He wouldn't let it happen for a second time. Only after he'd secured the final bits of evidence he needed to confirm the killer's guilt would Jon believe he had done all he could.

Then only would he go to the police.

IT WAS almost four by the church-steeple clock when Jon reached the Scarborough town green. He rounded it and headed east. After traveling for several miles, he turned north onto Cemetery Road. It was another mile and a half before he passed the old graveyard. In the fading light, long shadows from the tombstones stretched out mournfully in rows like silent legions of the dead.

Soon, along the right, Jon saw the ancient beech trees and, beyond them, on the hill, the home of Abigail Stives.

He brought his eyes back to the road again.

Then, as he approached the house where Mrs. Epsom and her husband lived, he slowed the car. At the roadside Mrs. Epsom was collecting mail from the postal box. She noticed the Range Rover and waved.

He waved back as he passed by, then accelerated and continued on.

When he finally slowed the car again, it was before a

grove of pine and cedar trees that he remembered from the last time he'd been on the road with Lorelei.

A twisting path of tire tracks, just wide enough for the Range Rover, led into it. Beyond the trees the farm itself began, separated by a barbed-wire fence. Jon turned onto the path and maneuvered the car in among the trees as far as he could go.

It was exactly as he hoped. From where he'd stopped, he had a clear view of the farmhouse and the buildings behind it. He reached under the seat, pulled out the binoculars and put them to his eyes. Magnified, the house seemed even more forlorn than Jon recalled. The clapboard siding that had once been white was now a chalky gray. Thin, listless curtains sagged behind the windows of the upstairs rooms.

One window of a first-floor room was boarded, the others showed no more than bare glass. The roof of the front porch listed slightly at one end, supported by a two-by-four where a wooden column had once stood.

Shifting the binoculars and readjusting the focus, Jon looked at the unpainted barn and long, low poultry building that stood behind the house.

Returning to the farmhouse, he moved the glasses slowly down along the rutted dirt driveway that connected the house and the road. The gate had been left open. Looking to one side of it, he saw the wooden farm stand, its shutters folded down across the front. Beneath them was the sign advertising eggs, poultry and farm produce.

That afternoon, on the drive back from Hartford, Jon had recalled Colin Hightower's remark about the girl, Gina, having worked the stand last summer. In past years, it had been run by teenage girls, students from the local high school. Once Labor Day arrived, they disappeared, except for one or two who filled in on September weekends.

But Jon also remembered driving past the farm in mid-

October and noticing the road stand was still open. He hadn't stopped; he hadn't even looked to see who stood behind the counter. Now he was certain that he knew.

Jon stowed the binoculars underneath the seat. He backed out onto the road and headed slowly toward the dirt drive that provided access to the farm. Turning in, he jounced along the ruts and parked on a flat stretch of bare ground near the front steps of the farmhouse.

He stepped out of the Range Rover. Glancing briefly at the barn and poultry house, he saw now what he could not spot earlier through the binoculars. Parked on the far side of the barn was the old white van. Until last summer, Jon had been one of the people to whom Bellkirk had delivered eggs. Then, after a routine physical exam, Jon's doctor had suggested eggs be discontinued, and he had switched to an egg substitute instead. Even so, the man now and then supplied farm produce or a roasting chicken on request. Often the delivery was made through the garage. In late October, Jon recalled, he had brought a roaster and a bag of apples to Jon's house. It had been a few days before Halloween.

Jon reached around to the backseat of the Range Rover and picked up the paper bag. He stepped out of the vehicle, carrying the bag, and walked up the steps of the house to the front porch. As he crossed it, he could hear the joists sigh beneath his feet. From where he stood, the house appeared deserted. The porch was now totally in shadow, as was the house itself. Yet no lights were visible inside.

To one side of the door was the doorbell, but it had been painted over long ago and when Jon pressed on it, it refused to move.

Jon gave a sharp knock on the door, waited, and then knocked again. Finally, from inside he heard movement.

Suddenly, from just behind the door, a raspy voice called. "Who's there?"

"Jon Wilder."

"Who?"

"Mr. Bellkirk—it's Jon Wilder. I'm sorry not to have called first, but I was driving by and thought I'd stop."

Jon paused, then added, "I have something to return to you."

He heard a door chain being slid across, a lock undone. The door edged open several inches.

Squinting out at him, Jon saw the owlish face of Oren Bellkirk. The round eyes behind the thick glasses appeared enormous in the dying light. Below them, the sharp nose hooked abruptly downward like a beak, so that the space between the nostrils and the upper lip could not be seen.

"What do you want?" Oren Bellkirk stared at him.

"As I said, I have something to return to you."

"To me? What?"

"It's a pie tin." Jon kept his voice friendly, natural. "I really apologize for bothering you this late in the afternoon. But I thought you might be out making your deliveries."

"I was. I just got back."

"It *was* good timing then," Jon said.

"What's this about a pie tin?" Bellkirk asked.

Jon displayed the paper bag. He reached inside and brought out the old tin, turning it from front to back.

The man peered at it, then glanced at Jon and shook his head. "It isn't mine."

"Oh, but I'm sure it is," Jon said. "It came with the mince pie you provided for Thanksgiving. The other pie, the pumpkin, had one of those new aluminium pans. That's what surprised me. This is the old type. Solid tin. Mrs. Bellkirk probably used this kind when she was baking years ago."

Bellkirk took the tin and studied it. His eyes blinked rapidly.

"As a matter of fact," Jon went on, "those pies you gave us for Thanksgiving were delicious. Almost as good as Mrs. Bellkirk used to make. Who bakes them for you now?"

"Another woman."

"Local?" Jon asked.

Bellkirk nodded, still examining the tin.

"Well, please tell her how much everyone enjoyed them."

"I will. Okay." Bellkirk started to close the door.

"One more thing," Jon said quickly. "I was noticing your poultry house in back. If I remember, you once told me you were hoping to add on to it."

The man's face darkened. "I was. I tried last June. They turned me down."

"Really? What a shame," Jon said. "At any rate, thank you again for the turkey and the pies."

"Okay," was all the other said.

Jon gave a half-wave, turned, and headed for his car. As he walked, he didn't hear the front door of the house close behind him. Bellkirk was still watching him.

Jon climbed into the Range Rover and began to turn around. As he did, he gave a quick glance toward the house. At the window of an upstairs room he saw a curtain part, then fall back into place.

He drove slowly down the driveway and stopped to check for traffic on the road, lowering the window as he did.

It was then that he became conscious of the sound. The loud shrill caws. The beating of a thousand wings.

Jon looked up through the windshield and saw them. There were hundreds of them. Crows—their swift black outlines etched against the twilight sky, a vast, shrieking river of birds flying toward the trees surrounding Bellkirk's farm.

It was the time of year when the crows gathered in communal roosts. At sunset every day during the late fall and early winter months, they would congregate in giant flocks, cawing as they flew, and swooping in among the trees in chase. Only as the darkness came would they begin to quiet, settling down into their nests at last to sleep.

Jon's sleep, on the other hand, would come much later. If it came at all.

SEVENTEEN

FIRST, HE PUT ON the dark jeans, then the black socks and black shoes. The darkest shirt Jon found in his dresser was one in navy blue. But rummaging through a shelf in his closet he discovered a black turtleneck sweater he'd forgotten he owned. It smelled somewhat of mothballs, but it would serve the purpose. He unfolded it and pulled the sweater on over his shirt.

For some time a north wind had been rattling the windows of the bedroom. The night would be colder than he had thought. But wearing a jacket or a coat would limit his mobility. And if everything went as he hoped he wouldn't be outdoors for long.

Before leaving the bedroom, he paused before the mirror above the chest of drawers. Seeing his own image dressed almost totally in black, he was reminded of old photographs he'd once seen of French Apache dancers. What Jon would do tonight, however, would be done alone, without a partner, or, for that matter, an audience. He took a pencil flashlight from a bedside table, slipped it into the pocket of his jeans, and left the room.

He had stopped momentarily in the kitchen for a small plastic bag and was heading down the hallway that led to the garage, when he heard the telephone ring. The answering machine was still engaged, and the last thing he wanted at that moment was a phone call. Still, he moved into the study, curious to know who the caller was.

Jon listened to his own recorded greeting, followed by a beep, then: "Hello, Jon... It's Lorelei. I'm calling from New York. It's about nine o'clock. I guess you're out or busy. I just wanted to tell you everything is fine with me and—''

Jon picked up the phone. ''Lorelei—I'm here.''

''You *are*. I'm glad.'' Her voice sounded pleased.

''I was just on my way out, actually.''

''At this hour on a weekday night?'' She gave a teasing laugh. ''I thought you were an early-morning lark, not a night owl.''

''Well...there's a movie playing at the theater in Mystic I've been wanting to see.''

''Really?'' Lorelei didn't sound convinced, but let it go. ''Then I won't keep you.''

''I should be here tomorrow.''

''Fine. I'll try to call you again when I can.'' There was a brief pause before she asked, ''Jon, are you all right?''

''Yes,'' he said at once.

''Okay. I'll call tomorrow. Have fun at the movies. Bye.''

He offered a good-bye, hung up the telephone and reset the answering machine.

Then he walked to the garage.

DRY LEAVES skittered across the headlight beams as Jon drove quickly toward Scarborough. The wind gusts buffeted the car and the low whistling sound around the windows made the Range Rover feel colder than it was. Jon increased the heater and rubbed his hands for warmth. He'd neglected to bring gloves, which he regretted now.

With almost no cars on the road, he reached the center of Scarborough in less than ten minutes. He rounded the town green and headed east.

He hadn't driven a mile when something in the rearview mirror caught his eye. It was the headlights of another car about a hundred yards behind. Jon dismissed them from his mind. But after several miles the car was still there, maintaining the same speed as the Range Rover. When Jon turned onto Cemetery Road, it turned as well. He accelerated slightly. The other car sped up.

Jon considered the remainder of the drive that lay ahead. He could approach his destination from the opposite direction, although it would add about five minutes to the trip. On the other hand, it hardly mattered. Where he was headed, no one was expecting him at any time. He hoped.

He checked the mirror, startled to discover that the car behind had cut the space between the two vehicles in half.

Jon focused on the road, remembering that it turned left several hundred yards ahead. He waited until he was close to the turn, braked suddenly, and swung the steering wheel left. Tires squealing, the Range Rover spun, recovered and shot forward as Jon pressed the accelerator hard.

He glanced in the rearview mirror again. The headlights of the other car were turning, too.

He passed the old town cemetery on the right; a short time after that came the line of beech trees that marked the beginning of Abigail Stives's land. Soon, along the left, the Epsoms' small frame house was visible.

Jon checked the mirror fleetingly. The other car was gaining once again.

Beyond the Epsoms' property, the road curved right, then left, and right again, reminding him how tortuous a country road could be, especially at night and at high speed. Then, without warning, the road suddenly became a single lane of tarmac sloping away steeply at the shoulders. In the drainage ditches bordering the shoulders, Jon could see pools of water that had accumulated from a heavy rain the day before. The ditches finally gave way to farmland bordered by fencing on both sides.

In the mirror, he could still make out the headlights of his pursuer's car. The gap between it and the Range Rover had again widened. But the other car was hurrying to narrow it.

Jon hit the high beams. Ahead, along the right side of the road, there was an opening in the fence line and what seemed to be the entrance to an unpaved tractor path between two fields.

He stood on the brakes, spinning the Rover onto the path. Lurching forward through the muddy ruts, the vehicle fishtailed wildly. The car behind him also turned onto the path, but unless it had four-wheel drive, it would almost certainly get mired in the mud. Before that happened, Jon hoped the driver had the good sense to give up the chase.

Looking in the mirror, Jon finally saw the headlights of the other car grow small, then disappear. He patted the dashboard gratefully, reduced his speed, and exhaled the breath he'd held since he turned onto the path.

The tractor path ended at what Jon was certain was the other end of Cemetery Road. He came to a stop on the paved apron. The road was dark and empty; there were no other cars in sight. He turned and drove toward Bellkirk's farm.

Approaching the entrance to the farm from this direction had one disadvantage. The grove of trees from which he'd studied the farm earlier that day was at its southern border. It would mean driving directly past the farmhouse before he could reach the sanctuary of the trees. Jon doubted the old man sat up at night counting cars along the road. Still, given the lateness of the hour and the rural nature of the area, Bellkirk, if he was awake, might hear the car and be suspicious of a trespasser. It was a risk Jon had to take.

Passing the farmhouse, he glanced quickly at the driveway leading up to it and saw the gate was closed. At last, the grove of pine and cedar trees came into view. He slowed and switched the lights to dim. Then, very slowly, he turned off the road and eased the vehicle in among the trees.

He killed the lights, turned off the engine, and climbed out. In the dark, a pine branch slapped across his face. He took the pencil flashlight from his pocket and pointed it at the ground. Grasping it at the front end, so as to concentrate the beam, he made his way through the underbrush to the barbed-wire fence that marked the boundary of the farm.

Extinguishing the light, he moved along the outside of the fence, feeling gingerly for a place where the wire might have rusted through. It didn't take him long. He stepped over the fence and looked in the direction of the farmhouse. It was dark, except for a meager yellow light that flickered through the curtains of an upstairs room. As he watched, he saw a silhouetted figure pass the window. Then the light went out.

Jon estimated that seventy-five yards of open farmland lay between him and the outbuildings behind the house. Scanning the field in the darkness, it occurred to him that in his reconnaissance of the farm, he had forgotten to observe what crop Bellkirk had been cultivating there. It obviously wasn't corn; whatever had been growing stood only a foot or so above the ground.

What he'd also neglected to make note of, Jon realized, was the condition of the field itself. Starting across it, he found the earth was deeply furrowed and slippery with wet mud.

He took another step—when something seized his ankles. He fell forward, hitting his head solidly against an object lying on the ground. Jon cursed, then pushed up on his hands and knees, at the same time disentangling himself from the thick vines that had caused his fall. He also saw what it was that his head had struck—a huge and somewhat rotted pumpkin. Jon stood up, wiped his hands against his jeans, and moved on cautiously.

His focus was now on the delivery van parked between the barn and poultry house. As the pumpkin field gave way to an area of hard-packed dirt, Jon sprinted for the van and crouched down behind it.

The poultry house was only twenty feet away. The building in which Bellkirk raised his chickens and collected eggs was a low, rectangular wood structure, sixty feet in length and thirty feet wide. Rows of small square windows extended down the longer sides. The end of the building nearest Jon was without windows. Instead, there was a single wooden door that showed a clasp and padlock. But the shackle had been folded back and the lock hung impotently from the clasp.

Jon ran to the poultry house and stopped beside the door. As he pulled it toward him, the rusted hinges squealed wildly. He let go of the door and glanced in the direction of the house. It remained dark.

He put his hand through the door opening and edged it open inch by inch. When there was sufficient space, he slipped into the building, leaving the door ajar.

The acrid smell of chicken droppings and the phosphate litter used to neutralize it overwhelmed him. He stood where he was for a few moments, letting his eyes grow accustomed to the dark. Hanging from the ceiling of the huge room, among the trestle beams, was a small bare bulb that provided almost no illumination. He guessed it served as some sort of night-light for the chickens as they slept. As his vision became better, he could make out several hundred of them sleeping on the roosting nests that occupied the center of the room. The roosts, long wooden slats with wire mesh beneath them, sat about two feet above the floor, stretching across most of the length of the building.

Everything was quiet. But as Jon listened, he could hear occasional contented clucking; perhaps from hens dreaming happy chicken dreams of freedom and of flight.

Against the long walls of the room, below the windows, were the wooden laying boxes where the birds deposited their eggs. Between these and the roosts were narrow aisles about four feet wide. Each aisle led to a door at the far end. Behind one of the doors, Jon assumed, was a storage room where Bellkirk kept the feed and general supplies.

He went to the aisle nearest him and started down it, the flashlight directed at the floor. The floor, he saw, was concrete, with a sand-and-sawdust covering. Running the length of the aisle also were sheet-metal troughs that held the feed. Large canisters providing water for the chickens had been placed alongside it.

Jon opened the first door he came to and shone the light inside. Large sacks of mash and grain were stacked against the walls. He was about to close the door, when he heard scuttling. He swung the light. From between two stacks of feed, a large rat poked out its head. The rat stared up at Jon, chattering at him as if annoyed at the interruption. Jon quickly closed the door.

The evidence he wanted was behind the other door, he was convinced. He went to it, opened it, and aimed the light into the room.

What he saw chilled him. It was the part of the poultry house referred to as the preparation room; the place in which the birds were killed and dressed. Despite its neat and orderly appearance, death was everywhere.

The room was windowless, with a small ventilation unit set into the roof. Along one wall were the instruments of death itself: large metal funnels into which the birds were forced, so that their heads and necks protruded from the base. The birds were then decapitated, or a long narrow knife with an upward-curving tip was thrust into the beak, so that the tip could pierce the brain, producing instant death. Below the funnels were the pails into which their blood drained.

On a table set against another wall, Jon saw a machine with a rotating drum and long protruding spikes. It was an electric picker. After its feathers had been loosened in hot, scalding water, the bird was held over the drum, so that the spikes removed the feathers. In the process, the feathers were occasionally mangled and the quill tips broken...just as the tip of the crow feather was that had been sent to Lester Fitch.

Directing the flashlight to the base of the picker, Jon saw some white feathers that had fallen when the dead chickens had been cleaned. Among them, also, were the black feathers of a crow that had suffered the same fate.

Jon took out the plastic bag he had brought with him, knelt, collected both chicken and crow feathers, and put them in the bag. He returned the bag to the pocket of his jeans and stood.

He left the room and retraced his steps along the aisle, keeping the beam of the flashlight pointed at the floor.

He was approaching the door that led out to the barnyard, when the beam of a much stronger flashlight swept the windows from outside. The light came from the direction of the house.

"Who's there?"

Jon stopped at once.

"Who's in there?" Bellkirk shouted. "Show yourself! I got a gun!"

Jon's heart beat wildly. There was no time to flee. He retreated to the aisle, ducked down, and lay flat, pressing his face against the floor.

The beam moved from the windows to the door, framing the edges of it in bright lines of light.

"I know you're there!" the voice rasped. "Come out with your hands high!"

Jon heard the squeal as the door swung out. A shaft of light arced through the poultry house.

He heard Bellkirk's footsteps crunch down on the litter as the man began to walk. He was moving slowly, carefully, along the aisle opposite the side of the roosting nests where Jon lay. The footsteps stopped, the light swung slowly over the rows of sleeping hens. Feathers ruffled briefly here and there.

Jon said a silent prayer: Please, God, let Bellkirk leave.

As if in answer, Bellkirk turned and started back along the aisle. But before he reached the door, he stopped again. The light moved over the sleeping chickens for a second time. He was trying to decide what to do next.

Then something wet and cold touched Jon's ear. He felt stiff whiskers brush his neck. Sharp claws pierced through the fabric of his sweater as the thing explored his back.

It was a rat.

Finding nothing edible, the rat squeaked shrilly, then leaped into the feeding trough with a loud thud.

"What the hell?" said Bellkirk.

The light went immediately to the roosting nests directly over Jon. He pressed himself as flat as possible against the floor.

He now heard Bellkirk's footsteps moving toward the aisle where he lay. There was a chuckle. "Well, well, well... It seems we got a fox inside the chicken coop at that."

Face still pressed to the floor, Jon was aware of the light moving up the aisle toward him. Up his legs. Across his back. His neck and finally his head.

"Whoever you are, get up!" Bellkirk said.

Jon heard the safety of a shotgun disengage. The slide handle was drawn back.

"Get up! *Now!*"

Jon rolled slowly to one side.

"Don't shoot," he said.

The light shone in Jon's face.

"Mr. Wilder?" The man's voice was incredulous.

Jon nodded.

"What the hell are you doing in my chicken house?"

"Put the gun down and I'll tell you."

"Tell me. And the gun stays. Get your hands where I can see 'em."

Jon did as he was told. The light blinded him.

"Tell me," repeated Bellkirk.

"I will if you put down the gun."

"I don't think so," Bellkirk told him. "What I think instead is that I'll kill you."

"Do that and you'll have something else to explain to the police."

"I'd be shooting an intruder on my property. He broke into my henhouse and I shot him." The man added, "I didn't know till later who it was."

"You're pretty good with a gun, aren't you?"

"Very."

"And a knife, too?" Jon said.

Momentarily, the light wavered.

"I know how to use both," Bellkirk said.

Keep him talking, Jon thought. Play for time. "Why did you take the knife from my garage?" he asked Bellkirk.

"It was handy."

"But you used your own knife to kill Ramsey. The one with the curved tip. What did you have against him? Was it because he disallowed the building application?"

"That and more."

"Like Gina?"

Jon heard a sharp intake of breath. "What do you know about her?" Bellkirk said.

"Gina lives here, doesn't she? Did Ramsey seduce her?"

"Ramsey was scum."

"But Bernie Benjamin? Did you kill him and set fire to

his restaurant because of the complaint he filed with the state?''

''The health inspectors cleared me,'' Bellkirk told him.

''After they investigated,'' Jon said. ''But that took a while. Meantime, word was out that you were selling tainted chickens to his restaurant. It must have hurt your business badly. But why Fitch?''

''They were all after me,'' said Bellkirk. ''Each in his way tried to ruin me. Ruin my life. Ramsey and the girl. Benjamin and the complaint about the chickens. Fitch and the zoning board. All of them were trying to drive me out; to make me sell the farm.''

''So you began to kill them.''

Silence.

''Listen—go to the police,'' Jon urged him. ''Tell them you were pressured. Maybe you can make a deal.''

''I'm not going nowhere,'' the man answered. ''But neither are you. Come out into the yard. I'm going to kill you there.''

The light that had remained on Jon's face wavered as Bellkirk began backing toward the door.

''Let's go,'' insisted Bellkirk. ''Time is up.''

Jon knew it was. His only hope now was to distract Bellkirk's attention. How?

''Walk toward me slow. Hands *out!*''

''I can't see where I'm going,'' Jon said. ''Get the light out of my eyes.'' Deliberately, he kicked the feed trough with his foot.

The noise startled Bellkirk; he shone the light down at the trough. As he did, Jon grabbed a sleeping chicken, hurling it at Bellkirk's face.

Startled, Bellkirk batted at it with his light.

Jon lunged.

He was too late.

He saw the gun barrel flash; his left arm screamed with pain. He clutched it, falling to his knees.

Suddenly around him everything was chaos—squawking chickens dashing wildly in panic, wings flapping desperately in an attempt to flee. A blizzard of white feathers filled the poultry house.

Dizziness swept over Jon. He rolled onto his back, still clutching his left arm. He could feel his own blood, wet and sticky, through his sweater where the shotgun pellets had ripped into his flesh.

His ears rang from the blast. But through it, he again heard the slide handle of the shotgun being drawn back. In a moment Bellkirk would fire for a second time. And this time he wouldn't miss.

Instead, the next sound Jon heard was the impact of an object striking something, followed by a gasp. Then came the clatter of the shotgun falling to the floor. Feet staggering. An unintelligible cry, and then a body pitching forward and collapsing on the nests.

There were men's voices.

A woman's sobs.

Light filled the poultry house.

"How are you, Jon?" a familiar voice asked.

Looking up, the face of Lieutenant Lydecker swam into Jon's view. The man was kneeling at his right.

"How are you?" Lydecker asked again. He shooed away some noisy chickens that were still running up and down the aisle.

"Lucky," Jon managed to say.

"Very lucky. Would you like a blanket?"

"No." Jon shook his head, then felt the pain. "What happened to Bellkirk?"

"He's dead," Lydecker said. "The girl stabbed him before he shot at you again. She got a knife and followed him out here when he came after you."

"She told you that?"

"We figured it out," Lydecker said. "The fact is, she's pretty incoherent at the moment. Won't even tell us her name."

"It's Gina," Jon said. "She's been living at the farm with Bellkirk."

Lydecker frowned, but took a notebook from his pocket and wrote down the information. As he did, a second police officer knelt at Jon's left side. He cut away the sleeve of the sweater from around Jon's wound and began to dress it.

Lydecker leaned over and inspected the wound. "You're also lucky Bellkirk was a lousy shot. It doesn't look like too much damage to your arm."

Distantly, a siren could be heard approaching. The policemen heard it, too.

"That's the ambulance," Lydecker informed Jon. "They'll get you to the hospital. In the meantime, use my jacket to keep warm."

The lieutenant stood up, removed his jacket and spread it over Jon.

"How did you know to come here?" Jon asked him.

"We didn't come here. We came after you."

"What do you mean?"

"Thank your friends, Mrs. Merriwell and Mr. Hightower. He was the one who called us," Lydecker explained. "Mrs. Merriwell phoned him from New York after she talked to you at home. You told her you were going to a movie in Mystic."

"Yes, I did."

Lieutenant Lydecker gave a small, triumphant smirk. "She knew what you didn't. The Mystic theater is closed for renovations. Has been for a month. Anyway, after Hightower called us, we alerted the officers out on patrol. One of them spotted the Range Rover passing the town green and followed you. He might have caught you, too, except for that quick shortcut you decided to take the tractor path. It took us fifteen minutes more before we found your car parked in the trees.''

''I'm glad you did.''

''Me too.'' Lydecker shoved the notebook into a rear pocket.

Red streaks swept past the windows of the poultry house as the ambulance came up the drive and stopped outside the barn. The siren died with a reluctant whine.

''The medics are here,'' Lydecker told Jon.

A young police officer entered the poultry house and said something to Lydecker. Jon heard the name Gina mentioned several times. Then the two policemen headed toward the door.

For Jon, the shock of what had happened was beginning to set in. He closed his eyes, and wondered if he might lose consciousness. Then lightly, for the briefest instant, something brushed against his cheek. It was so soft, he thought at first he had imagined it.

He opened his eyes and discovered he was staring up at the ceiling of the poultry house. Directly overhead, perched on a beam, he saw a large white hen, so plump that from below she looked like a lumpy ball of feathers delicately balanced on the beam. Somehow in the frenzy after the shotgun blast, she'd managed to get up there. Now, while he watched, the hen continued preening herself calmly, as if nothing in the least upsetting had occurred.

More feathers fluttered down on Jon. It occurred to him that over the years he had observed some of the rarest, most resplendent, most exotic birds on earth. But tonight, as he lay and looked up at the chicken, she was without doubt the most beautiful of all the birds he'd ever seen.

EIGHTEEN

COLIN STUDIED JON, at the same time making small harrumphing sounds. He nodded to the gray muslin sling supporting Jon's left arm.

"I'm pleased to say, Jon, you're looking remarkably chipper for somebody whose arm was grazed by pellets from a shotgun blast. Or, since you're an ornithologist, should I say 'winged'?"

Jon smiled. "Either way, I'm glad we can joke about it now. The other night was something else."

They were standing in the lobby of Scarborough Hospital. Jon carried a small overnight case in his right hand.

"By the way," Colin went on, "I have two gifts to give you. Here is the first."

He held out a soft package wrapped in tissue paper. "Shall I hold your case so you can open it? Or would you rather wait until you're home?"

"Now is fine," Jon said.

"Very well." Colin took the case, while Jon undid the paper and withdrew a folded piece of light-blue silk interwoven with gold threads.

"The silk is Indian," Colin explained. "It was purchased from a holy man in Amritsar, who assured me of its healing powers. You may use it to replace the thoroughly drab sling you're wearing now to hold your injured arm."

"It's wonderful," Jon said. "And thank you."

"You're most welcome," Colin said. "Now let's be on our way. The second surprise is waiting for you in my car."

Jon put Colin's package into a side pocket of the overnight case, and together they walked out of the hospital lobby to the parking lot. As Jon drew nearer Colin's car, he slowed his steps and stared.

"This *is* a surprise."

Lorelei rolled down a rear window. "Hello, Jon."

"I thought you were in New York."

"When Colin called and told me what had happened, I came back. He met me at the train a little while ago."

"Come, come, you two," said Colin, feigning impatience. "You can express your mutual delight when we get back to Jon's house."

Jon climbed into the passenger side, while Colin tossed in his cane, then squeezed behind the steering wheel. From the backseat, Lorelei leaned forward between them. They drove out of the parking lot and started on the road to Plover Point.

"So are you the man the newspapers are calling the Sherlock Holmes of the Henhouse?" Lorelei asked Jon.

Jon turned his head and gave her a wry smile. "I guess I am. Except Sherlock Holmes wouldn't have made the mistakes I did."

"Your only mistake," corrected Colin, "was in not telling anyone what you were up to. How can I be your Dr. Watson, if you insist on doing everything alone? You're an independent man by nature, Jonathan. We know that. But this time that independence almost got you killed."

Jon studied the road thoughtfully. "I guess independence isn't everything I always thought it was. Anyway, thank you both for worrying about me. And for getting the police involved. If you hadn't, I don't know what the outcome might have been."

Lorelei and Colin shared a glance. She looked again at Jon. "So what gave you the idea Bellkirk was the person who killed Ramsey and Benjamin?"

"First, the business of Ramsey's campaign button. I noticed it pinned to the sun visor of Bellkirk's van four days

after the murder. I also saw the van in town the same day
Gina first came to your shop. What confirmed it was finding
a white feather in your office the night we had the confrontation with the crow. There were a lot of crow feathers
on the floor, but there was also a white pinfeather from a
chicken. It had probably been on Bellkirk's sleeve when he
put the crow into your office through the broken window
of the door.''

"But how did you connect him with the crows?" asked
Colin.

"I couldn't at first," Jon admitted. "That's why I took
the old pie tin to him, pretending it was his. It gave me an
excuse to look over the farm.''

"And that's when you saw the crows," Lorelei said.

"Roosting in the trees around it, yes. He probably killed
some with his shotgun, or trapped them, and used their
feathers to send to Ramsey and the others.''

"But why put a live crow in my office?" Lorelei persisted.

"It was a warning," Jon explained. "As much to Gina
as to you. He knew she'd been visiting your shop and he
didn't want the two of you becoming friends. He was afraid
she might say something to you about him.''

"The word around Scarborough," Colin put in, "is that
the police had no idea Bellkirk was the murderer. In fact,
since the incident, Lieutenant Lydecker has been eating a
great deal of crow himself.''

"Maybe," Jon said. "But at least he's had the good
grace to admit it. He talked to me this morning in the hospital.''

"Did he say anything about the Scarecrows?" Lorelei
asked.

Jon nodded. "All of them confessed that they had pressured certain local landowners to sell out. The Standish
Corporation was behind it from the start. The money Stan-

dish paid the Scarecrows went first to Kittridge's bank, and then through Reverend Rill's church. Rill kept a secret set of books. Of course, Standish denies any involvement. Whatever may have happened, they blame on the middlemen—the straws. And by paying off the Scarecrows in cash, they've protected themselves pretty well.

"By the way," Jon went on, "Kittridge also admitted he hired Willie Trask to shoot at me that night along the shore. It was just meant 'as a warning,' Kittridge said, to intimidate me into ending my investigation."

"Outrageous," Colin snorted. "Do you have any notion of what the Scarecrows will be charged with? Conspiracy or coercing landowners to sell?"

"I suppose so," Jon agreed. "But Lydecker thinks they'll probably get the charges reduced with a plea bargain. He even passed along a rumor that Reverend Rill is giving up his ministry in Scarborough to become a television evangelist."

"Aha!" Colin chortled. "Now we're talking about *real* fraud!"

"What about Madeleine Thoreau?" asked Lorelei.

"As it so happens," Colin said, "I got her telephone number in Florida, and called to tell her what's occurred. She had no involvement with the Scarecrows' plot, apparently. But she knew enough of what was going on to be afraid. Particularly after Ramsey, and then Benjamin, were killed."

They turned into Jon's driveway and began the circuitous half-mile journey to his house.

"I've been afraid to ask about Gina," Lorelei said. "What will happen to her now?"

"She's been charged with killing Bellkirk, of course," Jon said. "I pity her. From what she's told the police, her life has been about as bad as anyone's can be. Her family lives in Providence; an alcoholic mother and a stepfather who abused her. She ran away last summer, came to Scarborough, and found a job working in the roadside stand at Bellkirk's farm. She started living at the farm, then met Rod Ramsey. They became lovers and when Bellkirk learned about the two of them he beat her; he even tried keeping her a virtual prisoner inside the house. After Bellkirk murdered Ramsey, he ripped the campaign button off the costume and pinned it to the sun visor of the van as a way of tormenting the girl. Finally, she knew she had no way of escaping Bellkirk unless she killed him.''

Colin slowed the car to a stop in the driveway turnaround. The Range Rover was parked along the side.

"How did your car get here if you were in the hospital?" Lorelei asked Jon.

"Lieutenant Lydecker again," Jon said. "He told me he owed me a few favors. He had the police bring it here."

Jon picked up the overnight case and stepped out of Colin's car. "Will you come in awhile?" he asked both of them.

"Thank you," Colin answered, "but I have to get back to the shop."

"You'll stay, won't you?" Jon asked Lorelei.

She looked uncertain. "You're just out of the hospital. Wouldn't you like to rest? Besides, I have to get my car at the garage."

"I'll drive you there later," Jon assured her. "I still have one good arm." He flexed his right, to demonstrate.

"Our friend is obviously eager for you to remain," Colin informed Lorelei. "Why don't you?"

"All right. A little while." She stepped out of the car.

"I'm on my way, then," Colin said. He gave a wave. "Call me tomorrow, Jonathan. Or better yet, come into town and the three of us can enjoy a celebratory lunch." He looked at Lorelei. "You'll be opening your shop, I hope."

She nodded. "I expect to."

"Good. The town hasn't been the same since your departure. Has it, Jon?" Colin added pointedly.

Without waiting for an answer, he swung his car around and headed up the driveway toward the road. Lorelei and Jon watched in silence as the car disappeared among the trees.

"Well..." Lorelei said, at last, "this has really turned out to be a nice day. Warmer than usual, I mean. You don't expect this kind of weather in December."

"No, you don't," he said.

An awkward silence fell between them.

"So," Lorelei asked, "would you prefer to drive me to the garage now, or what?"

"I'm sorry. I'm not being a very good host."

"And I'm a very pushy guest." She smiled. "Why don't we take a walk along the beach, at least. A short one."

"Good idea. I could use a walk."

Jon left the overnight case near the garage, and joined her as she continued to the terrace. They walked across it to the lawn, then down the narrow footpath leading to the beach. The pale autumn sun was dappling the water and a sea breeze caught Lorelei's hair, tossing it against her face, and resisting her efforts to brush it away.

Suddenly, they heard a whine. They turned and saw Jake staring up at them, a dirty tennis ball clenched firmly in his teeth. Jon knelt and patted the dog with his free hand.

"Thanks for the homecoming gift, Jake," he said. "But I'm not up to tennis yet. How about a game of catch instead?"

Jake wagged his tail. Jon stood and tossed the ball into the air. The dog leaped and caught it as it fell; but rather than return it, whirled and ran off with it down the beach. Lorelei and Jon laughed together.

"I'm afraid Jake has forgotten a few things from his retriever days," Jon said.

"A few," Lorelei agreed.

They began to walk along the beach.

"Really, I am glad you're all right," she said. "After Colin called me in New York and told me what had happened, I took the first train back."

"I'm glad you did," Jon said.

"May I ask you something?" she went on after a few moments.

"Sure."

"What you told Colin and me earlier... About independence."

"That it's not everything I used to think it was?"

"Yes. What did you mean?"

Jon looked out at the water, pondering. "I meant that maybe for too long I've lived by myself and for myself. Maybe for too long, Jon Wilder has looked at life the way he studies birds—with interest, curiosity, sometimes even fascination. But at all times from a distance. Now I think I'd like to change that, if I can."

"You once told me that if you could be any kind of bird, you'd be a petrel, free to go where the wind carried you. Has that changed, too?"

"I guess it has."

He smiled to himself, then looked at her. "On the other hand, I can't say I'm ready to become a perching bird. But I'll never be the solitary wanderer I was. Will that answer do for now?"

"For now."

A sudden wind gust caught her hair, flinging it across her face. She raised a hand to brush it back.

"It's getting cold, after all," Lorelei said. "Let's go back to the house and warm up."

Jon reached out his free hand and brought it to her face as well.

"That," he said, "would be a wonderful idea."

A random predator is terrorizing Southern California. After children start disappearing, it's up to the FBI's finest to stop a killer...

RANDOM ACTS

Criminal profiler **Laurel Madden** is at the top of her field. But Agent Madden has a dark side and even darker secrets—which is why she understands the criminal mind so well.

Claire Gillespie is a reporter assigned to cover the case. She has another more personal agenda: to rip away the veil of secrecy that surrounds and protects Madden. Claire has evidence that the FBI top agent committed murder—and got away with it...until now.

Dan Sprague is the veteran FBI agent who stands between the two determined women—torn by duty and loyalty to one woman and an intense attraction to the other....

From the bestselling author of *The Best of Enemies*...

TAYLOR SMITH

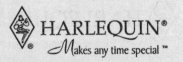